DIGGING UP DAISY

DIGGING

UP DAISY

SHERRY LYNN

BERKLEY PRIME CRIME
New York

BERKLEY PRIME CRIME
Published by Berkley
An imprint of Penguin Random House LLC
penguinrandomhouse.com

Copyright © 2023 by Sherry L. Rummler
Excerpt from *Murder Under the Mistletoe* by Sherry Lynn
copyright © 2023 by Sherry L. Rummler

Library of Congress Cataloging-in-Publication Data

Names: Lynn, Sherry (Mystery writer), author.
Title: Digging up Daisy / Sherry Lynn.
Description: First edition. | New York : Berkley Prime Crime, 2023. |
Series: A Mainely murder mystery
Identifiers: LCCN 2022058199 (print) | LCCN 2022058200 (ebook) |
ISBN 9780593546659 (trade paperback) | ISBN 9780593546666 (ebook)
Subjects: LCGFT: Detective and mystery fiction. | Novels.
Classification: LCC PS3617.U5643 D54 2023 (print) |
LCC PS3617.U5643 (ebook) | DDC 813/.6—dc23/eng/20221208
LC record available at https://lccn.loc.gov/2022058199
LC ebook record available at https://lccn.loc.gov/2022058200

First Edition: April 2023

Printed in the United States of America
1st Printing

Book design by George Towne

*Amy and Jean, I'll NEVER forget the
biggest surprise of my life, and your pop-in visit,
during the writing of this book.
Thanks for bringing my New England back . . .
Love you both, Xo*

Chapter 1

Kinsley Clark inhaled deeply. The salty sea air, along with a whiff of the nearby beach roses, sent a smile to her lips. The combined scent was intoxicating. She remembered planting the vivid fuchsia and white shrubs with her aunt Tilly soon after she'd moved into the caretaker's cottage behind her aunt's seaside estate. The Salty Breeze Inn, a mammoth cedar-shingled structure, weathered from the sea, stood proudly above the cliff walk. Trimmed in crisp white, the inn provided the perfect muted backdrop for a bounty of colorful floral hues. Kinsley turned to glance over her shoulder and eyed the scrub brush. The roses had grown wild along the coastline, their tendrils filling every crevice the untamed branches could reach. The silky blossoms fluttered in the cool wind yet pointed up to the light, as if sunbathing in the early-June sun.

At twenty-nine, Kinsley didn't realize how that season of planting would define her. Now, owner of SeaScapes, a thriving landscape design company in Harborside, Maine, she almost had to pinch herself. If not for the training her aunt Tilly had given her while she was growing up, Kinsley's entire career might have remained only a wish. Countless designers, landscapers, and artists only dreamed of working for the wealthy coastal homeowners of prominent Harborside. Because she was raised behind the Salty Breeze Inn, perched high above the well-worn cliff walk, the neighbors trusted her. They'd all witnessed the magic she'd created with the lush yet rugged southern Maine landscape, and the neighbors, wild with envy, wanted to replicate the picture-postcard splendor.

Sometimes good things do come out of the ashes, Kinsley thought as she turned her attention to face the sea. She returned the other half of an uneaten ham sandwich to the small wicker basket that held the rest of her lunch. She loved taking lunch breaks outside at her favorite spot—a hidden crevice, deep within the rugged rocks, that provided shelter from the crashing waves.

This was her office. And not for a moment did she take it for granted.

The sound of the waves had soothed her like a lullaby ever since she'd turned thirteen and moved permanently to Maine after her parents' passing. The lullaby had turned into a sweet song, as the sting of loss had been replaced by her aunt Tilly's unending, unconditional love.

Kinsley had certainly grieved her parents, but she didn't miss the constant household moves from her youth because of their ever-changing deployments. Her brother, Kyle, however, never tired of the changes. He'd enlisted in the Air Force, following in their parents' footprints, just as soon as he'd turned eighteen. Currently, Kyle lived on a base in Germany, and they didn't connect as often as she'd like.

She hadn't seen him in eight months yet prayed for him daily.

The numerous Air Force bases had never really felt like home to Kinsley. She, like a perennial flower, always longed for a steady place in which to put down permanent roots. Aunt Tilly's inn, perched high above the Atlantic, had given her that grounding. Years later, no longer a gangly teenager with a mouth full of braces, she still loved living in Harborside.

After Kinsley graduated from high school, her aunt had moved out of the caretaker's quarters that they'd shared and converted a room at the back of the inn for herself, leaving the cottage solely to her niece. Kinsley transformed the space into her own private oasis, where she resided and occasionally met with clients for SeaScapes. Although the caretaker's cottage came equipped with a fully functioning kitchen, Aunt Tilly still spoiled her with homemade dishes from the inn after an exhausting day of gardening work. Despite Kinsley's age, she didn't decline the hospitality her aunt so freely gave, or protest the occasional luscious meals packaged and secretly tucked within the confines of her refrigerator, waiting to be reheated at a moment's notice. Her aunt tended to show her love through food, and Kinsley willingly obliged.

Kinsley brushed the loose hair that had escaped her long blond braid away from her face with her forearm. Her hair would be bleached platinum by summer's end due to the many hours working outdoors. She then wiped her hands along her faded jeans to remove any remaining crumbs or mustard remnants from her sandwich. She hated to leave the comfort and the roaring sound of the ocean, but she had a lot more work to do. Kinsley had promised her aunt Tilly that despite her ever-growing list of clients, she'd replace the hydrangea bush that had perished last winter, clean up the yard, and place full, blooming containers throughout the property. The colorful containers were needed, as the summer perennials were not yet in full swing, and she needed to beautify the place before the big event that her aunt was participating in for the third year in a row—the Walk Inns.

The Walk Inns was an annual parade of homes, where several local bed-and-breakfast establishments signed up for an open-house showcase tour. Attendees obtained a map showing the participating homes and walked the route, going through the inns at their leisure. Since most of the inns that had taken part were now official SeaScapes clients, the event gave Kinsley a chance to showcase her work, too. Last year, she'd been featured in *Coastal Living*, standing alongside one of the stately Harborside homes. Kinsley hoped this year good things would come for Aunt Tilly, too—like a chance for the Salty Breeze Inn to be featured in the prominent magazine. But she'd better not get ahead of herself—though one couldn't blame her for daring to dream. She had always believed her aunt deserved so much more than Kinsley could possibly ever repay. Tilly's giving spirit was the heartbeat to not only her, but their community as well, as she volunteered for anything and everything, despite her own long hours of work.

Kinsley flipped the wicker lid closed on her lunch basket and then rose to a standing position. She stretched her arms high above her head and inhaled one last cleansing breath before grudgingly retrieving the basket and tuning her back to the sea. After dodging a few tidepools scattered with sea urchins, and navigating across several seaweed-covered boulders, she finally made her way safely atop the cliff walk.

The concrete cliff walk flanked the Salty Breeze Inn, traveled the coastline, and spanned miles in both directions from her aunt Tilly's estate. To the right, if she continued down the path for roughly half a mile, it would take her to the private sandy beach reserved exclusively for Harborside residents. To the left, the cliff walk would snake its way to the marina, where yachts and sailboats moored idly in the water, waiting for their captains to navigate them to the Atlantic Ocean. And beyond that, Breakwater Lighthouse jutted out from the mile-long rock jetty, ready to guide vessels safely home in the event the fog rolled in, or an impending storm broke. Which, in Maine, was quite common.

Kinsley promised herself that a boat would somehow be in her future. She hated to take that leap now, though, as the summer season was the busiest time for SeaScapes, and she wouldn't have time to enjoy that type of luxury. Although winter had its own appeal for her business, too. She loved the opportunity to decorate the wealthy Harborside homes and businesses for Christmas with live greenery, seasonal poinsettias, red roses, and dried hydrangea that she herself had cut when the summer blooms had faded and they'd had a lengthy time to hang upside down to dry.

The sound of a whistle caught Kinsley's attention, and her eyes, the color of the sky on a cloudless day, traveled upward to see her aunt waiting for her atop the wide flagstone staircase. The staircase, which wound directly from the cliff walk to a path, led guests to a wide porch that faced the sea. A favorite spot for Salty Breeze guests to relax after a long day in the sun.

"Oh, there you are! Something told me I might find you hiding out here." Matilda Hartwig stood atop the rock staircase with her arms wrapped around herself to prevent a light sweater from billowing in the wind. She quickly buttoned the sweater in an attempt to secure it. Her chin-length brown hair, highlighted with a hint of silver, also shifted with the changing breeze. She attempted to smooth her hair with one hand, but to no avail.

"Aunt Tilly, what's the matter?" Kinsley took the remaining flagstone stairs two at a time to greet her aunt with a half hug at the wide landing.

"Nothing, darlin'. I was just wondering if you wanted to share lunch. I'm taking a minute while many of my guests are off playing tourist, and I thought you might want to join me." Her hazel eyes, the color of toffee roses, sparkled with mischief.

Kinsley wondered what her aunt was up to.

"I was about to whip up something yummy for us to share, but it looks like you've already eaten." Tilly's smile faded as she gestured to the basket in Kinsley's hand.

"Trying out a new recipe? Or do you have something else you want to chat about? You know I always take my lunch breaks out here, any chance I get." Kinsley countered the twinkle in her aunt's eye with a raised eyebrow.

"I was hoping we could talk about the event. We've been like two ships passing in the night lately, and I was hoping I could run a few ideas by you. I love your input on these things, especially since you've had a sneak peek at some of our competition."

"Ah, I see." Kinsley knew there was something prompting this spontaneous lunch visit. It was uncommon for the two to share time during a busy workday. They scarcely saw each other in passing, both fiercely obsessive with their respective work. Some evenings, however, they would sit on the oversized white wooden rockers atop the wide wraparound porch overlooking the ocean. They'd catch up on the day's events over a cup of herbal tea or a late supper. But it had been days since that had happened.

Kinsley looped her arm through her aunt's and turned them in the direction of the inn. "Tell me what's on your mind. I can't really divulge much of what's going on with your competition, because I'm only working outdoors, but I still might be able to help. Do you have additional ideas for the floral decor? I've already decided instead of using your old containers the way they are, I thought I'd spray-paint them to freshen them up a bit before planting. I was also thinking about adding a floral garland to the posts on the porch. What do you think about that idea? Let's walk and talk, shall we?" Kinsley smiled. "I have sooo much to do."

Tilly patted her niece's arm as they walked. "No, I trust your judgment on the floral design. That's your wheel-house; I wouldn't dare touch it. Actually, I'm wondering what hors d'oeuvres to serve this year. Do I really have to serve a lobster dish *again*? Every event I host, we have lob-ster. Have you heard any chatter about what the other inns might be serving? I'm a bit lobstered out, to be honest." Her tone was weary, but then she smiled, causing her age lines to crinkle in the far corners of her eyes. Besides those lines, no one would ever guess her aunt was sixty-two. People often said she looked as if she were in her late forties, which always made Tilly throw her head back in laughter.

"I know you're about fished out, Aunt Tilly, but you have to remember, folks travel from all over for this event. They want the true southern Maine experience. Although you are blessed to have fresh lobster literally waiting for you in your backyard, most people don't have access to that. We're a bit spoiled here, you know." Kinsley grinned.

Tilly sighed. "Oh, I suppose you're right. I just want to stand out from my competition. Doesn't *everyone* on the tour serve lobster something or other?" She frowned, stopped midstride, and turned to face Kinsley, and then made funny fish lips at her.

Kinsley smiled at her animated attempt at a fish face but then turned serious. She placed her hands on her aunt's shoulders, looked intently into her eyes, and said, "I know how much pressure you put on yourself for everything to be absolutely perfect. Since you love to try new recipes, maybe you just need to create something different? Use the local ingredients but put your own spin on it. You really have a knack for that," Kinsley said, smacking her lips in anticipation of what her aunt might come up with.

"Thank you, darlin'. You're right, as always." Tilly moved a wisp of hair away from Kinsley's eyes, and Kinsley sensed the deep love in the gesture. "Maybe I'll make the usual lobster-type fare . . . but add a special finger food dessert." A new twinkle caught her eye.

"Exactly. And I'd be happy to sample test recipes—I haven't outgrown licking the bowl. You know, *someone* has to do the dirty work around here, and not just in the soil," Kinsley said, nudging playfully. "Let's face it. The other inns on the tour have *nothing* on you. Your delicious food and the hospitality you provide are the bee's knees," she added emphatically. "I can't help that I might be a little biased, too."

The two shared a wide smile and then they turned back toward the inn. Her aunt moved with a new urgency in her step and hurried a few strides ahead.

"Something deliciously chocolaty, and ooey gooey, and rot-your-teeth sugary," Tilly said in a faraway voice. "A finger food . . . something guests can grab and carry . . . but something they'll crave for days on end . . . something that will make them never forget their visit to the Salty Breeze Inn . . ."

"Now, that's the spirit!" Kinsley caught up to her aunt's pace before they made their way to the wraparound porch that faced the ocean. When they arrived at the bottom step, she handed her aunt the lunch basket. "Would you mind tucking the other half of my sandwich inside your refrigerator? I don't have time to run back to the cottage and put it in mine. I've got so much to do around here before sunset. I can pick it up later."

"I'll do one better; I'll eat it myself!" Tilly said with a laugh. "Then I can get going on digging into my recipe books to brainstorm and maybe kick some ideas around instead of wasting precious time making lunch for myself."

"Perfect. Help yourself," Kinsley offered, and then Tilly kissed her cheek and peeked inside the basket, as if in anticipation of what was inside, before walking up the grand wooden staircase, painted a crisp white, which led to the wide wraparound deck. The screen door closed softly behind her.

Kinsley noted the shovel she'd abandoned before her lunch break, waiting idly beside the withered hydrangea bush. She silently wondered how long it would take to remove the large bush, as she was anxious to dig into her own artistic juices and choose flowers that might work for the garland. In her mind, she had envisioned boxwood branches for the greenery base, with hints of sage and rosemary sprinkled throughout. And then adding pops of color using hot-pink and orange roses, along with white orchid flowers, and perhaps a touch of baby's breath to swag along the porch railing. The living garland was one idea she hadn't attempted before, and the inventiveness of mixing colors and textures was her favorite part of the gardening process—not necessarily the backbreaking work.

Although Kinsley was strong and capable, she'd recently hired a teen named Adam to help with the physical aspect of the job, as her client list had grown exponentially. She also hired out landscapers to keep up with maintenance after the initial design was in place. Today, however, since she was working at the inn, Adam was probably at home playing video games, and she was left digging on her own.

Kinsley plucked the work gloves from the ground where she'd abandoned them before lunch, laced her fingers into them, and immediately got to work. She pushed the round-pointed shovel into the earth, but because Harborside hadn't had a decent rain in over a week, the ground was tougher to maneuver than she'd anticipated. With shovel in hand, Kinsley walked over to the garden hose wrapped tightly on a large metal reel attached to the house. She decided to soak the ground before digging any further—an old trick her aunt had taught her when she was a young landscape gardener in training, and they'd removed a hearty overgrown juniper bush together.

As she was unwinding the reel and uncoiling the hose to adjust beneath the hydrangea, Kinsley noticed that the earth a few yards from the withered bush looked recently tilled, as if someone had dug into the soil there. It was unlike her aunt to do any of the digging around the shared property anymore; that had long been Kinsley's job. She wondered if her aunt had grown weary of waiting for her to do as promised and had attempted to work on the bush herself. As busy as Kinsley had been of late, she almost wouldn't blame her aunt for wanting to get a head start.

Perhaps something had been planted there. It was not the time for planting bulbs, though; that was done in the fall. Nor would there be any reason why seeds would be planted in that location, as it was tucked too close to other shrubbery. Whatever was planted there, it wasn't part of her landscape plan, so it would have to go. She did have a specific blueprint, after all, of how the landscape should appear, despite the work not yet accomplished.

Kinsley's curiosity won out and she walked over and forced the shovel into the fresh earth. When she did so, she hit something hard, but not a rock. She continued to thrust the blade around in the dirt, until something slowly surfaced that she couldn't initially place, something that didn't belong buried within the ground. A mud-caked pink high-heeled shoe emerged, the sparkles dulled by grime and soil.

Kinsley sucked in a breath, her mind flashing to the previous night's news report. The police had been searching for a shoe connected to a recent murder victim whose body was found a few miles from the inn.

Unfortunately, she'd dug up more than she'd bargained for.

The missing shoe.

A major clue in a crime the police had dubbed "the Cinderella murder" was sitting accusingly on her shovel.

Chapter 2

Bile rose in Kinsley's throat as she paced back and forth, her eyes never leaving the shoe. She knew if she told her aunt Tilly what she'd unearthed, there'd be no going back from that revelation and the implications of it. Surely it might suggest that foul play had occurred on their property. Had this been the actual scene of the crime? Was one of Aunt Tilly's guests somehow connected to the murder? Or worse, would the authorities look accusingly at her aunt? And assume that Tilly buried the shoe there? Each subsequent thought was worse than the last.

Kinsley's mind boomeranged to the previous night's newscast. The broadcaster had stood in front of yellow crime scene tape, shooting a live feed from a local potato field, roughly eight miles away. The tender potato shoots were barely peeking out of the soil. The body of a woman had been found. The victim had allegedly been shot with a gun. And she was missing a shoe. A sparkly pink high-heeled shoe. The broadcaster had held up a picture of the shoe, found exclusively at Mallards, an elite retail shop located in downtown Harborside, and the video feed zoomed into focus. His words still echoed in her mind: *"If we find that shoe, we find our killer."*

That shoe.

The thumping of Kinsley's heart was becoming keenly audible to her own ears. The sound pulsated, as if she could hear each physical beat like a soft throb. She stopped midpace and stared at the mud-caked heel. The filthy shoe had the potential to change everything.

Kinsley could already envision a problematic future. Newscasters from across Maine, or even nationwide— commentators peppered across the landscape, all pointing accusingly at the shoe. Not exactly the self-promotion she had hoped for, because it would smear the inn's stellar reputation for being a safe and beautiful place in which to vacation and find rest. After all, who would show up for the Walk Inns event if they found out a murder occurred here?

How on earth did it get here?

It was obvious the dirt was freshly moved. Kinsley knelt on one knee and sifted the dark soil through her gloved fingers. She held it to her nose. The dirt came from a different source—about this, she was sure. It was darker than what was inherently found in coastal Maine, and it didn't capture the same earthy scent. A potting soil, perhaps?

Kinsley weighed her options. What happened to the victim was tragic, no doubt, but she knew providing the shoe to the police *right now* wasn't going to bring the woman back to life. It might help with the investigation . . . but where would it lead? Found here, surely it would implicate Aunt Tilly as a suspect.

Maybe she could wait until after the big event, happening two weeks from Saturday, and then share her findings with the police. But that might be too long. Maybe someone had found it and placed it here to smear her aunt's inn's reputation in time for the Walk Inns? As a cruel, heinous joke? Her mind was racing in circles imagining the possibilities, making her erratic heart thump faster and her mouth grow drier.

What Kinsley needed was time to think.

She dropped to both knees and with her fingers dug frantically at the loose soil to create a deeper hole, hoping to a higher power that she wouldn't find anything more than what she'd already uncovered. Sweat dripped down her brow, and she wiped it away with her forearm. When she was convinced there was nothing else hidden beneath the earth, Kinsley dropped the shoe in the new hole, covered it with a mound of dirt, and patted it flat with her hands. She then looked desperately over her shoulder to be sure no one was watching. However, while she frantically covered the hole, it still bothered her that part of the soil was a tad darker than the rest, because she knew for a fact she wasn't the one who'd put it there. So, this was deliberate. Could the dirt have come from the potato field where the victim was found? It was the only thing that made sense, wasn't it?

"Kinsley honey . . . where are you?"

Kinsley's eyes flew to the sound of her aunt's voice, and she clutched her heart. She watched through what was left of the withered hydrangea bush as Tilly enthusiastically hurried down the porch steps and made her way toward her.

"Kinsley!"

"Over here!" Kinsley popped her head out from the brush. Had her aunt seen what she'd done? She rose and dusted the soil from her knees before greeting her.

"Sweetheart, are you okay? You look a little flushed!" Tilly reached a hand to touch the warmth of Kinsley's cheek, but her niece headed her off at the pass and brushed her away with one hand.

Kinsley forced a weak smile. "I'm fine. This hydrangea is just giving me a run for my money." She attempted to block her aunt from seeing the recently dug-up soil and kept direct eye contact so Tilly wouldn't grill her any further. Instead, Kinsley redirected with a question. "What's got you so excited?" She smacked her gloves together to rid them of the dirt and then put her hands to her hips and waited expectantly. Hoping sheer panic wasn't written all over her face.

"The press is coming! The *Maine Gazette* wants to highlight the Salty Breeze Inn in their next issue. The woman on the phone said she wants to do a story on the Walk Inns, and she's chosen me to interview! Can you believe it? Out of all the other inns she could've chosen, she wants to interview ME!" Tilly jutted a thumb to her heart. "Me . . . in the local *newspaper*! Finally, our little inn here is getting a chance!" her aunt gushed.

Kinsley's smiled faded and she quietly sucked in a breath. She began to chew nervously on the inside of her cheek. "When is she coming? Did she say?"

"Well, *now* . . . she's coming over right now!" Tilly raked her hands through her tousled hair. "Oh, I must be a mess, huh? Do you think she'll take a photo of me? Or the Salty Breeze Inn? Which photo will they highlight for the story, do you think?" She laughed nervously, as if the realization just hit, and she was nowhere near prepared for any kind of interview.

Kinsley cleared her throat. "I'm certainly hoping it's one of you. I'm not at all ready for any outside photographs of the inn. Any chance you could stall her, maybe? Give me a few more days?" Kinsley blew her breath out slowly as if deflating a party balloon. The last thing they needed was anyone eyeing the details of the yard. Or taking photographs.

Especially now. When everything seemed to indicate that either a crime had taken place on their property or they were being framed for murder.

"Oh. I'm sorry, I didn't think of that. I got so caught up in the idea that they want to interview me. Little ole ME! You know that I read the newspaper every single morning. It's the highlight of my day! This is a real treat! I didn't even consider the landscape not being finished. You don't have the containers planted yet, do you?" Tilly turned to regard the empty urns left in a heap beside the porch.

"No, I haven't. And as I mentioned, I was planning to spray-paint them first and let them dry overnight before I filled them. Are you sure you can't hold the press off for a few days?" Kinsley's arms dropped by her sides and her shoulders slumped in defeat.

"A few *days*? I don't think I can. The event is a few weeks away, and this would really be a good marketing plug for us. I've never had the privilege of an interview before. They've always chosen someone else . . ." Her voice trailed off, the disappointment now glaringly obvious.

"I know." The ham sandwich that she'd so enjoyed earlier began to gurgle in Kinsley's stomach. "I'm sorry, it's my fault I'm not further along by now. I had all good intentions today. I really did."

A lull fell between them as they both wrestled with their own respective thoughts.

"Wait. I have an idea!" Kinsley snapped her fingers. "Why don't you give her a photo from last year? Or one of those ones you used for advertisements? I doubt anyone besides us will notice a few changes to the landscape. What do you think?"

"Maybe . . ." Tilly shrugged, clearly not overly convinced.

"I thought we took a few with you standing out in front, didn't we?"

She could almost see the thoughts churning in Tilly's mind as her aunt slowly nodded her head in agreement. Kinsley nudged her aunt in the direction of the staircase leading up to the porch before Tilly had a chance to think more on it.

"You'd better hurry up and get ready, too. A bit of hairspray in your hair and a refresher of lipstick in case she wants a shot of you. I mean a photo of you—not a shot!" she added, nervously blinking her eyes in rapid succession.

Hadn't that reporter said the Cinderella killer used a gun?

Kinsley sensed her own growing agitation. She knew by the choice of her words she wouldn't be able to hide this secret for long.

Her mind flew back to the time she'd skipped school with her friends, and how her aunt had known, without her even uttering a word, that she had lied. The school had believed it when her friend had called it in and said that she was sick. But something about the way Kinsley had returned home that afternoon tipped her aunt off. Tilly had known immediately that Kinsley hadn't been where she was supposed to be. She wondered if she had the same dumb look on her face now. The one that had made Tilly finally corner her to tell the truth.

But how could she share this information with her aunt now? With the press on their way over? How could she possibly share that a very important clue to an ongoing investigation was beneath the earth on which they now stood? The stress was rising in every muscle in her body, but thankfully, her aunt seemed preoccupied with her own thoughts.

Kinsley nudged Tilly again with her arm. "Go on. It'll be fine," she said, feeling less than credible.

"Okay, I'll look on the computer for a photo from my marketing collection. I agree, that might work." Tilly slowly turned back in the direction of the inn.

"Aunt Tilly?"

"Yes, darlin'?"

"Can I ask you something?"

Tilly turned back to face her. "Sure, of course. What is it?"

"Have you been doing any work out here in the yard?"

"Don't be silly." Tilly waved a hand of dismissal. "That's your domain. I wouldn't dare touch it unless I asked you first. You know that."

"So, you haven't been doing any digging? Or have you noticed any of your guests messing around out here?" Kinsley leaned in closer and studied her aunt's reaction.

Tilly looked at Kinsley like she'd just fallen off her rocker. "What is wrong with you, child? That hydrangea bush died all on its own. These things happen sometimes . . . there's nothing you could've done to prevent it. Now, is that what you're so worked up about?"

"No, never mind, it's nothing. You better go and get ready. Every minute we stand out here talking is another minute of time you're losing. And time is of the essence. I'm sure you have a slew of fresh guests coming to check in soon, too. Are your rooms prepared? Three o'clock is only a few hours away, and now with a pending interview, you're losing valuable time." Kinsley pointed to her wrist even though she wasn't wearing a watch. "Hopefully no one is looking for an early check-in today. Go on ahead. I'll try to make myself invisible to the press, okay?"

"No worries. The *Gazette* might want to interview you, too. You don't have to make yourself scarce on my account. They have to know we're all working tirelessly to prepare for the Walk Inns." Tilly smiled, but her shoulders were hunched, and she walked back toward the porch with far less enthusiasm than when she'd come out.

Kinsley watched as Tilly moved up the steps and then over the threshold leading into the inn. She hadn't meant to burst her aunt's bubble, but the last thing in the world she wanted was to be interviewed by the press and have them share what she'd uncovered, or worse, tip off the local authorities and have them probing around the property with accusing eyes and damaging her landscape. One thing she was certain of from her aunt's reaction, Tilly hadn't buried the shoe. But that didn't mean people wouldn't suspect her of it, simply because it had been found here.

Kinsley studied the dirt she'd recently compacted and stood with her hands on her hips, chewing the inside of her cheek. Although it was against her better judgment, she knew she couldn't tell *anyone* what she'd discovered.

At least not yet.

Chapter 3

Even though a reporter from the *Maine Gazette* was en route to the Salty Breeze Inn, Kinsley decided to go ahead and move forward with her plans to remove the withered hydrangea bush. She had a limited amount of time to accomplish her work before the big event, leaving her little choice. The rest of the week, she was booked to design and execute the landscapes for several other entrants of the Walk Inns, and she just couldn't fall further behind. Besides, her adrenaline was pumping, and that would give her the extra muscle and nudge needed to do the job.

With the hose now soaking the roots beneath the bush, and the brittle branches cut back and removed so that Kinsley wouldn't scrape up her arms, she plunged the pointed shovel down into the earth. Instinctively, she encircled the roots and began to rock the shovel back and forth. She worked her way methodically around each side of the bush, but her eyes couldn't help but occasionally dart back to the newly compacted earth a few yards from her position. Kinsley hoped she was not contaminating a potential crime scene by continuing with her work. Nothing led her to believe that anything else occurred there, though, because the only evidence she'd uncovered was that awful shoe. And if she did happen to uncover anything else, she'd be left with no other choice than to immediately alert the authorities. However, she downright refused to leave a dead bush in the landscape for the upcoming event. Especially with Sea-Scapes' superior reputation for landscape perfection.

She couldn't seem to stop worrying about it, though. Maybe she was making a grave mistake by not immediately calling the police. Was her aunt in imminent danger? What if someone responsible for the crime *had* been a guest at the inn . . . or worse . . . what if that someone was still on the guest list? Was her aunt housing a killer?

She wished she'd paid closer attention to the newscast now. If only she'd recorded the nightly broadcast so she could rewind it on her DVR.

Kinsley shuddered.

Maybe she should inconspicuously peek at the guest list, to see if anyone could be a potential suspect. What did she know about the names on that list, though? Would anything even stand out to her? Not only that, but what connection would they have to the victim? She knew nothing of the poor woman who was left lifeless in the potato field. But she needed to be sure of her aunt's safety—this was of the highest importance. At the very least, she would convince Tilly to stay in the caretaker's cottage with her for a few days.

As her mind struggled to make sense of the situation, the hearty bush suddenly came loose, as if Kinsley were a dentist removing a tooth with a pair of forceps. She dropped the shovel and pulled at what was left of the root ball with a hearty tug.

"Hey, Kinsley!"

She was so preoccupied with her own thoughts that the sound of her name startled her. She dropped the root ball, sat back on her heels, and threw her soiled hands to her chest.

"Oh, Kins, I'm so sorry! I didn't mean to startle you!" Kinsley's best friend, Becca, stood awkwardly on her tiptoes trying to avoid digging her high-heeled shoes into the earth. Her hair, the color of velvety black petunias, was tied in a messy bun atop her head, but she still looked completely put together in a gray suit jacket, cream-colored silky blouse, and pencil skirt.

"No, it's not you, it's me. I'm so distracted with yanking this bush, I didn't see you coming. Sorry to be so jumpy." Kinsley recovered as she wiped the soil from her shirt and jeans and stood to greet her friend. She didn't dare reach for a hug, though, as she eyed Becca's work attire again. The suit looked expensive.

Becca must have noticed Kinsley's eyes pinballing the ground. "You certainly are a little distracted today, aren't you? Everything okay?"

Kinsley appreciated her friend's concern, but she wasn't ready to share. Instead, she redirected the conversation and gave her full attention to Becca. "Don't you look lovely today. New client? Or did you have a hot lunch date? Please tell!"

Becca nodded. "Uh-huh, thanks." She smiled, showing gleaming, recently whitened teeth. Then she looked down at her pencil skirt and plucked off a random piece of lint before smoothing the skirt with her hand. "Tilly said you were out here working, and I just thought I'd catch you for a moment."

"Wait. So, which is it? A date? Or a client? Who's got you looking all gussied up? Don't try and dodge the question. Inquiring minds want to know." Kinsley knew she was overreaching by getting chatty about Becca's latest lover, but the change of subject was warranted. Getting her best friend involved in what she'd recently unearthed would only compound the problem and drag Becca into the mess she now found herself in.

"A client."

"Ah, I was hoping you had a second date with that hot guy from the gym. What's his name? Jordy something or other? Has he called you back?" Kinsley removed her gardening gloves, tucked them into her back pocket, and then smoothed the hair off her face that had fallen away from her braid, yet again.

"Nope. And I'm not holding my breath. Thanks for bringing that up, though. It sure is nice to know I'm being ignored. I guess I'll have to find a new gym now, on top of everything else." Becca rolled her eyes and laughed.

"So . . . what brings you over? I'm surprised you didn't just shoot me a text."

"I was in the neighborhood, and I needed to ask you a favor."

"Well, I was hoping for sexy gossip to break up my workday, but I guess we're not discussing fun stuff right now," Kinsley teased. "What's up?"

"Hey, I'm totally up for discussing fun stuff. Speaking of . . . What's going on with you and Pete?" Becca shot back with an accusing finger.

Kinsley wasn't in the mood to discuss Pete right now, either. That conversation—a never-ending loop. She waved a hand of dismissal. "Oh no, we're not going there. I'd much rather hear about your shenanigans with men than chase after my own right now. Especially with everything I've got going on around here. I'm swamped. The last thing I have time for is dating." Kinsley's eyes zoomed back to where the root ball lay waiting to be tossed into the compost pile. "In fact, I really need to get back to work. Not trying to be rude, but my week is full. Overbooked, to be honest." She placed the back of her hand to her forehead and held it there as if suddenly totally overwhelmed.

"Okay, okay, I don't mean to scare you off by mentioning Pete's name." Becca grinned. "I know you're super busy, and I'm sorry to interrupt you. I wouldn't stop over to bother you if I didn't really need something." Becca's voice softened, and she tilted to one side on her tiptoes and almost lost her balance as she attempted to stop her high heel from sinking farther and deeper into the earth.

Kinsley reached out a hand to help Becca balance. "Yeah, sure, no problem. Anything for you, my dear. Now. Whaddya need?"

Becca paused before the words tumbled out of her mouth. "I might need your landscaping services. I'm hoping you have time and can squeeze me in. Pretty please? With sugar on top?" Becca put praying hands together and waited.

"*Me?* For what?" Kinsley removed her gloves from her back pocket, gave them a little shake, and put them back on.

"I just left a listing appointment with the Wilcoxes. You know the Wilcoxes? They own that oceanfront estate down the cliff walk?" She waved her hand as if to show the home was far to the left from where they stood. "Over on the marina side. They're thinking of selling, and as you know, summer is the optimal time for oceanfront property to go." Becca grinned. "I told them I'd stage the house with fresh florals right up until we're in escrow. I think they really liked the idea of the added special touch." Her golden eyes, the color of sunflower centers, danced with excitement. "Have you seen that house? It's a mansion! And *that* close to the marina? Can you imagine the buyers I would meet? I really hope I get this listing." She crossed her fingers. "They're interviewing two other Realtors and then they said they'd be in touch." It was obvious Kinsley's best friend was giddy with excitement.

"Yes, I've seen it, and it's a beautiful home. That would be terrific for you. What a commission if you land it! I really hope you get this one, Becca," Kinsley said, encouraging her friend with a nod.

"I was going to send over a floral thank-you as a reminder of what we could provide. So . . . if you could help me pick out some lavish flowers that would speak to the exclusive clientele? That's your sweet spot. What do you say? Will you help me with the floral staging, too, if I get the listing? I couldn't possibly find anyone else that tops your work. I mean, look at this place." It was then her eyes left Kinsley's and Becca scanned the yard, smiling.

Kinsley hoped she wouldn't ask what was recently buried not far beneath their own two feet. She felt a sudden rush of heat to her cheeks.

She shook her head as if to recalibrate her brain.

"Pleeeeze? If I get it . . . will you? Pleeezzze?" Becca sounded like a child at a grocery store, begging for candy. "Even if I don't get it, I'm still planning to send over a bouquet . . . it's professional and the right thing to do."

Kinsley hated to commit to anything else right now. But if it came to Becca needing something, she knew she would cave. "Of course you'll get the listing. I have complete faith that you will. And when you do, I'll certainly be there for you."

"You're the best!" Becca clapped her hands with excitement.

"I have just the right the array of flowers we could use . . . we'll make use of what's currently in season. It'll be beautiful, I promise."

"Oh, get those creative juices flowing, girl. This listing could potentially catapult my career!" Becca grinned and then pumped a fist high in the air.

Kinsley knew it wasn't easy for Becca to land the elite houses on a listing appointment. Most of her listings tended to be on the outskirts of town, or outside of Harborside altogether, mostly in the $300K range. Not like the million-dollar properties and mansions she hoped would one day fill her portfolio and client list. She'd tried on many occasions, but unfortunately the sellers had gone with a competitive Realtor—one who seemed to hold all the million-dollar listings in the area in his tightly buttoned pocket.

"Thank you so much for your willingness to do this, with everything else you've got going on. I really do appreciate it, hon." Becca reached out to touch her arm in gratitude.

"You bet. You'd do the same for me." Kinsley nodded, with a smile. "You've always been there for me when I needed you, ever since we met in swim class. Boy, we're really getting old, aren't we?" She grinned. "I wouldn't even be here if you hadn't saved me from drowning on more than one occasion," she said, teasing.

Becca shook her head and laughed. "If it wasn't for my water wings, we both would've drowned!"

"Good times, good times," Kinsley cajoled, and warmly reflected on the memory they'd shared and the beginnings of a lasting friendship.

"Since we've always been there for each other, can I

share something else with you that's really bothering me?" Becca's smile faded, and she turned serious. "Honestly, before my listing appointment, I really was hoping for some good news. I *need* this commission now more than ever. The last twenty-four hours have been rough going." Becca hung her head and shook it slowly.

"Oh no." Kinsley reached out for her friend. "What did I miss?"

Normally the two spoke every evening on the phone and kept up to date on the highs and lows of their day. Last night, however, Kinsley was beat, and they opted to catch up later. Now she wished she'd taken the time, as obviously something of great significance was bothering her best friend.

Suddenly the two were interrupted by the sound of conversation floating across the yard, carried over to them by the west wind. Kinsley assumed the *Maine Gazette* reporter must've arrived.

"Is that who I think it is?" Becca squinted, as if to get a better visual. Then her eyes grew wide like saucers, and she nudged Kinsley with her elbow. "Yeah! It is! Oh . . . MY . . . word! That's the guy from channel four news!"

"What?" Kinsley's head snapped in the direction of a man holding a microphone, and a camera man lagging not too far behind. Both were heading swiftly in their direction.

"What in the world?" Kinsley uttered. Her blood pressure was beginning to show signs of an uptick. She needed to contain herself, and quickly.

"Do you have any idea what they are doing here?" Becca leaned in, conspiratorially.

"No . . . I have no idea." Kinsley's stomach lurched. Yep, her blood pressure was officially rising. "Aunt Tilly mentioned someone was coming from the *Maine Gazette* for an interview. *Not* a reporter from the six o'clock news."

And not just any news reporter, but the one who broke the Cinderella story the previous night.

Kinsley's eyes darted to the newly compacted earth, to be sure nothing was peeking from the soil, and then back toward the men traipsing rapidly toward them, and sucked in a breath.

"Hey, here's your chance to meet a new guy . . . literally coming in your direction . . . dropped not far from your front doorstep . . ." Becca said out of the side of her mouth, and then subconsciously smoothed her skirt again. "I hear he's single . . . Don't blow it," she sang softly.

Kinsley swatted her friend with the back of her hand.

Where on earth was Aunt Tilly?

Finally, the two men were standing in front of them, and the one with the microphone switched hands and then jutted out his right one in greeting. Kinsley accepted his warm hand in hers.

"Roy Maxton, channel four news. Great to meet you." He pumped her hand like he was rapidly filling an old-fashioned water pump; hearty and strong. "I'm guessing you're Kinsley?" His eyes moved between the two women, and it didn't go unnoticed that he'd done a quick once-over of Becca before meeting Kinsley's eyes once again.

Kinsley must've looked like a deer in the headlights, because Roy added. "Your aunt Matilda is inside with the *Maine Gazette*. She told me I could find you out here digging in the yard. Let me explain why I'm here. I have an insider colleague over at the newspaper who suggested a quick piece on the Walk Inns, and I thought, what a terrific idea! The station is looking for more local feel-good stories. So here I am!" He leaned back and held out his arms dramatically. "I hear you're the one who handles the majority of the landscapes for these homes up and down the coast in preparation for the big event. How about an interview?" he said with a wide smile. Roy's auburn hair, the color of changing leaves in autumn, was full but hung neatly over his ears, and it looked as if he was wearing makeup. Kinsley couldn't help but study him. He wore more makeup than she did. Her style always leaned more to the natural. But then again, she wasn't a local television celebrity who needed to be camera-ready.

"Well? How about it?" he prompted.

"You want to interview me *now*?" Kinsley looked down at her soiled knees.

"Bad timing?"

"You think?" The words spilled sarcastically out of her mouth before she had a chance to retrieve them. It wasn't her attire or the lack of her own makeup that was the real issue, though. Kinsley's eyes lasered toward the loose earth. She hoped she'd done a decent job covering the shoe.

Becca held her lips with her fingers and slowly shook her head, as if to nudge her friend to lose the sarcasm.

Apparently, her comment had come out way more abrupt than she'd meant it to.

Roy reached into his black blazer pocket and flipped out a business card and held it between two fingers. "Give me a call when you're ready, okay? The sooner, the better, though, as the event is coming up fast, which is why I took the initiative. I won't do that again," he promised her.

The thing was, Kinsley was concerned about bringing needless attention to the Salty Breeze Inn. She wrestled with it, though, as it would be tremendous marketing for the inn, especially if he held the interview directly in front of it. In fact, her aunt was probably the one who pushed the idea to hold the interview right away anyhow, before the station would have a chance to change its mind.

"I suppose I could go and get cleaned up a bit, if you give me a minute," Kinsley said with hesitation.

"Hey, I understand. How about this. Why don't I go and grab lunch, and we'll meet you back here after?" Roy pushed, as his eyes confirmed the idea with the cameraman.

Kinsley gave an internal sigh of relief. "That sounds perfect. I'll meet you back here in say . . . an hour? And listen, I'm terribly sorry for my initial reaction, you just caught me off guard, and I have so much to do to prepare for this event." She hoped her comment brought the tension between them down a notch, but she could feel it rising in her shoulders, nonetheless.

Disregarding her apology, Roy patted the cameraman on the shoulder and then turned back to face her and said, "We'll be back." Then Roy and the cameraman turned on their heels and walked back in the direction of the inn.

"Wowza," Becca finally said when the two were out of earshot. "I can't believe you're going to be on TV. How exciting!"

"Yeah, thrilling," Kinsley said with far less enthusiasm.

"What's wrong? Camera-shy?" Becca nudged. "This will be great exposure, for Tilly, too, since it sounds like they're conducting the interview here. This is great publicity for the Salty Breeze. Your aunt is gonna be thrilled!" Becca said with a smile. After a moment her smile faded, though, and she added, "I should've asked Roy after the introductions . . . when I had the chance."

"Asked him what, exactly?"

"If he's heard of any updates regarding the Cinderella killer while he was hanging around the news station. Since he was the one who broke the story on the news last night, he might know more."

Kinsley's stomach flip-flopped. "Why on earth would

you ask him about that?" She placed her hands firmly on her hips and waited. "That would be a horrible thing to bring up!"

"Remember how a few days ago, I told you I was meeting a new client this afternoon?" Becca waited, and then she continued to prompt Kinsley's memory with a roll of the hand and adding, "The gal who potentially had deep pockets and was looking for oceanside property?"

"Yeah, I remember. I don't know what any of that has to do with this, though?" Kinsley sighed with relief as the two men stepped over the threshold and disappeared into the inn.

"Did she cancel on you?"

"No. Worse."

Kinsley waited for what seemed like an uncomfortably long pause and then she heard Becca's words echo hollowly in her ears.

"She's dead."

Chapter 4

"Wait. What? Hang on a second. What do you *mean* 'she's dead'?" Kinsley's eyes narrowed in on Becca and she held her breath waiting for a response. A response she dreaded to hear come out of her best friend's mouth.

"The gal who the police found. The one the broadcasters have been referring to as 'the Cinderella murder.'" Becca held up her fingers in air quotes.

Kinsley nodded and, with a sick feeling in her stomach, waited.

"Yeah, um, that just happened to be my new client. Her name's Daisy Davis."

"Oh no. Really?"

"Yeah, really. I didn't get a chance to tell you, because after I got your text last night, I figured you needed rest. I didn't think it would be fair to keep you up all night with that kind of news. Personally, I had to take a Benadryl to knock me out, I was so upset about it." Becca shuddered.

"This can't be happening—" Kinsley massaged her neck with her fingers before continuing. She almost blew the secret but stopped herself.

"What can't be happening?"

"Had you met Daisy?" Kinsley scrutinized the ground that had been recently compacted with her own two hands, and then returned her gaze to meet her best friend's.

"Once. We met over at her hotel room. And it was a brief encounter, as she mentioned she was super late for another appointment. Although I didn't really believe that. It seemed like just an excuse to get rid of me. Her eyes kept darting around the room and focusing on the closed bathroom door, as if there was someone in there she didn't want me to see. I dunno." Becca threw up her hands in frustration. "Maybe she didn't want to expose an affair, or something like that? She just seemed weird, you know? Cautious. In fact, before she arrived in town, I had suggested she stay here at the Salty Breeze Inn, but she refused and mentioned she didn't think your aunt's place would have enough security."

"Security? Huh, that's weird. It's not like she's famous. Is she? I mean, *was* she?" Kinsley let this thought marinate in her mind. "That was your only meeting with her, then. Did you have any other conversations or meetings set up?"

"Well, she asked if I'd run an online search of oceanfront properties and email them over to her. After she chose a few, I was planning on setting up a few showing appointments— and that's clearly not happening now." Becca blew out a frustrated breath that sounded like a whistle. "She had a very high budget, too. *Very* high. We're talking exclusive." To drive the point home Becca rubbed her fingers together as if showing cash.

"She stayed at a hotel?" Kinsley asked. "So clearly, she's not a local?"

"No, Daisy grew up around here but she's now living in New York City and just came to Harborside for a long weekend. I assume she works back in the city." Becca shrugged. "I mean, *worked* in the city," she added with a wince.

"Doing what? Do you know what she did for a living?"

"Boy, you seem to have a lot of interest in this person. What gives?" Becca's face scrunched, as if she'd just eaten a jalapeño. Her face always looked like that when she and Kinsley went out for spicy Mexican food and the salsa was a tad too hot for her.

Should she tell Becca her secret? Kinsley could feel the heat rise in her face. How could she? Her gnawing conscience didn't give her much of a choice. She reached out for her friend and clutched Becca desperately on the arm.

"I have to tell you something."

Becca's spine straightened, as she must've understood the significance of Kinsley's tone and the sudden death grip on her arm, because a new wave of alarm covered her face.

"What's going on, Kinsley?"

"Do you want to know the real reason why I'm not at all thrilled about the interview with channel four news?"

A pause fell between them while Becca waited patiently, and Kinsley looked around to make sure no one was in earshot—particularly anyone from the *Maine Gazette*. She pointed a shaky finger toward the loose earth.

"Over there." Kinsley's voice quavered.

Despite her pencil skirt and heels, Becca maneuvered in the direction of her friend's extended finger, careful not to plunge her heels back into the soil.

"What? Over here? Where?" Becca followed her lead when Kinsley moved and pointed, even closer to the dirt. "What is *wrong*? Clearly, you're upset, and this isn't about pulling out a sad-looking bush that's ready for the compost pile. Is it?" She frowned, and confusion riddled her face.

"I found the shoe," Kinsley whispered.

After uttering the words, the implications of the situation felt far more real. Especially when she saw the stunned look flash across Becca's face.

"What?"

"Beneath that mound of dirt over there . . ." Kinsley flicked her pointer finger rapidly up and down.

Becca's face remained perplexed.

"The shoe. The shoe!" Kinsley squealed, then covered her mouth with her hand to quiet herself. "I mean the other one—from the Cinderella murder. Daisy's shoe . . . It's buried under there."

Becca's face turned ashen. "You're kidding, right?"

"Oh, how I wish I was." Kinsley shook her head as she began to pace back and forth, her eyes lasered in on the earth.

"You found it *today*? Just now? Before I arrived?"

Kinsley nodded; she knew her eyes must've been laced with fear, because her friend was now mirroring them.

When Becca regained her composure she said, "No wonder you were acting so weird with Roy. It's not like you to snap at people like that. I think I could count on one hand the number of times you've reacted sarcastically. Why didn't you call the police?" Her tone was not accusatory, merely confused.

"When? How?" Kinsley said defensively. "I literally just dug it up, and then I hear the *Maine Gazette* is on their way over. Can you imagine the exposé? They'd be thrilled to break that type of story, I'm sure. And at Aunt Tilly's expense? I don't think so! Can you imagine the implication if they assumed my aunt was the one who buried it there?" Kinsley could feel the anger rising with each word, and she shook her head in defiance of any such idea.

"No, wait a minute." Becca held up her hands in defense. "Don't get upset, I hear you," Becca added soothingly.

Kinsley didn't know if she could stop this rolling emotional train. She was already moving past upset and rapidly into completely freaked-out mode.

"But what are you going to do?" Becca whispered. "You can't just leave it there and pretend you never saw it! It's a crucial piece of evidence in an ongoing homicide investigation."

"I realize that, but I can't call the police *now*. I just need to wait a little while longer. We can't have Roy from channel four coming back to the police scattered across the lawn!" Kinsley slapped her hand to her forehead. "I'm sure he'd love to do a piece on this, too!" Her voice rose to an uncomfortable octave. "The lawn would be covered with reporters from Maine to Boston and potentially across the entire United States! Do you have any idea how fast this kind of news travels? I'm sure the Cinderella murder will hit the national news if it hasn't already."

"Okay, I see your point. Not only that, but murders like this don't happen in Harborside. Did you hear during the news conference that they said this type of crime hasn't happened here in, like, forty years? It's really got the town on edge."

Kinsley flinched. "Yep. And now a major clue is literally beneath our feet."

"This is a real conundrum." Becca puffed out her cheeks like a blowfish and then slowly exhaled.

"I know, right?" Kinsley said, kneading her forehead for answers. "I honestly don't know what to do."

"It's not as easy as handing you my water wings for this one." Becca let out a nervous giggle to break the tension.

The comment did little to ease it, although she did crack a smile.

Kinsley's pacing halted and the two stared at the covered ground.

"What do I do? What would you do if you were in my shoes? There I go with a shoe comment." Kinsley slapped her forehead. "This could ruin everything for Aunt Tilly. Not only the Walk Inns, but this is her bread and butter! Who'd want to stay overnight here with the thought that a murderer could be lurking in the next bedroom! Or worse, what if someone thinks my aunt had something to do with this? Just saying it aloud sickens me!" Kinsley whispered.

"Yeah, I can see you're in a bit of a pickle." Becca winced.

"You think? Oh crud, Becs . . . What should I *do*?" Kinsley covered her face in her hands and her friend reached over and put her arm loosely around her shoulder and gave an encouraging squeeze.

"Kinsley, I know you feel responsible for your aunt's happiness. And I know you've always tried to compensate for that. But you can't do that to yourself now."

Kinsley wiped her eyes with the sleeve of her shirt. "What do you mean?"

"You told me a long time ago that Aunt Tilly's boyfriend Jonathan left her because she took you and your brother in after your parents passed. But that's not why he left, Kins. He left because he didn't have the same dream. Jonathan didn't want to run the Salty Breeze Inn, remember?"

"Yes, and if it wasn't for me and my brother, she would've met someone else and had kids of her own."

"You *are* her kids. Don't do this to yourself. She's always loved you as her very own, and you know that. She wanted to refurbish this old mansion and build a business and she wanted you and Kyle with her. And she followed that dream. Just look at this place." Becca swung a hand wide to demonstrate the beauty that surrounded them.

"Yeah, now you understand! This is exactly why I need to protect it. But more importantly, I need to protect my aunt. She's a mother to me, Becs, I can't let her down."

"Hellooo, ladies!" The two snapped their heads in the direction of the porch, where Tilly was now rushing down the stairs with the newspaper reporter on her heels.

Kinsley rapidly blinked, to clear her tear-filled eyes.

"You look fine," Becca encouraged. "Don't worry."

"Academy Award performance, Becca. Can you do that for me?" Kinsley whispered as she lifted the side of her shirt to dab her eyes one last time before the arrival of their guests.

"Oh boy, I'm not sure I like this. Now suddenly I'm an accessory to a crime! I've never been an accessory to a crime!" Becca said between clenched teeth, and then lifted her lips in a genuine smile and tugged to tighten her messy bun before greeting the oncoming women.

"Accessory to a crime? What do you mean? I didn't do anything! I didn't put it there!" Kinsley whispered. "This isn't my fault!" she added through her own gritted teeth.

"I didn't say it was your fault, but, girlfriend, you're withholding evidence. Surely that's considered a crime. I think you could actually do jail time for this," Becca warned. "I saw that on a TV show once. Someone withholding evidence went to jail . . . I can't remember what show . . ." Her voice trailed off.

Kinsley hadn't exactly thought about it that way. In her entire life, she hadn't so much as received a parking ticket or

incurred a fee for an overdue library book. This was a first.
Never had she broken the law. She was a law-abiding citizen!

Breaking the law had been the last thing that had crossed
Kinsley's mind until Becca had brought it up. Instead, she'd
been all too consumed with protecting the woman who
had always protected her, Aunt Tilly. But Becca's words
had merit. Kinsley knew the longer she waited, the worse it
would get. Without thinking clearly, she'd unintentionally
made a bad call by reburying the shoe. The shame coursed
through her body, but she ignored it, because her aunt and
the newspaper reporter had arrived in front of them.

Tilly's eyes held brief concern as, with a tilt of her head,
she looked at Kinsley. Kinsley brushed off her aunt's worry
by saying, "I had an eyelash in my eye," while encouraging
Tilly to return her attention back to the group.

"Well, ladies, I'm pleased as punch to introduce you to
Charlotte Cummings, from the *Maine Gazette*." Tilly beamed
as she looked lovingly toward her niece, who now held out a
hand in greeting. Becca greeted the woman next.

Charlotte was tall and broad-shouldered. Her gray hair
was cropped short, but she looked as if her hair had gone
gray prematurely, as not a wrinkle could be seen on her
olive complexion. Her smile was warm and inviting.

"Nice to meet you both." Charlotte's eyes, the color of
morning glories, moved between them.

"Charlotte was just finishing up her interview with me,
Kinsley, but I told her I'd be remiss if I didn't at least introduce her to the famous owner of SeaScapes. Seeing as how
you work tirelessly on many of the landscapes for the Walk
Inns participants, I thought it only fitting." Tilly beamed.

It was evident Aunt Tilly was proud of her, and the gush-
ing warmed Kinsley's heart, but she couldn't help but blush
at the compliment.

"I reminded her how you were featured in an exclusive for *Coastal Living* last year! I even showed Charlotte the article," Tilly continued.

"Yes, she did share that with me. And I must say, the landscape here is stunning!" Charlotte toured the property with her eyes, before returning to them. "Absolutely beautiful. You've done an amazing job here."

"Thank you for saying that. It's still a work in progress, but hopefully I'll have it ready in time for the Walk Inns," Kinsley answered quietly.

"It sure is evident you take pride in your work. I might need you to come and give me an estimate," Charlotte said under her breath, as if she was churning the idea in her head in real time.

"Kinsley could make time for you, for an informal quote, isn't that right? But it might not be until late this afternoon," Tilly said as she wrapped her arm around her niece's shoulder and gave a quick squeeze. "Especially since channel four will be coming back soon. Did you hear my niece is going to be on the news tonight?" Tilly gushed. "It's an exciting day around here!"

Charlotte headed her off at the pass, "Oh, I'm glad Roy decided to take the tip, that's wonderful. Unfortunately, I have another pressing meeting to which I can't be late, so I really need to get a move on."

Kinsley gave an inward sigh of relief. She couldn't remember a time when so much attention was put upon her and her aunt. And she did not need reminding . . . the timing just couldn't be worse.

Kinsley held back her fears with a swallow, and smiled. "Yes, and truly I'd need to see your property firsthand before I could quote you. I would love to take a peek, though, whenever you're ready."

"How about I give you a call after the Walk Inns event to set up a time? I'm sure we're both booked up until then." Charlotte glanced at her Apple watch. "I really need to run," she added apologetically.

"Sure, no problem," Kinsley agreed. "Just Google Sea-Scapes and my phone number should pop right up for you. I wish I had a business card on me, but they're back at my house." She patted her pockets for verification but was certain she'd neglected to bring some along.

"No worries, I'll find you." Charlotte regarded the three of them with a smile, and then directed her attention back to Tilly. "I'll look forward to your email with the photo of your grand estate. Please don't forget. I'm under a strict deadline." She pointed to her watch.

"Yes, of course. I'll get right on it," Tilly promised with a vigorous nod of her head. "In fact, I'll send a few, and you can choose whichever one you'd like."

"Thank you. Again, it was a real pleasure, and I appreciated the tour of your lovely inn. It's so peaceful here." Charlotte's eyes traveled longingly out toward the sea. "You own a beautiful piece of property."

Kinsley shot Becca a warning glare. All she could think of was how this peaceful property was now potentially part of an ongoing crime scene. Though neither she nor Aunt Tilly had heard any gunshots, so she couldn't be sure. Aunt Tilly surely would've shared that if she'd heard something.

Charlotte then reached for Tilly's hand for another handshake. "The story on the inn should run early next week, and I'd be happy to send you an extra copy if you'd like."

"That would be wonderful!" Tilly shook Charlotte's hand enthusiastically.

"Okay then. I'm sorry to have to run off like this." Charlotte jutted a thumb in the direction of the inn. "Do you mind if I stop back inside and grab my laptop bag off the dining room table on my way out?"

"Absolutely not. You go right ahead!" Tilly said. "I'm right behind you, and I'll get on those photos right away!"

Charlotte turned on her heel and started out across the lawn and as soon as she was out of earshot, Kinsley turned to her aunt asked, "How'd it go?"

"Wonderful!" Tilly cooed. "I'm so tickled about this, and I can't wait to read the article. It'll be so fun, and it's great publicity for the inn!" She clapped her hands in delight as if she'd just won the lottery. "And now you? I'm over the moon that Charlotte wants to hire SeaScapes, too. And you'll be on the news tonight! Life couldn't get any better!"

"Aunt Tilly?"

Kinsley could sense her aunt immediately deflate at her tone.

"Yes, my sweet?" Her brows came together in question.

"There's something I need to tell you."

Chapter 5

"Look, Aunt Tilly, I'm sorry I haven't been sharing in your enthusiasm regarding the press rushing over here like ants to a watermelon today. There's a perfectly good reason why, though, and I think I have no other choice than to explain." Kinsley rubbed the back of her neck and then dropped her hands limply to her sides.

"My dear, if this is about the landscape, don't worry that it's not finished. I'm not fretting about that hydrangea bush, nor should you. Charlotte said it's no problem if we use a photo taken last year. In fact, she was quite happy about it, as she doesn't have to send the photographer over here for a new one." Tilly laid a hand of comfort on Kinsley's arm and softened her tone. "Now. I know you're overwhelmed, but you'll fill that hole lickety-split. You're being too hard on yourself. We must take advantage of the publicity. Honestly, Kinsley—"

Kinsley finally cut Tilly's response short with a raise of her hand. Her aunt took a step backward in surprise, and confusion riddled her face.

"What is with *you*?" Her eyes then traveled to Becca, who remained unusually tight-lipped and whose glance seemed to remain on the ground. Kinsley wondered if her friend was looking for additional clues.

"Did you happen to catch the evening news last night? Did you hear about the local murder?"

When Tilly responded with only a creased brow, Kinsley continued.

"I'm talking about the woman's body that was found out in that potato field."

"Ah, yes." Tilly raised a hand to her heart and clucked her tongue. "I know, isn't that just horrible news. We haven't had that type of monstrous crime in our area in an awfully long time. Honestly, I can't remember a time when . . ." She moved her hand to her cheek and shook her head with a drawn-out sigh. "Yes, it was very difficult news to hear, for sure. Is that what has you so upset?" Tilly reached out a hand to comfort her niece. "I know how sensitive you are. But I didn't realize that news touched you so deeply."

Kinsley lowered her voice to a whisper. "I found the shoe. The shoe they were talking about. Remember how they referred to it as the Cinderella murder?"

"What did you say?" Tilly raised a finger to her ear as if she were hard of hearing, which she was not. "I don't understand what you're trying to tell me, Kinsley," she reiterated slowly, as if still completely confused.

Kinsley pointed to the recently compacted soil, and Tilly followed with her eyes. Her glance then bounced between the two, before landing back on the dirt and scanning the area. "What are you saying? I don't see a thing."

"I dug it up, and then reburied it. I didn't mention it until now because the newspaper reporter was on the way over here. Then channel four showed up." Kinsley rolled her neck to remove the kinks, but it did little to alleviate the growing tension. She just might need a visit with the chiropractor after this one.

"Are you absolutely *sure* it's the shoe the police are looking for, and not one of Edna's that maybe her dog buried? You know Baxter has a habit of taking her shoes. That dog has a real foot fetish, I'd say!" Tilly smirked. "Edna told me once that he'd destroyed a few of her Louboutins!"

Their neighbor had a gorgeous Australian shepherd that frequented their yard almost daily. It wasn't uncommon to find Baxter galloping across the property with his tongue lolling as if smiling at the fact he was unleashed and ruling the roost. That didn't explain the change in soil, though, or the exact match to the missing shoe.

"Oh, she's quite sure it doesn't belong to Edna. Right, Kinsley?" Becca finally opened her mouth and then closed it again when Kinsley gave her a disgruntled look, as if she were being no help at all.

"Well, if you're sure, then why didn't you call the police? We need to get on that right away! Kinsley, why on earth would you bury it back up if . . . ? Well, if . . ."

"And expose you and the inn to that kind of publicity?" Becca defended.

"Right before the Walk Inns?" Kinsley added in a panicky voice. More panicky than she'd meant it to be, because the last thing she wanted was to pass on undue alarm, and she could tell from Tilly's expression that she'd already done so. Her aunt's shoulders sank, her eyes doubled in size, and then she wrung her hands nervously. This made Kinsley feel horrible.

"We need to call the police, and right away . . ." Tilly said under her breath, and then put her head in her hands. "We really don't have a choice. Do we? We can't wait for the Walk Inns. That's weeks away!"

"Do you know what finding that shoe here implies? Think long and hard about it. I'm concerned that this murder investigation might lead back to one of your guests. Living right under your own roof! It might not be safe, Aunt Tilly. You probably should stay with me over at the caretaker's cottage."

"I'll do nothing of the sort. I'm not leaving my home over this. Besides, I'm sure it was an isolated incident."

"Well, what if the authorities think you have something to do with this horrific crime!" Kinsley shrieked.

"Now, look at me. Do you think the authorities would believe I'm capable of hurting someone like that?" Tilly said, defending herself. "And as far as my guests, they were at their class reunion at the time of the murder. From what I gathered watching the news, they found the woman's body yesterday morning. According to rigor mortis, they stated the murder took place the previous night, while my guests were partying until the wee hours. And besides, I'm a very light sleeper. I would've heard something."

"You didn't hear gunshots?" Kinsley asked, hoping to confirm at least this.

Her aunt shook her head vigorously. "Not a one."

"Then how did the shoe get there? Look, Aunt Tilly, I was in no way trying to make things worse by reburying it. I'm just trying to protect you. I promise you that." Kinsley hung her head.

"It's not like we can bring the poor girl back from the dead. The shoe's not going anywhere . . . I'm beginning to agree with you, Kins, it's safe exactly where it is," Becca continued, which only made Kinsley's throat tighten as she held back tears. She was humbled her friend was now coming to her aid. Even if, Kinsley now realized, she had made an error in judgment. It was nice to know her friend would defend her just the same.

"Oh, I know, and I appreciate your intentions, I really do. However, it won't help the police in their investigation if we ignore it," Tilly said. "They need to know what's going on over here. We need to do the right thing," Tilly added, lifting her chin and solidifying their decision.

"Again, I'm really sorry. I didn't mean to hide anything from you, I was only trying . . ."

"We'll figure this out, not to worry." Tilly snapped her fingers. "In fact, I've got an idea."

"What's that?" Kinsley asked.

"Do you still have Rachel's number?"

"You mean Rachel Hayes? Kyle's ex-girlfriend? The cop, right?"

"Yes, do you have it?"

"I'm not sure my brother left her on the best of terms. I heard she was disappointed when Kyle took orders for Germany. I think she assumed he wouldn't reenlist and would stay here in Harborside and settle down instead," Kinsley answered. "Honestly, I'm not sure reaching out to her is the best idea."

"What does that matter, Kinsley?" her aunt clucked. "She's a professional. I heard she was recently promoted to detective." Tilly rested her hands firmly upon her hips. "Give me her number, I'll explain everything and see if she can stop by, in an unmarked car, until we figure this out. I'll go and do that straightaway and then tend to my guests. I still need to send those photos to Charlotte, too," she added, more to herself than the group.

"I have it," Becca piped up as she scrolled through her phone. "I'll text it to you, Tilly."

"You have it?" Kinsley asked with a hint of surprise.

"Yeah, she's in my contacts because she's been house hunting for a while now. I thought I told you that. It must've slipped my mind." Becca shrugged.

"Ah, I see. I think Kyle will be surprised to hear that she's been house hunting here. I think my brother was secretly hoping she'd quit the local police force and join him in Germany. Not so, I guess, if she's looking for permanent housing. Neither one of them seems to want to budge."

"Perfect. Thank you, Becca," Tilly said with a decisive nod of her head. Clearly oblivious to Kyle's love life and reopening that can of worms. "I'll get right on it."

"Can you at least wait to call Rachel until after my interview with channel four news?" Kinsley asked. "I think the last thing we need is breaking news right here on your front lawn. And whether she's in an unmarked car or not, one of the neighbors might get suspicious. Someone might recognize her! And we just don't need that right now."

Tilly nodded. "Justice can wait. Just a little bit longer, I guess . . . with hopefully no harm to the investigation. And no harm to the inn. I don't want to alarm my guests yet, either. This is their home, too, for the next few nights. I really don't want to be the one to ruin the time that they've had to reconnect over this—they've been having such a fun time. In any event, we still don't know how the shoe got there."

"Thanks," Kinsley said, deflated. "Hopefully, we can minimize any fallout."

"Not to worry, we'll figure this out," Tilly said, squaring her shoulders and giving another decisive nod before retreating to the inn.

Kinsley was surprised at how stoically her aunt had taken the news. Tilly didn't panic, instead her aunt thought it through and made a plan. Though Tilly had no other choice, as new guests would soon be arriving and she had to keep up good impressions. Her very livelihood depended on it.

Becca excused herself soon after, as she'd almost missed a closing appointment with one of her sellers at the bank. Kinsley wasn't the only one having trouble focusing due to all the recent commotion; her best friend had gotten sucked into it, too. The friends agreed to meet for drinks at the end of their workday, as they seemingly had a lot more to talk about. And even though it was the middle of the week, a strong drink was clearly just what the doctor ordered.

Hopefully, Becca could shed more light on the victim's past. Maybe Kinsley could find out if there was a connection between Daisy and any of the recent guests at the inn. She thought about this as she rushed across the lawn to ready herself for the big TV interview.

Chapter 6

Kinsley shed her dirty gardening clothes, slipped on a newer, sharper pair of jeans and a light blue SeaScapes polo shirt before a quick glance in the full-length mirror. She figured that although her attire was casual for an interview on the evening news, she was after all being interviewed for her business—and this was her business. She looked down at her shirt to regard the floral logo Aunt Tilly had embroidered on the side of her left shoulder, encircled with the company name.

Kinsley unbraided her hair, slid a brush through the long blond tangles, and then began to rebraid it as she abandoned her bedroom and stepped into the small living space. She wished she'd had time for a hot shower and a flat iron, but that wasn't in the cards. Normally, she might invite Roy and his crew into the caretaker's quarters, to view for themselves the headquarters of her operation. But as she looked around, she noted the place was a complete mess. In no way would she encourage an interview inside her home right now.

The open-concept room allowed for the entire living area of the bungalow to be viewed all at once. The white-washed paneled walls and heightened paneled ceiling made the space appear larger than its one thousand square feet. Kinsley had been meticulous with her choices and decorated the home with a maritime feel. Washed-up seashells from the beach filled the glass lamp bases, and larger shells, along with sand dollars, lined the fireplace mantel crafted from driftwood. Smooth rounded stones balanced on top of one another in perfect harmony and flanked each side of the small wood-burning fireplace. The process of finding and stacking stones, an act she'd found truly methodical, relaxing, and almost spiritual, had become part of her weekly ritual. Although most times she'd left her creations somewhere along the cliff walk, or on the beach, for others to enjoy.

An antique lobster trap had been topped with heavy leaded glass and transformed into a coffee table and placed in front of a comfy denim love seat. On one wall, a large wooden oar that had washed up on the shoreline hung by boat cleats, never to be reclaimed by its owner. Kinsley had taped a note to the abandoned oar and left it on the beach for two weeks before shaking the sand off and dragging it home. Another wall showcased a large painting of a gorgeous view of sunset at sea, splattered with vivid hues of blues, pinks, and purples. She'd found it at a local art fair, and the over-sized painting was one of her favorite splurges.

On the east side of the house, a round porthole streamed light at first dawn. The nautical-style window looked as if it belonged in the belly of a large ship and really added to the character of the home. The caretaker's quarters had been built intentionally small, but it was efficiently perfect.

Kinsley's eyes scanned the kitchen, where she regarded a butter knife, soiled with mustard. And breadcrumbs, spilled across the counter and onto the floor—evidence of where she'd haphazardly thrown together her lunch. Dishes from the previous night lined the sink, as yesterday she'd had a full day and hadn't taken the time to wash them, either.

The kitchen was compact and useful but lacked a dishwasher. Normally, Kinsley didn't mind soaking her overworked hands in the warm suds to wash the dishes, as she found the task somewhat meditative and soothing after a long day. Sometimes, she would load her dirty dishes into her aunt's dishwasher, especially when the meals were leftovers from Tilly's kitchen. Yesterday, though, she did neither. There was no time now, as she heard a hard knock upon the front door.

She quickly kicked a set of pruning shears out of the way beneath the love seat and decided she'd put them in the truck later, when guests weren't patiently waiting.

As she greeted Roy and his crew, she slipped out the painted wooden front door and closed it quickly behind her. For some reason, the thought of the news crew filling her personal space seemed invasive, not only because of the disarray. Something more was gnawing at her.

Maybe Kinsley was just being paranoid, but she decided that, moving forward, the only people she would allow in her private space would be Becca and Tilly—at least until they found answers regarding the Cinderella killer. What if a serial killer, or someone from Harborside, was involved? It was a shame, really. She used to feel so safe in her community, and now she was having second thoughts.

Kinsley encouraged Roy to host his interview out on the flagstone staircase leading to the cliff walk. She thought it would give enough of a backdrop of the Salty Breeze Inn, and wouldn't give away too much of the landscape that was truthfully not up to par. It also helped that they'd be located many yards away from a significant piece of buried evidence.

When they arrived at the suggested location, Roy was busy fiddling with his microphone, tapping it with his fingers to test the sound, and the cameraman was looking at his live feed or adjusting something on the camera.

Kinsley took this moment to take a deep breath of the salty air. Immediately she was cleansed and renewed. She focused her ears on the nearby waves and counted them in her head, like a meditation. A storm might be brewing, as the more intently she listened, the louder the roar inside her head.

The wind kicked up a notch, and she noted Roy smoothing his perfectly groomed hair with his hand. Seagrass fluttered in the wind, causing the reeds to sing out, like violinists playing the melody in an orchestra.

"This might not work after all," Roy said with a smirk.

It was obvious Roy didn't handle many interviews out in the elements, as he looked annoyed. Or at the very least, he didn't enjoy it. Kinsley thought he was kind of handsome, in his own way, but couldn't see herself partnered with a guy who most likely went to a salon for more manicures than she did. She instinctively looked beneath her own fingernails, where dirt and grime remained tucked in deep, even though she wore garden gloves most of the time.

Kinsley overheard the cameraman utter to Roy, "What do you want to do? Head back toward the inn, out of the wind?"

"If we head down the steps closer to the cliff walk and stand at the bottom, it might break the wind a bit. Maybe you can still get a shot of the inn located in the background? If you tilted the camera up a bit?" Kinsley suggested with a shrug.

"She has a point." The cameraman waited for approval from Roy as he readjusted the camera on his shoulder.

"Well, we're here. Let's give it a try, and we'll see." Roy ambled down the staircase ahead of them, holding the side of his head the entire time, in a paltry attempt to keep his hair flat along the journey. The sight of him made Kinsley smile. Clearly the newscaster was concerned with his looks more than anything else. She wondered suddenly if he approved of her own casual attire for an evening broadcast.

As they walked, Roy said over his shoulder, "I'm just going to ask you a few questions and keep it simple. I don't like to tell my guests exactly what questions I'll ask ahead of time, because then the interview comes off unnatural and rehearsed. Viewers don't appreciate that."

Kinsley wasn't sure how she felt about this as she made her way down the steps. It's not like she was exactly comfortable standing in front of a camera. The only thing that was propelling her forward was the thought of additional marketing for her aunt's business. As far as SeaScapes, she was overbooked to begin with, and word of mouth proved to be her best asset, but this certainly wouldn't hurt, either.

The cameraman held his equipment at eye level and then leaned back. "This should work, but I can't hold the camera in this position too long, so we're going to have to make it quick," he said as he looked down at the precarious steps he was taking to get the perfect shot. He was balancing his weight on a large boulder not far from the cliff walk, and one wrong move might dump him into the roaring sea.

Kinsley glanced at the backdrop the newscaster had chosen, and approved. Their back wouldn't show the sea, instead the polished flagstone steps that led up to the Salty Breeze Inn. She hoped the inn would also be caught in the wide-angle shot. And the waves lulled along with their voices, like background music.

Kinsley heard Roy say, "Testing, testing." And then she saw the cameraman give a thumbs-up. Without warning they were filming.

"Greetings! We're coming to you from the Salty Breeze Inn. I'm here with Kinsley Clark, owner of SeaScapes landscaping, and she's here to tell us a little bit about the Walk Inns event coming up in a few weeks. Isn't that right, Kinsley?" He jutted the microphone in her direction.

Kinsley nodded and smiled but didn't say a thing. She panicked. It was like words were stuck in her throat and she couldn't get anything out. Roy must've caught on quickly because he recovered. "Last year, your business—SeaScapes—was chosen for an exclusive article in *Coastal Living*. That's quite an accomplishment. Congratulations," Roy gushed enthusiastically as he tapped her on the shoulder, encouraging an answer to come out of her mouth.

"Thank you." Kinsley smiled.

"You know, your interview with the magazine really put Harborside on the map! Now the buzz has started that the Walk Inns event will be bigger and brighter than ever this year. I hear many of the parade homes involved in the event are your clients. Isn't that right?"

Kinsley nodded.

"What's your secret to getting these businesses to look like something we'd find on a postcard? Or in an art studio? I've heard you try and keep the natural seascape while adding pops of color for surprise."

Looked like Roy had done his homework.

Kinsley cleared her throat. "Yes, that's true. I try and use the natural elements as my backdrop, and plants that are native to Maine. And then I get to play with color, almost as a painter plays with color on a canvas. The landscape is my canvas. It's a very rewarding job." She grinned.

Using a point of his finger, Roy encouraged her to turn her head in the direction of the cameraman so they would get a face-on shot of her.

"Well, you heard it here first, folks! It's time to roll out the red carpet for the incoming tourists and prepare for the Walk Inns event. Let's show people what kind of exceptional community we all reside in. People travel from all over the country to join us here in Harborside."

Roy did a large sweeping motion with his hand and then continued, "The Salty Breeze Inn, located behind us, is just one of many gorgeous properties guests will have the privilege to walk through. Time to spruce up those landscapes. Isn't that right? Can you share with my viewers the exact date of the event?"

"Yes, two weeks from Saturday, June twentieth." Kinsley nodded.

"Mark your calendars, folks. June twentieth for the Walk Inns. The parade of businesses participating in the event will be provided on our website. Thank you, Ms. Clark, it's been a pleasure. Back to you in the studio!" Roy shot a pretend gun in the direction of the camera and winked. Kinsley hoped to God she didn't roll her eyes and get caught with her reaction on the feed.

The cameraman released the camera from his shoulder and immediately navigated off the rocks.

"Well, that's a wrap!" Roy said as he patted Kinsley on the shoulder. "See, that wasn't so bad."

Apparently, Roy had caught on to Kinsley's less-than-enthused attitude. She should have been grateful for all the attention, but after the day she'd had, and the adrenaline pumping in overdrive, she was quickly growing weary. She tried to recover by saying, "Thank you so much for the interview and sharing my aunt's business in the process. I really do appreciate it." She forced a smile.

"No. Thank *you*, Kinsley. It's just what we needed on the air tonight. We're ready for a 'feel-good focus.'" He held his long fingers out in air quotes while managing to not drop the microphone.

"The local murder on the outskirts of Harborside has everyone on edge," Roy continued. "My boss is hoping that taking the focus off the Cinderella murder for a bit will bring back some normalcy. Did you know we haven't had an investigation like this in many years? It's practically unheard-of! You've heard about the Cinderella murder, right? It's all we've been covering; you'd have to be a hermit to have missed the story."

Kinsley could feel the heat rise from her neck to her face. She quickly stepped away from Roy and headed up the flagstone steps to avoid his gaze. "Yeah, it's awful," she said over her shoulder. "I agree, you'd have to live under a rock to not have heard about it. Seems we're all on edge, it's terrible."

"It's quite a story. That's for sure. But we certainly don't want the folks of Harborside to hide indoors, or people to avoid traveling here for the big event. We can't have one tragedy dictate how we run our lives."

Kinsley hadn't thought about that. Would the recent murder in their town deter visitors from coming to the Walk Inns event completely? She really hoped not, for her aunt's sake. Besides that fact, why was Roy referring to this as a news story? It was more than that. He was referring to a victim of a senseless crime. The hard evidence found on her aunt's property made her stomach churn with anger. And she'd do whatever it took to protect Tilly's name and fortify the inn's stellar reputation.

Chapter 7

Not long after Roy and his television crew had departed, while Kinsley hurried to finish tidying up her aunt's property, she caught sight of Rachel Hayes out of the corner of her eye. The detective was walking with purpose toward her, and Aunt Tilly was close at her heels.

Kinsley straightened her shoulders and tried to compose herself. Her mind immediately replayed the last conversation she'd held with her brother before he'd departed for Germany.

"Hey, just because Rachel's enlistment is up, doesn't mean I'm supposed to jump on board with her plan," Kyle had defended as he'd stuffed his USAF-issued duffel bag with the remainder of his belongings to prepare for his new post in Germany. *"I never promised her I'd move back here. It's not my fault she fell more in love with Harborside than with me."*

Rachel and Kyle had met in a classroom on an Air Force

base, both training to become MPs—military police. On several occasions while on military leave, Kyle had brought Rachel home with him. It was obvious she'd fallen in love with Maine and decided one day, if given the chance, she'd make Harborside her permanent home. Kinsley guessed that Rachel thought her brother would jump at the chance to return, too. But like their parents, he couldn't stand to be planted in one place for long. He reminded her of dandelion seeds blowing in the wind; they could never land on the grass and take hold. And the military always provided his next move. Kyle had told her once that he wanted to travel the world. Kinsley tried to convince her brother there were alternative ways to travel instead of being relegated to an Air Force base. But Kyle insisted, as if he were holding his stance with an M16 at his post, that he preferred the safety of the base and the ability to immerse himself in the community in which he served. He was so noble, like their parents. Kinsley secretly wondered if her brother was self-sabotaging his relationship with Rachel, though, because of what had happened to them. If he and Rachel were married and stationed at the same post, was there a chance they could . . . repeat a bad ending in history? Their mother wasn't even on duty at the time of the attack, yet somehow, both their parents had perished in a military accident. The records had been sealed by the Air Force, and Kinsley had been told on more than one occasion that it had been fate. Fate, as if that were a perfectly acceptable explanation. But she couldn't use fate to explain away the loss of her parents in a horrific tragedy.

"Hi, Kins, good to see you." The sound of Rachel's voice interrupted her thoughts when the detective appeared, suddenly within arm's reach.

Kinsley studied her. Rachel seemed to have aged since the last time she'd seen her. The lines around her hazel eyes, the color of Sweet Tea heucherella leaves, spoke volumes. And deep shadows hollowed them. Her hair was colored, like beach sand streaked with platinum, and bluntly cut, as if she were still in the military and didn't have time to braid it or tuck it beneath her military field cap.

"Hey, Rachel, how's it going?" Kinsley removed her garden gloves and stuffed them into her back pocket. She then reached to greet Kyle's ex with a quick hug. "Good to see you," she added genuinely after stepping back from their embrace.

"You're looking good, Kins. You know . . . I have to ask . . . How's your brother?"

Rachel certainly didn't waste any time. Kinsley shared a look with her aunt, who smiled sheepishly. She wondered again if it was such a good idea calling her over. "He's good, I think. I haven't heard from him in a few weeks, I guess he's been busy." Before Kinsley had a chance to back out and call someone else from the police station, she was cornered with a pointed question.

"Tilly mentioned you have something important to show me. Something that might help a case?"

Kinsley looked for a response from her aunt, who replied with a shamefaced shrug.

"You didn't tell her?"

"I thought I'd leave that up to you." Tilly forced a smile.

Just then a bit of commotion caught their attention. "Hellooo? Where do I check in?" A woman wearing a sundress, waving a matching sun hat, sang out from the porch. The guest looked as if she'd just been transported from a film set back in the 1950s in Charleston, South Carolina. She looked beautifully put together. Kinsley self-consciously looked down at her recently soiled polo shirt and wondered if she could ever pull off that kind of ladylike prettiness.

"Oh dear." Tilly's eyes moved between the guest and her niece before landing on Kinsley. "Can you handle this? I need to go and tend to my guests."

Kinsley nodded. "Absolutely, I've got it." She laid a comforting hand on her aunt's shoulder. "Go on ahead and we'll catch up about it later."

Tilly zipped her lips before moving away. Kinsley assumed her aunt meant to keep this whole ordeal among the three of them, but she didn't think that would be possible after sharing this kind of news with Rachel.

Kinsley led the plainclothes detective to the spot where the shoe was buried and looked over both shoulders to be sure they were out of view before reaching for the shovel and unearthing the evidence. She heard a gasp over her shoulder and gathered Rachel was just as stunned as she, Becca, and Aunt Tilly had been. Because, based on the sound that emerged from Rachel's lips, it was clear she knew whom the shoe belonged to.

"We've been searching for that. How'd you find it?" Rachel pointed to the shoe.

The gems of the victim's discarded shoe were catching the sunlight and glaring accusingly at Kinsley.

"Yeah, I know, I heard that on the news last night. I dug it up shortly after lunch," Kinsley admitted. "But then we had the news media here on the property, so I buried it until we knew what to do. Please don't judge me, Rachel, I was just trying to protect my aunt." She tossed the shovel aside to land on the ground with a thud.

"No, no, not at all." Rachel surprised her with an understanding tone as she knelt to take a closer look. "How did it get here, though?" she added, distantly.

"That's the million-dollar question. It makes no sense

whatsoever. How did it get from the potato field, where she was murdered, to our yard?"

"Actually, the evidence points to the fact that the victim's body was placed in the potato field and the murder occurred elsewhere. We're just not sure *where* exactly . . ." Rachel stopped herself short and rubbed her hand slowly over her mouth, as if she'd already shared too much.

"Well, it didn't happen here at the inn, I can promise you that! I didn't hear gunshots, nor did Aunt Tilly, her guests . . . None of us heard a peep! And I'm sure one of her guests would've said something if they witnessed anything. My aunt is certain they were all attending a class reunion at the time of the murder."

"You wouldn't have heard gunshots; that's not how she died. The victim was strangled."

"That's not what was reported on the news!"

"Right. That. Yes, a shell casing was found. But that shot came from a farmer who had killed a coyote a week prior. It had nothing to do with the murder. See how gossip flies? Another reason not to believe everything you hear," Rachel added with a huff.

"So, you don't think she was strangled at the potato field?"

"Look, we can't be sure of anything right now, Kins. My job is to follow the evidence where it guides me and then make my determination. I think you better take a step back; this could potentially be a murder scene." Rachel scoured the area with fresh eyes after plucking a pair of rubber gloves from her pocket. She began lifting branches and looking under rocks. And left no stone left unturned.

Kinsley did nothing but look on in dismay.

After watching Rachel for what seemed a lengthy

amount of time, Kinsley pushed ahead, hoping the detective would share more. "I know my Maine dirt, and I can tell you that where the shoe was found, the soil isn't the same. You may want to have that tested. By the way, what makes you think that the murder didn't happen at the potato field, where someone found her?"

"Hardly any evidence was left at the crime scene. No marks in the dirt or anything to indicate an altercation had taken place there. The only thing we found was an earring on the ground, not far from her body. So little evidence was there, in fact, that we haven't had much to go on—until now." Again, Rachel regarded the shoe. And then her eyes grazed the area, as if begging for more evidence to show itself. "I'll have the crime scene unit out here to get a sample of that soil and have it tested, because I'm not seeing anything else of value here."

"An earring? How do you know it didn't belong to the victim? Or it hadn't just dropped there, from someone else?"

"In a potato field? The farmer claimed it wasn't his." Rachel chuckled. "It didn't come from our vic because she was already wearing studded hoops and didn't have any other body piercings. Besides, the earring wasn't covered in dirt or anything, and it was found too close to her body to be coincidental. The diamond glared up at me in the sun, sorta like that shoe is doing right now."

"Oh well, that makes sense. Look, I'm sorry, I would've called the police right away; it's just I'm trying to protect my aunt's reputation here. We have a huge event coming up, and I don't want the media catching wind of this—"

Rachel put up a hand to halt her from sharing anything else. She lowered her voice to a whisper. "Listen, Kins, we don't want *anyone* getting ahold of this information any more than you do. Trust me, I'm glad you waited."

Kinsley finally allowed herself a sigh of relief and let her shoulders sag. "Really, why?"

"This piece of evidence could be the only thing that will lead us directly to the killer. Better for no one to know, so we can sift the perpetrator out."

"So, you're planning on keeping the shoe a secret?"

"Not exactly. I need to bag it for evidence. But rest assured, I'm not planning to announce what's going on over here. It's not like the property will be covered in crime scene tape, either, if that's what concerns you. I will, however, be sending over a crime scene investigator, and they'll take a vial of the soil. But I'll ask that they be discreet until we find the actual crime scene in this case. Because I'm pretty confident the murder didn't occur here. I'm not finding anything that leads me to believe otherwise. We'll keep this on the down-low, for now."

"Rachel?"

"Yeah?"

"Honestly, right now, my biggest concern is Aunt Tilly's safety. What if one of her guests had something to do with this? It's not out of the realm of possibility, if you're saying the crime didn't happen where her body was found. My aunt is convinced they were all at a class reunion, but what if one of them slipped out, murdered Daisy, and then returned to the reunion? Creating the perfect alibi?"

Rachel's eyes narrowed. "How do you know the victim's name? We haven't yet released that information and won't until we notify the next of kin."

"Becca."

Rachel rolled her hand to prompt Kinsley to continue.

"Daisy was one of her clients. Apparently, she was looking at real estate in the area before she . . ." Kinsley gulped. The thought of the poor woman found in the nearby potato field, a field that she herself drove past at least once a week, brought a bit of bile to the back of her throat.

Rachel took in this information. "So, Becca had met with her then, on several occasions? Where was she staying? She wasn't a guest here at the Salty Breeze, correct?"

"No, Becca mentioned a hotel, as she said Daisy needed security. Anyhow, I think you'd better reach out to Becca. I don't want to misinform you of anything." Kinsley bit her lip and stopped short. Now her best friend was sure to be questioned by the police. She hoped Becca wouldn't be upset that she'd shared this bit of information. "But what about Aunt Tilly? Is she safe? Be straight with me, Rachel."

"Rest assured, I'll have background checks and alibis confirmed on everyone who is currently on this property before day's end. And the police will handle this on the down-low. We're not going to share with anyone that we've found the shoe out here. We don't want our perpetrator to know we've got a lead. It's a secret between us." She waved a finger between them. "Because right now, it's the only lead we have."

Chapter 8

The Blue Lobstah, a restaurant perched atop the cliff walk, and a stone's throw from the marina, was Kinsley's favorite hangout. The indoor-outdoor bar provided a sweeping view of the Atlantic and the nearby yachts that bobbed idly in the water. Breakwater Lighthouse was also not far from view.

The oversized deck hosted a platform where local bands played on the weekends during the summer months—often for a large crowd, well past midnight. Deep inside the restaurant, the nautical feel continued. Oversized lobster traps with glass tops and mason jar candles lit with white lights were available for intimate seating. King-sized navy booths lined the wall, where colorful buoys hung between each one, adding pops of color. An enormous blue metal lobster, tinted with a purplish hue, which had been constructed by a local artist, hung prominently in the room. The walls had been built from rustic barn boards, as if an old farm had been deconstructed, moved, and reconstructed into a weathered boathouse. All this made it feel as if the newly erected restaurant had stood the salty test of time, for decades.

The eatery's owner, Pete O'Rourke, had transplanted up from Boston. After attending culinary school at Johnson & Wales University in Rhode Island, Pete had then spent a few years working tirelessly for Atlantic Fish Company in downtown Boston. His accent was thick and the name of his restaurant intentional. He'd shared with them that the blue lobstah was rare, like the culinary dishes he'd planned to *off-ah*. Kinsley didn't tell him the locals were only mildly interested in his fried calamari dipped in hoisin sauce. Or his Fourchu lobster. People came because they liked him, and he served the best lobstah roll in Harborside. (Yes, he'd even kept to his roots, using the New England pronunciation of lobster in blue letters on the side of his restaurant *and* inside his menu.) Kinsley didn't dare share any of this, though, for fear of bruising his ego.

Not unlike herself, Pete was a ferocious worker, dedicated to making his business along the wealthy coast thrive. On one occasion he'd shared that he, too, spent his summers sailing the harbors of Maine as a child, and it was always his dream to plant himself back where fond memories prevailed. Kinsley wasn't sure how old Pete was, or the underlying current about his former life that made him a bit mysterious. What about his past made him want to escape to a place that held fond memories? She'd thought about this on more than one occasion while sipping the house wine. While waiting for Becca, planted in their familiar seats, she tried to guess his age once again as she watched him handing amber bottles across the bar. On numerous occasions, Pete had joked with them that he was going to have nameplates attached to their stools because they often waited for each other at the exact same spot at the end of the bar.

Pete's light hair was cropped short and buzzed to his neck. He often stepped in as head chef and shared several times that he didn't like to wear a hairnet. His eyes, the color of blue asters, shone with a hint of mischief. His skin was ruddy, like that of a California surfer, from hanging out on the outdoor bar and extended deck all summer long, chatting with patrons. He wasn't a hands-off owner. He seemed to thrive out in the trenches, either mixing drinks behind the bar or, with a smile, delivering meals to a table. Kinsley caught his eye, and he winked as he pointed out Becca entering, while someone held open the door for her.

"You started without me?" Becca teased after she slipped onto the stool beside Kinsley. She waved to Pete, and he smiled wide and sent her a nod, meaning he'd bring a glass of the house wine immediately.

"How old do you think he is?" Kinsley leaned over and whispered to Becca's ear, for fear Pete might overhear.

"You know, I'm not sure." Becca ticked off fingers while watching him. "A couple of years in culinary school, a few years working at Atlantic Fish Company. He's so vague, I don't know if we'll ever get his true age out of him. But definitely datable age—if that's what you're asking," Becca teased.

Kinsley swatted her friend on the arm.

"What? Don't think I haven't noticed the way you look at him."

"And what way is that exactly?" Kinsley defended.

Becca just smiled and then turned her attention to the fresh glass of wine that appeared in front of her. "Thanks, Pete! You're the best." She grinned, and his expression mirrored hers.

"No problem," he answered, then removed a rag from his shoulder and wiped down the bar in front of them.

Pete tossed the rag back behind the bar and turned away from them.

"Wait!" Kinsley piped up. "May I please have a refill?"

Pete pivoted and then locked eyes with her friend before doing a double take in Kinsley's direction.

"What?" Kinsley asked, holding her hands out in a defensive stance.

"On a school night?" Becca asked, shocked.

Pete rested his arms comfortably on the bar and leaned toward Kinsley. "Yeah, what's up, buttercup? You never ask for a refill unless it's a weekend and we have a good band playin'. What gives?" He jutted his chin in her direction and then eyed her with deep concern.

Before Kinsley could answer, Becca pointed to the TV located behind the bar, causing them all to turn their attention in that direction. "Turn it up! Turn it up! Look, Kinsley, it's your interview!"

Kinsley could feel the heat rise in her face as Pete turned to grasp the remote. She leaped from the stool and reached across the bar to stop him. "Please don't do that!"

"Oh, come on, we wanna hear it," he said conspiratorially, looking at Becca with a sly smile and then turning the volume up slightly so others in the restaurant wouldn't turn their heads, but the three of them could still hear.

Kinsley looked at herself on the television and shuddered. She wished now she'd worn a SeaScapes baseball hat, as wisps of hair had escaped her braid again. What she was witnessing was a hot mess. If only she could crawl beneath the bar and hide.

When the interview was over and they turned to gauge

her reaction, Kinsley let out a sigh and put her head in her hands, trying to escape her embarrassment.

Becca threw her arm around her and squeezed. "Look at you! Our latest Harborside celebrity! I can't believe I have the privilege of sitting next to you! You're famous!" she teased with a wide grin and a raise of her glass.

Pete seemed to look at Kinsley with fresh, approving eyes.

She tried to get the attention off herself by redirecting Pete and, with a pointed finger, reminding him of her second glass of wine.

"Yes, ma'am, I'm on it!" He saluted and swiveled on his feet, as if he were doing an about-face, just like her brother, Kyle, often did when in town. For the first time, she wondered if their friend Pete had also spent some time in the military and just hadn't mentioned it.

Just then, Kinsley's deepest competitive rival in the landscaping world approached out of nowhere. Denny Davenport was constantly vying for her landscaping jobs and did everything in his power to mess with her—she'd even caught him purposely pulling out plants one time at the Pierces' property. Denny leaned his elbow on the bar, curled his lip, and ran a hand through his slick dark hair with a silver streak in it that reminded her of a black garter snake. He looked pointedly at her and said, "Just 'cause you made the nightly news doesn't mean you're gonna win this year's Walk Inns, Kinsley Clark."

"What are you talking about, Denny?" Kinsley asked flatly. "There's nothing to win here." Kinsley swirled the last bit of wine remaining inside her glass and downed it, wishing that Pete had already fulfilled her refill request and she could take a larger gulp.

Denny jutted a thumb to his chest. "I'll be the one making the cover of *Coastal Living* this year," he mocked. "Not you." He then flung his fingers from his chin in her direction. "You only get the local business around here because of your aunt's place. Let's just call it what it is," he added flippantly while flagging Pete's attention for another drink.

"Oh no, not that again. When are you going to get over the fact that your company didn't make the cover of *Coastal Living* and mine did? Sorry you weren't chosen, Denny, but you really ought to let that go. And by the way, the Walk Inns isn't a landscape competition, it's an event for the local bed-and-breakfast establishments and has little to do with us. You really need to get over yourself."

"First you get the *Coastal Living* cover, and then you get notoriety on the nightly news. What's next? Jimmy Fallon? All this attention on SeaScapes is undeserved, in my opinion. I'm just sayin'."

"Whatever."

"And by the way, who do you think you are undercutting the Stapleton job by two thousand dollars, huh? You can't provide a breathtaking landscape that cheap!" Denny tilted the amber bottle to his lips and took a swig. "What are you gonna do? Scatter cheap marigold seeds around the perimeter?" he taunted.

"The Stapleton job? First of all," Kinsley defended, "I've designed a beautiful landscape that I'm very proud of, and one I know they'll love when fully executed, and secondly, I didn't even know you were quoting them. That's news to me!" Kinsley paused to inhale sharply. "And lastly, they've been an ongoing customer of mine for three years now!" Her voice rose an octave. "Oh, and one more thing, marigolds are beautiful, especially the vanilla ones, but you wouldn't know anything about those, would you? Maybe you should do your homework!"

"Don't you worry, I'm going to lowball them and half your other clients, too, because you're undercharging them by the thousands! But I'll take the hit, just to put SeaScapes out of business, once and for all." Denny huffed. "I guarantee I'll bury you," he sneered before downing the remainder of his beer, slamming the bottle on the bar, and sauntering off, not waiting for Pete to return with his refill.

"What was that about?" Becca asked.

Kinsley didn't answer because an eerie chill ran down her spine. She couldn't help but question the choice of Denny's words.

He'd bury her.

Chapter 9

The hollow sound of the foghorn blared rhythmically, causing Kinsley to refocus and grip her coffee mug tighter. She turned her head in the direction of Breakwater Lighthouse, but couldn't make the beacon out, save a tall outline. The rolling fog was so thick in front of her that Kinsley couldn't even determine the horizon line. She squinted and averted her eyes away from the pewter ocean and noticed she could no longer distinguish where the cliff walk was located behind her, either, because her surroundings were as thick as pea soup. The damp air prickled at her skin and covered her hair in a mist of droplets. The beach roses seemed to dip their heads in disgust as the heavy air weighed them down.

Kinsley took a sip of her tepid coffee and then set the mug beside her. It wasn't often she took the time for her morning brew facing the Atlantic. But after a restless night, she'd traipsed out to her favorite spot in search of answers.

She'd hoped the caffeine fix, along with the waves, would help her refocus. The last twenty-four hours had been a whirlwind, to say the least, and she couldn't wrap her mind around why a murder had taken place in their safe little town of Harborside, or who could possibly be involved in it.

Unfortunately, her mind remained as unclear as the tumultuous sea.

Kinsley hugged her knees and turned her head to let the wind blow the hair away from her face. She closed her eyes and listened intently to the water. The waves thundered into the shore. After a few moments, the sound of a whistle interrupted the waves' rhythm. Then she heard clapping hands and "Baxter! Baxter! Where are you?" The voice was familiar, and instantly she knew who it was.

"Edna?" Kinsley asked as she abandoned her favorite refuge and went in search of the voice. She met her neighbor Edna Williamsburg out on the cliff walk. Edna's white hair, which was usually coiffed and perfectly hair-sprayed, was blowing in the breeze in an unruly fashion. It was the first time Kinsley could remember seeing the older woman without makeup. Edna looked much different from the dressed-to-the-nines prominent member of society who typically stepped out of her house. This woman, out on the cliff walk in her bathrobe, was almost unrecognizable. Kinsley thought she looked much younger without the mask.

Edna's loved ones had come from old money. The Williamsburgs had resided along the cliff walk for generations and had held one of the first properties erected there. In fact, they had been instrumental in the creation of the cliff walk and had sold the properties adjacent to it over time, the Salty Breeze Inn being one of them.

Her family had ties with Alexander Graham Bell, who'd

invented the telephone, and money had been invested in the New York Stock Exchange, solidifying the family's bank account for years to come. Edna Williamsburg knew everyone in Harborside, but more important, everyone knew her. And she was Aunt Tilly's dearest friend.

"Are you okay?" Kinsley asked, reaching for her now and growing genuinely concerned.

"No, I'm not okay," Edna snapped, and then hastily recovered. "I'm sorry, honey, I'm just at my wit's end. Baxter has been missing for a few days now, and I've been going out of my mind trying to find him." Her face crumpled. "Have you seen him?" she added eagerly.

"No, I'm afraid not," Kinsley admitted. "Why didn't you call us? We could've helped you look for him."

"Because I know Tilly is getting ready for her big event, I didn't want to bother her. And besides, Baxter has done this to me before, but he's never been gone for this long." She sniffed and then plucked a tissue from her bathrobe pocket, giving her nose a hard blow.

"Have you tried calling animal control to see if they've seen him or picked him up?" Kinsley knew that Harborside had a strict leash law, one that Edna seemed to ignore from time to time. Baxter was treated more like a human companion than a dog, and Edna was often lenient with her furry friend. She even dressed Baxter up for various holidays. And he *always* sported his own adorable custom-made Halloween costume come October 31st, to greet the children who would frequent her doorstep.

"I wouldn't dare call animal control; they'd take him from me for sure!" Her hands clenched into balled fists, and she threw her arms to her sides defensively.

"When did you let him out?"

"I didn't let him out," she said hastily. "A delivery man did that injustice!"

More than anything, Kinsley wanted to help find her neighbor's dog. She knew Edna would be absolutely devastated if anything should happen to her most prized pet.

Edna continued, "Oh, this is just an awful week. Baxter . . . Daisy . . ." She put her head in her hands, but when the wind caught the inside of her bathrobe, she hurried to secure it tight with a knot.

Kinsley's ears perked. "Daisy? You heard about that?"

"Heard about that?" Edna's eyes, the color of forget-me-nots, doubled in size. "Why, of course I heard! It's my fault she's dead!"

"You can't possibly mean that, Edna. What are you talking about? Surely, a woman being murdered is not your fault." Kinsley secretly wondered if her neighbor had mixed up her medication or had suffered a nightmare and was still in the process of sleepwalking.

"It most definitely is my fault. I am the one who brought her here." Edna sniffed.

"To Harborside?"

"Yes, it was my idea she come." Edna's shoulders hunched, and her glance fell and landed at her slippered feet.

"I don't understand . . . ?"

"The class reunion committee had been looking for someone to sing along with the band they'd hired. They specifically wanted one of the songs from the musical that they'd won an award with the year they graduated."

Kinsley must've looked confused, because Edna continued.

"You of all people should remember that our high school's drama department is one of the best in the state. In fact, it's what led to Daisy winning roles on Broadway! She, too, graduated from Harborside, but she graduated a few years after the reunion committee. She's one of the few to make it in New York! And that's no simple feat."

"Wow."

"Yes, it's because of Harborside's standing that she was invited to audition in New York in the first place. Each year, high school theater companies from around the country compete. Our high school drama department is *renowned*, as one year we presented the musical *Cats* and took first place in *USA Weekend*'s nationwide competition for best American high school production." She jutted her chin proudly and pursed her lips. "Well, the year this reunion class graduated, the drama club won an award for *West Side Story*. Daisy was coming to perform 'One Hand, One Heart' with my grandson, as a surprise to the reunion members. But she never showed. Instead, she was murdered!" she shrilled. "And it's all my fault, because I'm the one who brought her to Harborside." Edna's face scrunched before she put her head in her hands.

Kinsley knew the bulk of Edna's time was spent at the Harborside Playhouse, where she was a board member and a frequent front-seat guest for all the performances. She could understand why someone would ask her to find a special guest to perform for the reunion. The biggest surprise, though, was that Daisy was to perform with her grandson.

"So, Luke had met her then?" Kinsley's mind began to wander and piece together things she didn't want to think about. Such as, what if Edna's grandson was the last person to see Daisy alive? Because if he was, it could potentially make him a prime suspect in the murder investigation.

"Of course they'd met. They've been rehearsing all week to prepare a flawless performance for the night of the reunion. They wouldn't just go out there cold." Edna stated this as if Kinsley should know better, and she did. She just didn't like the implication of the news.

"Right, I see." Kinsley nodded. "Anyway, I heard that Daisy wasn't up here for just the performance, so I wouldn't take the blame of her being in Harborside on yourself. Becca mentioned that she was looking for real estate, too. I think she planned on purchasing a summer home here or maybe even becoming a transplant."

That comment was met with shock because Edna's eyes doubled in size yet again. "I didn't think they'd fallen in love *that* fast. Fast enough that she was looking to relocate! My, oh my!" She shook her head in disbelief. "I had no idea."

"Fallen in love?"

"It was obvious my Luke had eyes on her. They had gone to grade school together, so it didn't take long for them to reconnect. The way my grandson got flustered in her presence was so unlike him." Edna wagged a finger at her. "Even though I'm old, I'm not ignorant to love, you know. He certainly didn't waste any time, though!" She frowned. "Of course, his biological clock is ticking away, he knows we need an heir!"

Kinsley was at a loss for words. The idea that Edna's grandson was involved with Daisy added a whole new twist to the story. She'd have to seek Luke out and have a talk with him, see what he knew.

Edna rubbed her hands up and down her arms. "I'm getting cold. I need to get back inside for a cup of tea to warm these ole bones. Clearly, Baxter is not out here." She sighed sadly.

"Yes, of course." Kinsley was suddenly transported back to the present. "Let's get you back home, where it's not so damp." Kinsley led Edna by the arm, up the stamped-concrete staircase. Leaving her coffee mug behind, to retrieve later, on her lunch hour.

"Thank you, dear," Edna said when they reached the top of the stairs and the gate that led to her property. She looked forlornly out toward the sea and muttered, "Oh, Baxter . . . where *are* you?" Tears pooled in the older woman's eyes.

"I'll help you find him." Kinsley patted Edna's hand gently to console her. "Instead, how about this? I have work in town today so why don't we make up a few flyers, and I'll ask around? I can even tape some to a few prominent places where people will be sure to see it."

"Oh, my dear!" She wadded the tissue and clasped her hands together. "You'd do that for me?" Edna's facade melted as she tenderly placed her head on Kinsley's shoulder.

"Of course I will."

"What do you want me to do?" Edna asked. Her eyes now searched Kinsley's eagerly.

"Go straight inside, and before you put the kettle on send over an email of the best picture you have of Baxter, and I'll handle the rest."

"Oh, thank you! Thank you, dear!"

Edna threw her arms around Kinsley before she disappeared into the pea soup.

Kinsley turned and looked out toward the sea, but still she could see nothing. And she'd solved nothing in her mind. If anything, more questions plagued her.

She prayed Aunt Tilly wasn't too far off, and maybe it had been Baxter who had escaped to a crime scene and buried a very important piece of evidence in their yard. And she hoped Edna's grandson, Luke, didn't have any buried secrets of his own.

Chapter 10

Summer blooms with a heady perfume greeted Kinsley as she stepped from her SeaScapes work truck in downtown Harborside. The hanging hayrack baskets that she'd recently planted along Main Street needed fertilizer. Kinsley had strategically chosen the red, white, and purple petunias so that by the Fourth of July the blooms would cover the pots outside the storefronts and transform them into patriotic globes. She texted her teen employee, Adam, to get right on it. He replied with a thumbs-up emoji, so she tucked her cell phone into her back pocket and moved in the direction of Toby's Taffy.

During the summer months, downtown Harborside was typically flooded with so many tourists that you could barely walk the sidewalks. It was still early in the day, however, and the early-morning fog seemed to have kept the tourists at bay.

The taffy shop, owned by Toby McNeil and his wife,

Jenna, had been an iconic hangout, at least for Kinsley. It was the first place she'd run to, and into the arms of the owners, when she'd moved to Harborside while grieving her parents. Jenna would stroke her hair, and Toby would hand her a fresh piece of taffy and wipe her tears. The two were like extended family, and she loved them dearly.

The building originally looked like a standard white-shingled house. With its bright red door and a candy cane–striped awning covering the front entrance, it had been renovated to be more welcoming. The large front window allowed passersby to view, in real time, the long glistening ribbons of sugar being transformed into taffy. Beachgoers would soon line the walkway around the corner to buy boxes of the smooth, sticky treats to stuff into their suitcases before returning home from vacation.

Kinsley also handled the floral arrangements outside Toby's Taffy, along with the flowers in front of several other businesses along Main Street. In the winter, she was the go-to hired hand to decorate these businesses for the holiday season, too. She was proud of overseeing the transformation of downtown Harborside into a festive, welcoming community that tourists and locals alike could all enjoy. And couldn't wait to return to.

Before entering Toby's Taffy, Kinsley looked to the whiskey barrels that she'd recently planted, and stopped short with a gasp. The ruby geraniums looked sickly, the begonias sad and leggy, and the trailing ivy that had spilled over the sides was nearly dead. "What in the world?" She shook her head in disbelief. She'd specifically chosen that combination of flowers because they liked to dry out between waterings and she knew she'd watered this whiskey barrel after planting. Now, however, it looked as if it hadn't been touched in weeks. She looked over each shoulder, as if someone outside could provide an answer. When met with nothing, Kinsley opened the door, causing a jingling bell to sing out.

"Mornin', Bumpkins!" Jenna looked up from the translucent counter filled with treats and smiled as she wiped her hands on her apron. Jenna's graying hair was atop her head in a heaping bun, rarely released down her back. Her hair could almost reach her waist if given the chance. Her eyes, the color of dark lilacs, always danced with a hint of mischief. Bumpkins was the nickname lovingly given to Kinsley by Toby in her youth, and it stuck like the sticky treats the two created.

The inside of the taffy shop was just as jolly as the outside. Candy cane–looking cushions dotted a few intimate tables in the corner. A few years ago, they'd purchased the insurance agency next door and taken down the wall between the businesses, creating one big room. The expansion allowed them to offer cupcakes and ice cream, too, which encouraged tourists to linger.

Kinsley handed her a flyer.

"What's this?" Jenna's eyes scanned the page.

"Have you seen Baxter? It seems Mrs. Williamsburg has lost him."

"Again?" Jenna clicked her tongue. "Edna certainly has a hard time keeping track of her dog. No, I haven't seen him. You can hang that in the window, though, if you'd like." Jenna handed back the flyer, and Kinsley tucked it under her arm with the rest of them.

"Here I thought you'd stopped in to sample our latest flavor. Toby came up with one he's calling strawberry cheesecake. Wait till you try it, it's a keeper!" Jenna reached atop the counter for a candy dish and held it out for Kinsley to take a sample.

"Don't mind if I do!" Kinsley unwrapped the candy and immediately popped it in her mouth. She rolled her eyes in ecstasy. "Oh my word, what are you doing to me?" she teased as she reached for another and tucked it in her pocket for later. "That'll be a favorite flavor, for sure!" she said between chews. "I'll take a box of assorted for Tilly, if you don't mind. Just make sure and add those to the mix." Kinsley reached into her pocket and placed a ten-dollar bill on the counter. "Keep the change."

Jenna smiled proudly. "Toby's pretty excited about the new flavors he's been working on. Keep your money, you have to stop doing that," she said as she made change and attempted to hand it over.

"I insist." Kinsley shook her head and waved her hand to refuse the change. "Keep it. It's for all those free samples you've given me over the years." She grinned. "It's probably still not enough, I probably owe you a million at this point," she teased.

Jenna rolled her eyes. "You're like one of our own, my sweet."

"And I love you, too." Kinsley smiled wide. "Hey, by any chance, did you or Toby water the geraniums out front? They like to dry up a bit before watering, otherwise they look sickly. And the ivy looks about dead . . . I just don't understand it."

"Nope, that's your department, Bumpkins." Jenna brushed her hands together, as if she were wiping them of the matter. She moved a strand of hair from her brow and gazed in the direction of the door, where patrons would soon be lining up. "You said you'd handle everything this year, and I'm taking you up on the offer," she added, and then moved from behind the counter in the direction of the window and peeked outside.

"Adam's across the street, maybe he watered them?" She turned to face Kinsley.

"Oh, he is? I must've caught him already working downtown when I asked him to fertilize." Kinsley left the box of taffy on the counter to retrieve later and spun on her heel. "I'll be right back," she said over her shoulder. Kinsley threw open the door and walked directly into Roy, the broadcaster from channel four news. The flyers under her arm flew into the air like confetti and littered the ground around them.

"Whoa! Someone's in a rush." He put an arm out to stop himself from tumbling over after Kinsley crashed into him.

"Goodness! I'm so sorry!" Kinsley gushed as she grabbed ahold of the sleeve of his shirt to help steady him on his feet.

Jenna let out a giggle and then turned on her heel. Kinsley could hear her chuckling from a distance as she disappeared into the back room behind the counter. Kinsley was secretly wishing Jenna had stuck around so she wouldn't have to face her embarrassment in front of Roy alone.

"We meet again, Ms. Clark! Way to plow me over." He cackled, and then ran his hand through his perfectly combed hair and patted it against his head.

"Yes, I guess, we do . . . meet again . . ." Kinsley's face grew hot, and she hurried to regain composure. "I'm really sorry, I didn't mean to crash into you like that." She winced. "Are you okay?"

"All good," he said as he straightened his tie and wiped his hand down his sleeve, smoothing the wrinkles now present in his light blue dress shirt.

Kinsley reached down to collect the flyers, and Roy stood there watching. He didn't offer to help or even ask her what was on the sheets of paper.

Instead he asked, "Did you see the newscast last night? You're becoming quite popular. The segment was loaded to our website and people are commenting left and right." He folded his hands across his chest and waited for an answer. "You might even say you're trending."

Kinsley wasn't sure quite how to respond. "Is that right?" She could feel the heat rise to her face again. Normally, she'd love the extra publicity, but the fear of exposing the shoe at the inn had her rethinking anything that might draw attention to her business, or her aunt's.

"Yeah, except it seems you have an anonymous Internet troll that isn't your greatest fan." He frowned, causing his makeup to crease. Kinsley wondered if he'd recently been on the air and was unable to remove it, due to a later broadcast. "The person calls themselves anonymous 455."

"Troll? What exactly are they saying?"

"That you work in a highly competitive market and you aren't necessarily the 'girl next door.' That people don't really know what's beneath the surface . . . stuff like that."

Now Kinsley's face was officially red-hot, like a skillet left on the stove. "What? You're kidding me."

Roy shrugged and then waved a hand of dismissal. "I wouldn't worry about it, happens to me from time to time. You know, being in the public eye and all . . ." He looked at his manicured fingers and then dropped his hand. "I wouldn't give it the time of day, it's not worth it. Besides, you seem nice enough to me."

"Really, *Denny*, you'd stoop that low?" Kinsley muttered through gritted teeth.

"Who's Denny? You think you might know the person who's harassing you online? You should probably report it then. These things have been known to get out of hand occasionally." He grimaced.

"I'm sorry, did I say that out loud?" Kinsley covered her mouth with her hand and then pressed her brow with her fingers. She could feel a slight headache coming on.

"If it were me, I'd wanna nip that in the bud. See what I did there? Nip and bud?" Roy chuckled. "Get it? Being in the floral biz, I thought you'd think that was cute," he added with a grin. Clearly, he was quite proud of his own wit.

Kinsley smiled at Roy's musings. "Denny's harmless, he's just going about his business the wrong way. I don't think it's something I need to report, but thanks for the suggestion. It's just that competition for my line of work is pretty fierce around here."

"Oh, you don't have to explain that to me. I'm up for news anchor, and I'm pretty sure I'll get the raise I've been after real soon. Being a reporter has its perks, but the anchor position for the nightly news is highly coveted. But I'll get there," he added confidently.

"Okay, well . . . I don't want to take up any more of your time, I'm sure you're a very busy man." Kinsley planted a smile on her face. "If you'll excuse me." She backed out the door of the taffy shop in search of Adam, across the street.

After he set down the watering can, Kinsley caught the teen's attention and waved him over. Seemingly, he'd been doing just as she'd directed and had already been fertilizing the petunias. He looked both ways and then jogged across the street to meet her.

"I just started." Adam threw a thumb over his shoulder. "I still got a ways to go," he added, gesturing to the hanging baskets.

"No, it's not that." Kinsley pointed to the whiskey barrels. "Have you been watering these?"

Adam's freckled nose wrinkled in confusion. "Was I supposed to?"

"No." Kinsley laid a reassuring hand on the teen's shoulder. "I was just wondering who did. They're not looking so good and I can't figure out why." She frowned.

Adam shrugged and wiped his hand along his T-shirt, leaving a grime streak across the front of it. "You told me to water downtown on Mondays and those weren't here then. Were they? I can't remember," he added absently.

"No"—Kinsley nodded—"you're right. I planted these on Monday evening. No worries, Adam, thanks for your hard work. You can get back to it. I might need some help this afternoon finishing up some planters at Salty Breeze. You in?"

"Yeah, sure, I can help." He smiled, showing his silver braces.

"All right. Well, thanks. I'll catch you later. Give me time to stop at the greenhouse, though, I need to pick up a few plants before I return. I can text you."

Adam gave a thumbs-up before trotting back to his watering can and stepladder.

Kinsley plunged her finger into the soil to test it and then rubbed her fingers. She gave her fingers a whiff. If she didn't know better, there was a hint of vinegar. Vinegar was something she didn't use as a fertilizer. She plucked one of the leaves from the geranium and took a closer look. After studying the leaf and rubbing it through her fingers, she noticed a sticky substance, like a residue of dish soap, was stuck to it. She had used a mixture of dish soap and water to kill aphids from time to time for petunias. But a combination of vinegar, salt, and dish soap could be lethal to plants. Someone had been using homemade weed killer on her flowers. She was almost sure of it. And she had a pretty good idea who.

Chapter 11

After a trip to the local greenhouse and loading the back of her pickup full of colorful annuals and perennials, Kinsley returned home to fill the planters around the Salty Breeze Inn. Adam texted and asked if she still needed him because his mom had asked him to babysit his kid sister. Knowing Adam's mom, who worked tirelessly to provide for her children on a single income, Kinsley said she could handle it. As much as she cared for Adam, and though it was no fault of his own, she thought she might need to hire additional help, as he couldn't be as reliable as she'd initially hoped when she'd taken him under her wing. And so much needed to be done before the Walk Inns event.

Kinsley was in the process of unloading the back of the truck when her aunt came to greet her.

"Hey, sweetheart, how you holdin' up? I didn't see you sneak in and snag something from the breakfast buffet this morning. Did you eat?"

Kinsley greeted Tilly with a half hug. "No, I skipped breakfast this morning and settled for a granola bar instead." She didn't dare admit to her aunt that she was hungry, as Tilly would drop everything and make her stop for a bite, and neither of them had time for that. "Speaking of food, did you find a recipe for the event?"

"I sure did! Busy as a bee is always me!" She tapped her fingers together conspiratorially. "I thought about what you said, and I'm keeping on track with the local lobster fare. However, I did find a chocolate finger food dessert option to add to the menu," Tilly said, and then, swayed by the hues of color, she leaned in and peeked inside the back of the truck. "Are all of these for me?" Her hands then flew to her heart and her lips curled upward in a genuine look of gratitude.

"Yep, I plan on filling all the planters today. Remember how I mentioned I was planning to spray-paint the old ones? I changed my mind. I thought with the time constraints, it would be better to splurge for new. Hope you don't mind," Kinsley said as she lifted one from the back of her truck. "You like 'em?" She displayed the new flowerpot on her knee before lowering the heavy container to the ground.

"Why, I love them, but you can't afford that! Those oversized pots this early in the season cost an arm and a leg." Tilly threw her hands on her hips and shook her head disapprovingly. "Add it to my bill then," she said finally.

"What bill?" Kinsley teased. "Since when have you paid me to keep up the yard?" She chuckled.

"Oh yeah, good point. Well, take it off your rent money for next month then," she said resolutely. "Or six months' rent, I don't care! It was your idea for me to charge you rent in the first place. If it were up to me, I'd cancel it altogether."

"It's my responsibility. You raised me, Aunt Tilly, but you don't have to be burdened with me for the rest of your life. I'm a grown woman," Kinsley said as she organized the flowers in the truck bed into groups based on where they were going to be planted around the yard.

Tilly interrupted her with a stern look and wagged a finger under her nose. "Now, I'll have none of that. You've never been a burden to me, my sweet, we're *family*. And if you don't know by now that you're the apple of my eye, well . . . then . . ."

Kinsley reached to embrace her aunt again, to stop her from rambling. And then held her at arm's length. "I know that. I just think sometimes you forget I'm an adult now, and this is me adulting. So, no worries, these new planters are my treat." She grinned and sent her aunt a wink as if she'd officially won the war.

"Thank you."

"You're very welcome. Besides, this is my home, too, you know!" Kinsley continued. "Now, let me tell you, if it takes me the rest of today to finish up this plot of land, I'm doing it. I'm really hoping for minimal interruptions this time, because I'm not moving on to the next property until the Salty Breeze looks perfect."

Tilly beamed. "I didn't expect anything less!"

"By the way, totally off subject, but I called Rachel on the way home, and she confirmed I can plant something where the hydrangea was located. The crime scene investigator removed a soil sample and since they didn't find any other evidence over there, she's releasing the property back to us. I bought some Shasta daisies, they're perennials, too, so they'll come up every year. I think I'll add some begonias in front of them for when the flowers recede. Anyway, I hope you don't mind—it seemed fitting."

Tilly's smile faded. "Oh, Kinsley, I think that's very special and kind of you. What a sweet gesture. Of course I don't mind." Tilly blew out a slow sigh. "I still can't get that poor girl out of my mind, what an absolute tragedy."

A tragedy indeed. Kinsley didn't know what else to say, except she couldn't let it go, either. She didn't share this with her aunt, though, for fear Tilly might push her to stay out of it. Which, at this point, wasn't really an option in her mind.

A quiet lull fell between them.

"By the way, did you hear that Baxter is missing?"

"*Again?* I wondered that since I haven't seen him around, but then again I've been busy this week." Tilly searched the property, as if she might see him hiding under a bush or behind a tree somewhere or even happily galloping in their direction.

Kinsley chuckled. "Seems that's the consensus—no one is surprised by his sudden disappearing act. Speaking of Baxter, Aunt Tilly, you mentioned it before, but do you really think Baxter would be capable of going all the way to that farm field, then coming back and burying that shoe at the inn?"

"Anything is possible. Edna has told me that he's destroyed several of her favorite shoes. I guess we can't rule out the possibility, now, can we? Did Rachel happen to mention anything else about the investigation when you spoke?"

Kinsley shook her head. "She was kinda tight-lipped. Except I forgot to tell you, they found an unidentified earring at the crime scene. One that they didn't think belonged to Daisy. Other than that, there was very little found at the field. At least, that's what Rachel shared with me."

"Oh . . . Well, I'm sure she's not able to divulge too much."

"I suppose. To be honest, I was surprised she shared as

much as she did." Kinsley loaded her arms with annuals and set them on the ground. "Hey, I'd love to chat more, but if you want the yard spruced up today as much as I do, I need to get back to it. Let's catch up on the porch when I'm finished. You have any lemonade?"

"I sure do, my love! Just made a fresh batch this morning." She swatted Kinsley lovingly on the backside with the dish towel that had hung over her shoulder, as if she were still ten years old. "I'd better get back to work, too. I'll meet you out on the porch in a bit," she added before turning on her heel.

"Sounds perfect," Kinsley said, and then moved to lug the oversized garden planter to its final location. Once placed, she abandoned the containers and instead focused on planting the Shasta daisies in the victim's honor. She dug a hole in the soil and set them carefully in front of where the hydrangea had been removed. Then she circled the daisies with red and pink begonias, tapped them into the soil, and watered them in.

When finished, she laid a hand across her heart as she stood back and uttered a silent prayer for Daisy. Even though the shoe was now in Rachel's care, Kinsley couldn't help but feel curious. Was any DNA found on the shoe? As soon as the workday was finished she would reach out to Rachel again and prod her for more information, see if any new evidence had come to light. She had to. After all, it was her job to protect her aunt's well-being, and her livelihood. And *nothing* would stop her from that.

An unnerving feeling, as if she were being watched, suddenly came over her. She turned her head and after looking over both shoulders, Kinsley chalked it up to paranoia. This murder in Harborside really left her feeling on edge. She shook it off and went back to work.

Kinsley returned to the flowerpots and filled them with purple fountain grass in the center for height and added a colorful arrangement of salmon geraniums, sweet alyssum, and blue lobelia to spill over the sides. She then stepped back and with her cell phone took a picture of the planter to add to her website. The photo also allowed her to see the arrangement with fresh eyes in case anything looked out of place and any adjustments needed to be made. Which it did. After setting her cell phone aside, she replaced her work gloves and added a bit more lobelia until the container was full. Kinsley had just removed her garden gloves once again and wiped her brow when she heard a voice over her shoulder.

A woman Kinsley didn't recognize caught her attention by saying, "Wow, that's stunning! What's the grassy thing called?"

"Oh, thanks. It's called purple fountain grass. I like it, too, as it fills in nicely by the end of summer and dances in the breeze. We're lucky to have those windy days, being out here close to the water." Kinsley smiled. "Hence, the Salty Breeze Inn . . ."

"Yes, I can see how that would dance." The woman mimicked her smile and then did a little wiggle to demonstrate, causing the two to share a chuckle.

"Are you staying here for the reunion?" Kinsley thought she knew the answer, but decided to play dumb, in hopes of pumping the woman for information. She dropped her gloves to the ground and wiped her sweaty hands on her shirt, then landed her hands on her hips. Her mouth watered at the thought of her aunt's homemade lemonade.

"Yeah, I'm leaving the day after tomorrow," she answered with a groan. "I'm not ready to leave this place, it's magical. When I grew up in Harborside, I lived in town. It was always my dream to come back someday and live oceanside. So far, that hasn't happened because it's so incredibly expensive." She sighed. "That's life," she added with a shrug, before the two looked longingly out toward the sea, where the fog was now burning off and a hot summer sun was taking its place.

Kinsley wasn't sure how to respond. She knew she was incredibly blessed to live on her aunt's property, and she rarely took it for granted. Instead, she said, "I'm sorry, I didn't catch your name?"

"Oh, I'm Abigale, but my friends call me Gabby. The name fits, as I have the gift of gab, or so I've been told." She grinned.

"Nice to meet you. I'm Kinsley." She looked down at her soiled hands and held back. "I'd shake your hand, but despite the gloves, I still seem to get the dirt beneath my nails."

Gabby laughed. "No worries. Have you worked here long, Kinsley?"

"This is actually my aunt's inn; I live back in the caretaker's quarters." Kinsley pointed out the cottage, and Gabby followed with her eyes.

"Oh, you are so lucky! I would die to live here," Gabby said, and then she took a step backward, stunned at her own choice of words. Then she lifted her hands to her cheeks. "I didn't mean that . . . Oh boy." She cringed. "Bad timing for a comment like that."

"You're fine." Kinsley chuckled, trying to keep the mood light. Hoping to make her feel comfortable and prod Gabby for more, Kinsley continued lightly, "I'm glad the fog is finally lifting, great day for the beach."

"Oh, it sure is." Gabby looked to the horizon and then back at her. "I was just on my way inside to change into my swimsuit and meet the others down there." She smiled.

"Not to rub it in or anything; looks like you have been working hard out here. I'm sure you could use a beach day."

"Oh, it's all right. I love what I do. Trust me, I take my moments when I can. How long is everyone else in your group staying at the inn?"

"When we booked, we all decided to add on a few extra days after the reunion to really catch up. Honestly, we all agreed no one wanted to be on a plane with a hangover." She grimaced. "That would make for a long trip."

"Yeah, I suppose it would, wouldn't it?"

"Anyway, I think the others are staying even longer but unfortunately, I gotta get back the day after tomorrow. Duty calls." She frowned.

Gabby turned away, and Kinsley put out a hand to stop her. "I know you're probably in a rush for the beach, but can I ask you something?"

"Sure." She pulled the hairband off her wrist and fastened her dark hair into a makeshift ponytail while she waited for the question.

"Do you know if anyone lost an earring? I found one, and I was just wondering who it belonged to. I thought if someone changed clothes, it might've dropped. It looks kinda expensive, so . . ."

"Ah," Gabby self-consciously checked both ears with her hands. "Mine are still there." She smiled. "I haven't heard anyone complain of missing one."

"Oh. Did anyone noticeably disappear from the reunion that night? To change clothes or anything?"

"The only one I knew that left for a bit was Stacey."

"Stacey?"

"Yeah, someone spilled an entire glass of red wine on her dress. I felt so bad for her. She came back, though, after she changed. She didn't let it dampen her evening. What a trooper!"

"So, she came back to the inn then? To change clothes?"

"I'm assuming she did. She lives here in Harborside, but since we all knew we'd be drinking like the good ole days, even the locals are guests here this week. Plus, we all wanted to stick together as much as we could since we haven't seen each other in ages. Anyhow, you'd have to ask her." She shrugged. "Why? Where'd you find the earring? Out here in the grass?"

Kinsley dodged the question and instead said, "No one else disappeared for a noticeably long period of time?" She waited with bated breath, hoping Gabby might share a minor detail she had forgotten to share with the police. Or a slip of the tongue. *Anything* that might give Kinsley a lead or direction on where to dig next.

"Why do you ask? If this is about the murder, I guarantee no one from our class had anything to do with that. None of us had met the victim or knew that she was supposed to perform that night until we were questioned by the police. Awful, though, eh? So incredibly sad."

"Someone must've known Daisy was going to perform in order to book her for the event, no? A coordinator, perhaps? Who oversaw the planning?" Kinsley didn't share that she knew Edna was part of it. She wanted to see if Gabby would drop either her or Luke's name into the mix.

"I suppose. I know Ginger was hit hard with questions. I didn't think about that, I should've asked her," Gabby said, more to herself than to Kinsley, and then returned her attention with a grimace. "It was awful to be interrogated like that, to say the least! I've never encountered a situation like this. I lead a boring life," she added with a chuckle.

"Yeah, I can't imagine what it would be like to be questioned by police, especially after a time when you all should be celebrating."

"Kinda put a damper on the reunion, to be honest. Was that all you wanted to ask me? I really should get going . . ."

Kinsley used her hand to tent her eyes from the sun. "My apologies, I've kept you long enough from the beach, and I'm sure your friends are wondering where you are. Enjoy the rest of your stay!"

The woman's eyes looked longingly toward the cliff walk. "Yeah, I'm sure they are, I better get a move on. Have a good day!" Gabby turned and took the porch steps two at a time.

Kinsley couldn't help but think Gabby's former classmate Stacey might know something about the murder. She hated to jump to conclusions, but was it possible the spilled wine on her dress was just a ruse to leave the reunion? With little to go on, Kinsley needed to dig into that further, to see if Stacey was the person who might be missing an earring.

Chapter 12

"This might be the best glass of lemonade you've ever made," Kinsley said as she wiped the condensation from her glass and then took another huge gulp.

"Glad you like it, but you say that all the time." Tilly smiled as she rocked slowly on one of the oversized rocking chairs that filled the long porch. Her legs barely reached the ground, and she had to tip her toe to keep the chair in a rocking motion.

"I can't help it. It's so refreshing on a hot day like today."

"Sometimes I think you work too hard out there. You need to take breaks, especially when the sun burns off the fog. It sure is turning into a hot one," Tilly added, fanning herself with her hand. "I don't handle the heat as well as I used to. I'm getting old." She clucked.

"You're not old, you're still a spring chicken," Kinsley rebuked. "I will admit, I probably wouldn't work as hard if you didn't spoil me so much." Kinsley reached for the lobster roll her aunt had left on a side table. It was made with the leftover lobster meat Tilly had fed her guests the previous day, and Kinsley couldn't wait to take a large bite. "Thank you, this is sooo good," she added after she'd swallowed and licked her lips.

"I don't know how you don't get sick of eating that stuff all the time." Tilly then reached for the bag of salt-and-vinegar potato chips beside her, popped it open, and dug her hand into it. "I almost can't stomach lobster anymore," she added between chews. "Maybe it's 'cause I cook it all the time."

Kinsley didn't dare point out that her aunt constantly ate vile vinegar chips—to each his own. Instead, she said, "Hey, as long as you're saving me the leftovers, I'll gladly eat it." Kinsley winked before taking another large bite. "I'd take laboring out there in the yard over toiling away in the kitchen any day of the week," she added through chomps. "I hate cooking."

"Although it's hot on the porch today, I'm glad the sun came out so the guests could head to the beach. I've got some serious cleaning to do while they're gone. I probably should get a move on but I'd rather not. I'm enjoying your company." Tilly reached out to pat her on the hand but missed and hit the arm of Kinsley's chair. "After this event is over, promise me you and I will do this more often."

"I have no problem with that." Kinsley grinned.

"I wonder if we should invite Rachel over here from time to time to join us for dinner. She's a nice girl, even if Kyle is too dumb to see it. Isn't it our duty to welcome her to Harborside properly? After all, she hasn't lived here that long. I'm sure she'd love the company."

Kinsley grew serious and lowered her voice. "About that." She wiped her mouth with a napkin and tucked the empty plate back on the side table after literally scarfing her lunch. "Rachel's team supposedly interviewed all of your guests to check their alibis at the time of the murder, but did she know one of them left the reunion?"

"How do you know that someone left?"

"I was talking to Abigale, who is part of the reunion group, and she mentioned Stacey came back to change clothes. Do you know who Stacey is?" Kinsley thought that a rhetorical question because her aunt had the memory of an elephant. Upon check-in, Tilly instantly knew her guests by name, as if she'd birthed them herself. She'd told Kinsley once that she purposely made a point of remembering people's names for two reasons: one, it made them feel instantly at home, and two, it would keep her from getting Alzheimer's, and she didn't want to repeat her own mother's fate.

"Did you happen to see Stacey that night?" Kinsley pressed.

"No, but . . ."

"What room is she in?"

"Why?"

"Because I'm going to clean her room while she's at the beach. It'll give me a chance to snoop. I need to see if I can find something."

"You'll do nothing of the sort!" Tilly stated firmly.

"Okay, then. We'll do it together. If you insist, *you* can clean and I'll do the snooping." Kinsley grinned.

"Kinsley, my dear girl. I offer my guests the utmost of privacy. I would never, *ever*, snoop in their room," Tilly said, adding a disgruntled clucking from her tongue.

Kinsley pointed upward to the ceiling of the porch and lowered her voice. "Really? Even if you could be housing a killer right there under your own roof?"

"I don't see how that's possible. Rachel vetted them, didn't she? And I trust her."

"Yes, she did. But what if Stacey didn't admit to leaving? And what if the police didn't learn that fact? Maybe no one thought to share this little tidbit of news. What if they held back? It's not out of the realm of possibility, you know."

"How can you say that when you heard the same thing right out here in the yard! Of course Rachel would've heard that detail. Phone her right now and ask her," Tilly said with a decisive nod. "Then we'll know for sure."

Kinsley plucked her phone from her pocket and dialed Rachel. After receiving her voice mail, she hung up without leaving a message. "She's not answering. And we're running out of time. What if someone comes back from the beach? We need to get a move on! Just let me in there for a few minutes, it won't take long. Come on, Aunt Tilly, trust me."

Kinsley could see her aunt weighing the options. Kinsley put out praying hands to beg and used her best puppy-dog eyes to drive the point home.

"Oh, all right. But don't disturb anything." Tilly's brow furrowed. "You put everything back *exactly* how you find it. Understood?"

"Absolutely," Kinsley said, rising from the chair.

"What do you really expect to find inside that girl's room that will turn this investigation on its head?"

"One lonely earring. The one I told you about. Maybe I can find its match," Kinsley replied as she threw open the screen door. "And then we'll find the killer," she added over her shoulder.

Her aunt slowed down their pace by picking up the

soiled lunch dishes and stacking them in her arms. "I'll meet you up there. I'm bringing these to the kitchen first."

"Which room?" Kinsley held the door so that Tilly could step through with her arms full. She didn't dare stop to help her aunt with the lunch dishes like she normally would, for fear Tilly would change her mind.

"I think she's in Schooner, but you might want to check the reservation desk to verify," Tilly said over her shoulder as she headed in the direction of the kitchen.

Twenty-five rooms made up the Salty Breeze Inn, and zero were numbered. Instead, maritime names had been assigned to each room, with a corresponding sign above each door. How her aunt could remember which guest was in which room always astounded her. But nine times out of ten, she got it right. Kinsley rushed to the reservation desk by the front door, logged into the computer, and confirmed the room, if only to ease her aunt's mind. She then grabbed the spare key and dashed up the wide navy-carpeted staircase.

The Schooner room was one of the first guest rooms located at the top of the stairs, which made it easy to slip in and out of. This was the first thing Kinsley noticed as she stepped over the threshold after unlocking the door. She decided to leave the door ajar so Tilly could join her. The wallpaper was of muted sailboats and the grand king-sized bed like something you'd find on a fancy cruise ship. Stacey's suitcase was set atop the bed, with clothes strewn across the white bedspread. How Tilly kept the bedspreads looking as pure as the color of white carnations was also something Kinsley thought miraculous.

Kinsley moved to the long dresser located across from the bed in search of the earring. Instead, she found a bottle of suntan lotion, a pack of mint gum with a few missing pieces, a crumpled name tag, seemingly from the reunion, a pen, and a Salty Breeze stationery notepad. The top page looked as if something had been written there and then torn off. She tried to make out the message but couldn't. But after studying it further, it read, *Blue Lobstah*, and a time. Stacey must've been meeting someone there . . . Kinsley's eyes scanned the room, trying to decide where to look next.

The sound of footsteps and a happy whistle caught her attention. It couldn't be Tilly, as in all the years she lived with her, she never heard her aunt whistle.

Like a deer in the headlights, for a moment Kinsley was too stunned to move. Adrenaline pumped through her veins and she dropped and rolled herself beneath the bed. She held her breath and then waited. Seconds ticked by, feeling like long minutes. She chanced a peek by lifting the bed skirt and noted a familiar pair of sandals moving toward the dresser. Why was Gabby in Stacey's room? Gabby exited as quickly as she'd entered and closed the door behind her. Kinsley finally took a breath, causing her to cough. She willed herself from beneath the bed and smoothed her rumpled clothes.

After hearing footsteps again, Kinsley rushed toward the door and flew out to the hallway. She took in a sigh of relief when she noticed her aunt round the corner, and then follow her into the room.

"I thought you were cleaning up the lunch dishes."

"I figured I'd better join you in case Stacey returns. I really feel terrible letting you in here—it's not right," Tilly whispered. "What's in your hair?" Tilly plucked a wad of dust from her head.

"I was under the bed . . . Never mind . . . Wait, did you just run into Gabby?"

"Gabby?"

"Sorry, she probably checked in as Abigale."

"Oh yes. I just passed her on the stairs. Why?"

"Did she have anything in her hands?"

"No, just a beach bag over her shoulder."

"Oh." Kinsley couldn't help but wonder if Gabby had been tipped off from their conversation and came in to see about the missing earring. Kinsley returned to the dresser and noted the bottle of 30+ sunscreen was missing. Stacey must've asked her to pick up the lotion before heading to the beach.

"Did you find anything?" Tilly asked.

"Not yet. But I think I figured out why Gabby popped in . . . and it wasn't about the earring, because she was in and out of here like a flash."

"See, I told you! Rachel was adamant she was going to make sure all our guests were safe at the inn and that I wasn't housing a murderer. Don't you think she's smart enough to do her job? You're not going to find that earring match here, I promise you that. These rooms have been thoroughly searched."

Kinsley shrugged in defeat and blew out a frustrated sigh. "I guess I just thought I'd find something that would help, is all. This murder happening in Harborside has made me feel so helpless. I just want to be sure you're safe. You're everything to me, Aunt Tilly! And what's happened on our property is so unfair. I don't want any connection to this awful thing!"

Tilly reached for her then and enveloped Kinsley into her comforting arms. "I know, darlin', it'll be okay. It's understandable to be a little shook up over this but we'll get through it." She soothed Kinsley, patting her on the back softly. "But you really need to get out of here in case Stacey returns."

As Kinsley hugged her aunt, her eye caught something

poking out of a suitcase pocket. Curiosity made her back away from their embrace to investigate. She pulled out a professional program, as if from a Broadway production. After opening the *Playbill* for *Wicked*, she instantly noticed the name of the actress who had played the leading role. It was Daisy. And the *Playbill* was signed. A photo fluttered from inside the program and Kinsley reached out a hand to grab it before it hit the ground. A photo of Daisy, alongside another woman with a matching grin, stared back at them.

"Is that Stacey?" Kinsley asked.

"Yes, that's her," Tilly answered. "It looks like Stacey knew the girl who was murdered."

And the photo of the two of them had been taken in front of the Salty Breeze Inn.

Chapter 13

Prior to her friend stepping fully inside the Blue Lobstah, Kinsley caught Becca's attention with a wave of her hand. As soon as they were within distance, Kinsley looped Becca by the arm and directed them away from their typical seats at the bar to a table located outside on the outer deck. With the tourists most likely crowding the bar, she didn't want anyone to overhear their conversation.

When they located an empty table, Kinsley dragged it a bit farther away from the others just to be certain they'd be out of earshot.

"What are you doing?" Becca asked, tossing her oversized purse onto the table and causing her cell phone to spill out.

"You and I need to talk about this crime that's happened practically on our doorstep, and I'd rather this conversation remain private. This murder investigation is hitting a little too close to home, and I don't think Rachel is any further along in solving this case. And the suspects are stacking up like cordwood. I need your help."

"What do you mean?" Becca asked. She slid into the seat beside Kinsley and leaned on her elbows, so they could be closer.

"I found out one of the guests at the inn had met Daisy before she was murdered."

"How'd you find that out?"

"I discovered a signed *Playbill* in her room. Did you know that Daisy had the leading role in *Wicked* on Broadway?"

"Okay, so maybe she had the *Playbill* signed in New York, while attending *Wicked*? Sometimes actors will do that after a performance."

"I don't think so," Kinsley said adamantly. "There was a photo inside, taken of the two of them, right outside the inn."

"I'm still confused," Becca replied.

"Daisy was a surprise guest, asked to perform at the reunion with the band, but supposedly she never made it to the reunion. So how would Stacey's *Playbill* be signed, if only a select few on the reunion committee knew she was supposed to perform? And have her photo taken with her?"

Becca raised a brow. "Maybe this girl Stacey was the one who'd asked Daisy to perform at the reunion in the first place, maybe she's the one who planned it? Or maybe Stacey ran into her at the inn and asked that she pose for a picture and sign her *Playbill*."

"Well . . . yes and no. Yes, maybe she just ran into her, but I know for a fact she wasn't the one who handled the planning."

"How do you know that?"

"Someone on the committee named Ginger organized it.

But also, Luke was supposed to perform with her. Anyway, Edna was the one who had asked Daisy to come to Harborside."

"Edna?"

"Yeah, I'm guessing this Ginger person reached out to Edna, as she has so many connections in the thespian world and is so involved with the Harborside Playhouse. And even though the reunion attendees didn't graduate the same year as Daisy, it's a pretty big deal she made it all the way from Harborside High to performing on Broadway."

Pete appeared at their table and tucked his head between them. "What's going on here, ladies?" he asked with a raised brow and a grin that lit his face like fireworks on the Fourth of July.

Kinsley thought Pete's animated smile only added to his charm. She wondered if that was why everyone in the community seemed to embrace the Bostonian. Every time the man smiled it looked as if all the muscles in his face participated. His disposition was, in a good way, contagious.

Pete interrupted her thoughts when he added, "Two nights in a row? I'm happy to see you both, but . . . What exactly are you doing here?"

"We needed a private place to talk," Kinsley answered.

"'Bout what?" His eyes ping-ponged between them, finally resting on Kinsley for an answer.

"Aren't you the nosy one?" Becca teased, swatting him on the arm.

"Hey, I appreciate your patronage, but clearly something big is going on here." He frowned.

"What makes you say that?" Kinsley asked.

"You two never sit out here. And believe it or not, the stools are open at the bar. I think even the tourists are afraid to sit in your assigned seats." He turned his head to verify, and Kinsley and Becca followed with their own eyes.

When he turned back to them, he continued, "Besides, I can't remember a time when I've ever seen either of you two nights in a row. Are we drinking tonight, ladies? Or are you here for dinner?" he asked, flinging a towel he'd held in his hand over his shoulder.

"I'm not hungry. Tilly fed me a late lunch. But she might want something," Kinsley said, gesturing to her friend.

"Should we ask him? Maybe he's heard something?" Becca asked.

"Ask me anything, I'm an open book." Pete leaned back and flung his hands out wide like Fonzie from *Happy Days*.

"Not really, we still don't know how old you are," Becca teased.

Pete responded with a wink and a wagging finger. "Age is but a number. Once you reach thirty, you stop counting. Believe me, birthdays don't hold the same excitement as they used to."

"See, he still won't give it up. At least we know he's over thirty now," Becca said, shaking her head in mock disapproval. "It's my best guess."

"Okay, enough about my age. What's up? What do you want to ask me?"

Kinsley gestured to the bar owner to come closer, until their heads were almost touching. "Have you heard anything about the Cinderella murder?" she whispered.

Pete's demeanor turned instantly serious. "That's what you two are here to discuss? The girl found out there in that farm field?"

"Yeah." Kinsley looked at Becca while her friend studied Pete.

"Why are you digging into that?" he asked.

Kinsley found Pete's choice of words a little interesting. She wouldn't confide in him about the shoe—Rachel swore her to secrecy. But she sensed Becca thought his word choice was interesting, too, as she sank deeper in the chair, moved away from him, laced her arms across her chest, and tightened her lips.

"Well, we haven't had anything like this happen in Harborside in a long, long, time. I just figured, with so many tourists hanging out around the bar, you might've overheard something . . . anything . . ." Kinsley prodded.

Pete waved his hands as if he wanted nothing to do with the conversation. "I try and keep my distance from anything regarding the law." His face tightened. "I wouldn't touch that with a ten-foot pole. No way." He took a step backward.

Kinsley was mildly surprised by his reaction, but she pushed ahead anyway. "Had the victim, Daisy, ever come here? You ever see her?"

She shared a look with Becca before they both returned to study him.

"Yeah, she was in here. Pretty little thing, too. Darn shame." He hung his head and shook it slowly. "She had a whole life ahead of her . . . Awful what happened to her."

"Hey, O'Rookie!"

The three turned to see a woman with a big grin splashed across her face waving at the bar owner. "You said if I came in tonight, you'd make me that special candy-kiss drink, *remem-bah*?" She puckered her rosy lipsticked lips and pouted.

Pete held a up a finger for the patron to wait a minute. "I'll be right there, Justine." He then turned back to Kinsley and Becca and said, "Look, I gotta skedaddle. A friend of mine is up here on vacation from Boston, and I promised her a drink. But if you want to stop in sometime, right before I open when the bar isn't flooded with patrons, I guess I'll tell you what happened with that girl." He tapped his hand on the table twice then swiveled away from them before Kinsley had a chance to stop him.

Chapter 14

A few days had passed, but the rolling calendar did little to erase the murder investigation from Kinsley's mind. If anything, she'd spent the bulk of her time planting flowers and developing scenarios in her mind, trying to unearth the truth. She'd overheard her aunt Tilly handling a reservation cancellation, and she couldn't help but start to panic about that, too, thinking word might be getting out. Had people decided after hearing about the recent murder that Harborside wasn't the safe, quaint place to visit? She was anxious to return to the Blue Lobstah to prod Pete for more info, too, but her tight schedule hadn't allowed it. However, it was high on her agenda, and she would make a point of it, even if she had to work overtime to make it happen.

Kinsley was en route to the Stapleton property when an animal limping alongside the road caught her attention. She slammed her foot on the breaks in the middle of the tree-lined street, which caused her tires to screech, and most likely leave a streak on the road. She winced as she looked in the rearview mirror. Thankfully, there hadn't been an automobile following her. But something far more important had caused her to stop.

"Baxter!"

After navigating her pickup to the side of the road, Kinsley reached for the apple that had rolled into the passenger seat. It wasn't a dog treat, but it was the best she had on hand to lure her neighbor's dog.

"Baxter!" she called again as she leaped from the truck. She held her hand down for the dog to investigate a chunk of apple she had bitten off for him. The Australian shepherd came toward her slowly, with a limp. His eyes, the color of crystal blue sea glass, looked up at her hungrily for more and she obliged. His mottled pattern, normally in shades of red, was covered in briars, and he was filthy from head to toe, as if he'd rolled in a mud bath. It looked as if he'd been bleeding, too, as dry blood was caked on the top of his head and traveled between his eyes. Kinsley pushed the fur aside to get a better look at the injury, but none could be found. The dog didn't flinch as she examined him. Upon further investigation, she realized the blood was only on top of the fur, as if poured on top of him. Human, perhaps?

Kinsley plucked the water bottle from her truck and offered some to the animal. The dog sucked down the tepid water as if he couldn't get enough of it. Meanwhile, with bits of apple, she lured the Australian shepherd into the passenger seat of her truck and closed the door. Immediately, she phoned Edna and asked which veterinarian's office to take him to and suggested they meet there.

Minutes before arriving at the vet's office, Kinsley's hands-free device sang out inside the cab of the truck. She connected the signal while looking over at the passenger seat to check on Baxter, whose sad eyes looked up at her as if he was exhausted.

"Rachel, I found Baxter."

"Baxter?"

"My neighbor's dog, he's been missing."

"Okay?"

"Anyhow, I'm just pulling into the vet's office, the one off of Cove Road. Can you meet me there?"

"What's this about, Kins? I'm kinda busy."

"There's blood on him, but I can't find an injury. It might be a stretch but is there a chance Baxter may have been at the crime scene? My aunt mentioned that our neighbor's pup has a bit of a shoe fetish. Maybe Tilly's right and Baxter is the culprit who buried the shoe in our yard. Is it possible that whatever is stuck on his fur could hold a clue?"

"I see."

"I just parked in the parking lot out front. Should I wait to take him inside? I don't want the vet to wash him off if there is even a hint of possibility that something of value or evidence could be on him. I'll wait for you, okay?"

"You've been watching too much *CSI*." Rachel chuckled. "But, yeah, hang on, I'm on my way."

Kinsley parked the truck and stroked Baxter's back. "It's okay, buddy," she said, soothing him. "You'll be home soon." He lifted a limp paw to the console in response. The briars that were stuck atop his paw looked painful. Her heart sank for the dog. She really hoped he was only minorly injured and this was the worst of it.

Before long, Rachel pulled an unmarked car into the space beside the truck. Kinsley was thankful Edna hadn't arrived yet. She rolled the window down and Rachel stuck her head inside. "Hey, fella. What a cutie. Look at those eyes," she said as she reached for the dog. He snuggled against her and licked her hand. "What a lady-killer you are," Rachel added, and then blushed, as her timing for that comment was horribly off. Kinsley didn't dare call her on it. After all, the detective spoke the truth, Baxter was a gorgeous dog, and anyway, she knew what she'd meant.

When Kinsley finally spoke, she said, "Thanks for coming, Rach, I know it might be a stretch but look at his head. Is that human blood?"

Rachel leaned in closer to examine the dog. "It's possible. Sure looks like blood to me. In any event, it doesn't hurt to take a sample that we can test later, if need be."

Edna's car pulled in, with Luke behind the wheel. Within minutes the two joined them.

"Oh, Baxter!" Edna gushed as Kinsley opened the passenger door and the dog went to greet his owner. "Are you hurt?" The older woman knelt to look him over after he rushed to her legs. "Oh, my poor, poor baby," she cooed. "He's hurt!"

"He was limping, and really thirsty," Kinsley said. "We'd better hurry and get him inside."

"Grandma, I'll be back to pick you up, okay? I need to run an errand," Luke said, and looked toward Baxter, as if the dog were a wrinkle in his plans.

"I can take her home," Kinsley suggested. "I want to be sure Baxter is okay before I leave, anyhow. Don't worry, your grandmother is in good hands."

"You sure?" Luke asked. His dark eyes, the color of the center of a black-eyed Susan, narrowed in on her. He was dressed as if he was heading to a business meeting, but as far as Kinsley knew, he traded stocks online from the privacy of a home office. She wasn't sure why the tall, dark, and handsome man was dressed to the nines. His gaze landed on Rachel, and he seemed to try to place her, and then he said, "Hey, I know you. What are you doing here?"

Rachel shared a conspiratorial look with Kinsley before answering, "I'm here to pick up my cat."

"Ah, I see. Any progress in the case?" Luke's eyes had lasered in on Rachel, studying her intently.

"You two know each other?" Kinsley asked with more surprise in her tone than she'd meant.

"I wouldn't take it that far. If you include being inter-rogated by her, then, yeah"—Luke chuckled—"I guess we know each other pretty well, now, don't we?" Luke's eyes traveled from Rachel's head to her feet, and then back again.

Rachel didn't answer, she just stood there with rigid shoulders and a blank expression.

"Rachel's an old friend of mine; she dated Kyle. Luke, have you ever met my brother, Kyle?" Kinsley rambled. "Rachel, we'd better go check on your cat, right?" She el-bowed the detective in an effort to continue along with the ruse before chuckling and saying, "Small world, eh?" Kins-ley was afraid that if Luke had anything to do with the mur-der and he knew what they were up to, he'd toss Baxter inside the back of his SUV and scrub him down so fast their heads would spin. How could she think this of her neigh-bor's grandson? Suddenly, everyone's motives were suspect. A shudder crawled down her spine, but she straightened her shoulders to ignore it.

Luke turned his attention to Kinsley before she had a chance to walk away, and said, "Thanks for taking her home." He then redirected his attention to Edna but contin-ued to ignore the injured dog at her feet. "Grandmother, I'll stop by later for dinner, okay?" He kissed Edna on the cheek before disappearing into his SUV. Luke peeled out of the parking lot so fast, Kinsley wondered if he was worried that she might change her mind about taking his grandmother home.

"What happened to your cat?" Edna looked to Rachel with concern.

Rachel shot Kinsley a look.

Kinsley chewed her cheek and waited to see how the detective would respond.

"I'm here on official police business. I might need to take a closer look at your dog," Rachel said.

Edna's eyes doubled in size, and she gasped. "My Baxter? Whatever for?"

"As I'm sure you've heard on the news, we're trying to locate a shoe from our murder victim. I hear your dog has a bit of a shoe fetish. We're following any and all leads," Rachel said.

"Well, I certainly don't have it!" Edna snapped. A little too vehemently, in Kinsley's opinion.

"I didn't say you did," Rachel said calmly, and then looked to Kinsley. "I'm taking a sample of his fur for the record."

"What record?" Edna asked. "What does my dog have to do with that poor girl found out in that field? Is that where you found my Baxter?" Edna's eyes narrowed in on Kinsley, seeking confirmation.

"Now that you mention it. Yeah, I found him not far from the potato farm where the victim's body was found. It's a possibility Baxter visits that farm to hunt for small animals in the fields," Kinsley said, taking the dog by the collar and redirecting him to the door of the vet's office.

"Are you going to prohibit me from extracting a sample? Or will I need to go through the proper procedures and get a warrant?" Rachel asked. "If I do that, I'll have to ask the vet not to touch your dog until I have the paperwork I need. It might take a few days."

"She can't do that. Can she?" Edna looked at Kinsley helplessly. "I'm taking my dog home today!"

"Wouldn't you want them to take a sample of fur, or look him over, if it can help in any way?" Kinsley encouraged as she held the door for them to walk inside. "Maybe Baxter can be the key to solving this. He could be Harborside's hero!"

"I suppose there's no harm in it," Edna said, slowly mulling it over and looking to Kinsley, as if she was thinking the repercussions through.

Kinsley just hoped for Edna's sake that it was indeed Baxter who had buried the shoe and Luke had nothing to do with the crime. What if Luke had the means— What if he was the last one to see the victim alive? If he had unrequited feelings for Daisy, that was a potential motive . . . Kinsley needed to do whatever it took to clear Edna's grandson from the suspect list, as that suggestion surely wouldn't sit well with Aunt Tilly. Not for a minute.

Chapter 15

After meeting with the vet, Kinsley was relieved to hear that other than a minor injury to his paw, Baxter was released to Edna with a clean bill of health. Edna had been given strict instructions on how to care for his injured paw and told to keep the dog on a leash moving forward. She doubted her neighbor would take all the sound advice the vet offered but wondered if this last scare of losing Baxter for an extended period would change things. In any event, it was a relief to be heading home with her neighbor and the dog in tow. A cleaner version of Baxter sat between them inside the cab of the truck as they rambled along the road. She knew how much the dog meant to her neighbor and she was happy he was soon to be returned home, safe.

Kinsley phoned Adam with instructions, and the teen assured her he'd take up the slack and move the begonias to the other side of the yard over at the Stapleton job. Adam often rode his bicycle to jobsites, and that one, luckily, was close enough for him to take on.

When she clicked off the phone, Edna patted Kinsley on the shoulder and said, "Thank you again, honey, for saving my Baxter. You could've driven right by or called animal control, instead you took care of him for me. I'll never forget that." Her hand moved to stroke Baxter on the head. "Mama's gonna spoil you rotten when you get home. I'm even going to let you nap on my bed," she cooed. "My poor little puppy."

"You know I couldn't do that. I know how much Baxter means to you and, honestly, to all of us. Aunt Tilly will be thrilled to learn he's home safe and sound, too. She's been worried about him and looking everywhere." Kinsley reached over to scratch the dog's neck and he licked her hand.

"Well, I can't thank you enough, Kinsley dear. I'll have my cook bake you a pie."

Kinsley smiled. It was Edna's way of repayment, to have someone else bake a pie. "No need to have the oven on in this heat. It's no bother, really."

"An ice cream cake, then? You used to love those when you were a child, I do remember that." Edna snuggled closer to her dog on the seat. Baxter then cocked his head between them, causing Kinsley to grin.

"No thanks, I don't need ice cream cake, either. Really, I'm happy to help. And besides, you'd do the same for me." Although as soon as the words were out of Kinsley's mouth, she wondered. She loved Edna dearly, but her neighbor tended to put her own needs above others. If it was on her agenda, then she'd participate, but if it wasn't, she tended to ignore Aunt Tilly completely. Kinsley had shared her feelings with her aunt, when Tilly would go above and beyond for Edna time and time again, but Tilly would defend Edna to the end.

"Did you know Luke was questioned by the authorities?" Kinsley asked tentatively.

"I wouldn't say questioned," Edna said. "You make it sound as if my grandson is a suspect. They asked any of us who had met with Daisy for information. It was just information sharing. Trust me, that is *all* it was," she corrected. "Besides, Luke was with me the night of the murder," she said firmly. "He has a solid alibi."

Kinsley chose her words carefully. Since Luke having an alibi was most likely part of Edna's agenda, she didn't dare push it. "So, you spoke to Rachel about Daisy, too, then?"

"Of course I did. She came by the house and talked with everyone, even the staff. Didn't you?"

"I never met Daisy, so no, I didn't. Only Becca had met with her. Remember I told you, she was one of her clients?" Kinsley didn't dare bring up the fact that Rachel had asked her questions about the murder. Questions that would lead her back to the shoe. "Who do you think had a motive to kill her? Have you wondered about that?"

"I have no idea—some psychopath!" Edna said. "Certainly not my grandson or anyone else in our circle," she added firmly. "I can't even believe you would insinuate that."

"I'm not implying that at all. I just know the police like to look at those closest to the victim first. Please forgive me, Edna. I watch too many crime shows in the winter months when my business slows down. I'm just going by what I know, is all."

"It's all right, honey," Edna soothed. "But you should really change your habits. Documentaries are so much better for your brain." Edna reached over her dog and patted her on the arm to drive the point home. "Anyhow, Daisy and Luke weren't that close, I can assure you that. Just because she was buying a house here, doesn't mean she was planning to date my grandson. That was only *his* imagination working overtime." She rolled her finger to her temple, to insinuate Luke was crazy to even think it.

That was the opposite of what Edna had said the other day out on the cliff walk. It seemed as if she was trying to take her grandson completely out of the equation now, distancing Luke from Daisy. Kinsley didn't think she would get much more out of Edna and didn't want to further upset her neighbor, so she decided to drop the subject entirely.

The two remained quiet on the remainder of the ride, until traffic came to a complete stop. Cars lined up ahead of them and a billow of smoke filled the air. Once she realized they would be there awhile, Kinsley had no other choice than to put the truck in park and turn off the engine. She had forgotten to fill the tank and they were running on fumes.

"Oh dear! I do hope no one is badly injured," Edna said, deep concern lacing her tone as she rolled down her window. The smell of smoke seeped in, causing her neighbor to close the window back up.

"Yeah, you know what? I'm going to check it out, you wait here. I'll go see how far the line of cars is up ahead. I might have to turn around and take an alternate route but I wanna check first, as this is the fastest way home. Before my truck runs out of gas."

"Yes, honey. You do what you need to do to get us home," Edna replied, snuggling into Baxter.

Kinsley hopped from the truck and jogged ahead to see what had happened. She gasped when she saw Luke in the middle of the road, waving his arms helplessly while shooting flames licked from his expensive SUV.

"Luke!" Kinsley shouted, and ran toward him. When she reached his side, she looked him over carefully to be sure his clothes weren't singed. She didn't initially see any fire damage to the poor man. "What on earth happened?"

"I have no idea. I was driving along and noticed smoke coming from the hood, so I stopped. As soon as I got out of my car, it erupted in flames!" He shrugged and looked toward the melting steel, put his head in his hands, and then crouched to the ground as horror filled his face.

A shiver ran down Kinsley's spine. She couldn't help but wonder if Luke's SUV, now engulfed in fire, was no accident. After all, how often does one see an automobile randomly catch on fire? Especially a rather pricey SUV. Had someone sabotaged his car because he knew something? And maybe now he was the next target?

A worse thought crossed her mind and she swallowed hard to push it down. Rachel mentioned that Daisy was not murdered in the field, she was placed there. Was Luke taking matters into his own hands and destroying crucial evidence in front of her very eyes? No! It absolutely couldn't be. That thought she would emphatically deny.

She searched him again, looking for answers, and Luke shook his head as if in shock and utterly disgusted. Kinsley just wasn't sure if he was playacting for the crowd or honestly shocked that his SUV was up in flames.

Chapter 16

The next day, after dropping off a floral bouquet for Becca because she'd officially gotten the listing and wanted to continue to woo her new clients, Kinsley stopped in at the Blue Lobstah in hopes of cornering Pete and talking him into sharing what had been left unsaid. She didn't see him behind the bar, though. Instead, his bartender, Raven, was slopping drinks and making light conversation with sunburned tourists. Kinsley waved for Raven's attention as soon as she noticed she'd hit a lull.

"Hey, girl, what can I get ya?" Raven's friendly smile lured Kinsley a step closer to the bar, and she leaned her weight into it.

"Oh, how I wish for a drink after the week I'm having," Kinsley said with a laugh.

Raven's eyes, the color of goldenrod, held her attention. "That bad, eh?" she asked with a grimace.

Kinsley shrugged to downplay her comment while Raven wiped her hands on the apron that hid her narrow waist.

"Pete around?"

"You just missed him. He ran out about a half hour ago to deliver a waterside pickup over at the marina. He'll be back in a few if you want one on the house while you wait. I won't tell him." She put a conspiratorial finger to her lips and smiled.

"That's very kind of you, Raven, but I still have a full day ahead. I need to keep my head in the game. Thanks, though," Kinsley answered, but her shoulders sank. She'd really hoped to speak with Pete.

Obviously, her disappointment showed because Raven asked, "Everything okay? You seem a little upset. Maybe there's something I can help you with?"

"I'm okay. It's just the murder here in Harborside has me totally on edge, I can't seem to shake it." Kinsley drummed her fingers atop the bar, wondering what she should do next.

"I hear ya, girl. It's so awful. I even told Pete to take the late shifts from now on. I'm not walking to my car alone at two in the morning. No sirree! Not with some lunatic traipsing around our town!" Raven shivered and then shook her head, causing her dark ponytail to swing like a horse's tail aiming at flies.

"It's terrible. Unthinkable, really. I've never felt unsafe in Harborside, until now. It's just hitting a little too close to home for my liking," Kinsley said as she scanned the bar to see if they were in earshot before continuing. "Did you meet her?"

"Who?"

"Daisy."

"The woman that was murdered, you mean?" Raven asked.

"Sorry, I thought by now everyone knew her name was Daisy. It's all anyone in Harborside seems to be talking about. Everywhere I go, the bank, the vet, the greenhouse . . ."

"Yeah, I've heard mumblings about it here at the bar, too, but mostly people are calling her Cinderella. I think that guy on channel four news did a disservice by calling her that because it certainly stuck." Raven gestured for Kinsley to come closer and then pointed toward the other end of the bar. "She and Luke sat cozied up to the bar one night, talking among themselves about her being famous. I heard she was an actress?" She shrugged. "On second thought, maybe he was just drunk and slurring his words." Raven smirked. "The drinks definitely kept coming that night."

"Is that right? Any chance you remember what night that was?" Kinsley wondered about the note found in Stacey's room. Had Luke summoned both Daisy and Stacey to the Blue Lobstah that night? If so, why?

Raven cringed. "It wasn't long after they'd been in here that I heard she'd been found out in that field. Come to think of it, I think she was wearing the same dress she had on that night! And I couldn't help but ogle those shoes . . . The way they sparkled!"

"Oh? She was wearing the shoes?"

"Hard to miss. I wondered where she bought them, and then I heard from the newscaster that they were purchased from Mallards. Apparently, a one-of-a-kind pair, as they were made exclusively for her. I can't imagine having shoes made exclusively for me, can you? Sounds extravagant." Raven plucked a rag from beneath the bar and began to wipe long strokes in front of her.

"Did you see Luke with her on more than one occasion?"

"Nah, just the one time."

"They seemed to get along okay?"

"I think so . . . Why?" Raven's eyes turned the size of quarters, and she lowered her voice. "Is Luke, like, a *suspect*?"

Kinsley swiftly shook her head to deny it. The last thing she wanted was to spread gossip about her neighbor's grandson. Even though the fire coursing through his SUV had left a burning image in her mind. "No, Edna told me Luke was with her that night," she said adamantly.

"Phew!" Raven wiped her brow and shook her hand out dramatically. "That would've been awkward! The guy comes in here, like, all the time. I can't imagine finding out I'd been waiting on a *murderer.*"

"Can I get a Coors Light?" A man wearing a polo shirt and matching shorts, as if he'd just stepped off the golf course, slid over to the bar, interrupting them.

"Duty calls," Raven whispered. "Take care of yourself, girl, I'll see you soon."

Before Raven fetched the drink, Kinsley asked, "When you see Pete, can you tell him I was looking for him?"

"You bet!" Raven answered before turning to greet another customer, who slid beside Kinsley at the bar. It was Denny.

Kinsley inwardly composed herself before greeting her competitor after Raven stepped away from them. "Denny," she said, acknowledging him with a curt nod and forced smile.

"Oh, hey, if it isn't Kinsley Clark." Denny returned the smile. "I'm glad I caught you. About the other day—"

Kinsley put up a hand to stop him in his tracks. "It's nothing. Just drop it, okay?"

"Look, I owe you an apology. Anytime I drink, it's kinda like 'loose lips sink ships' and all that." He grinned as he absently stroked his beard shadow.

"I accept your apology. But what are you doing here in

the middle of the workday ordering a beer? Not busy?"
Kinsley sent him the dig and then inwardly chastised herself for acting so childish. Why did she allow herself to
stoop to his level?

Denny gave her a once-over. "If I'm not mistaken, you're
in here looking for a cold one, too, so I'm guessing we're
even. Can I buy you a beer? What do you say we call a
truce, Misssss Clark?"

"I'll toast to that." Kinsley held up an imaginary glass in
cheers. "Thanks for the offer, but really, I need to get back
to work. Maybe another time." She wasn't sure why she'd
said that. The very last person on earth she'd share a drink
with was Denny Davenport. Ever.

"I'm sure you do," he rebuked. "I mean, you're waayy
too busy to share a drink with a guy like me. I'd hate for
you to compromise your standards."

Kinsley didn't have time for this nonsense. "You take
care, Denny, and stay away from my plants, you hear?"

"Like I'd bother with them!" He snorted.

"I'm watching you," she said over her shoulder as she
skidded out the door.

The strong wind rolling off the ocean hit Kinsley hard
as she meandered down to the marina. Seagulls squawked
and dove for food, circling her head, like she was one peck
away from being lunch. One of the gulls even scooped up a
random French fry along the cliff walk and flew rapidly
away, as if to protect its prized possession.

Kinsley brushed the hair away from her face and allowed the wind to do the rest. The stirring smell of salt and
kelp caused her to breathe in willingly and center herself
after her encounter with Denny. No doubt, he was incorri-
gible, but she needed to let it go. No sense letting the childish man get under her skin, yet again.

After removing the sunglasses that hung from her shirt, Kinsley adjusted them over her eyes to keep the blinding sequence of sparkles bouncing off the water at bay. The smell of the ocean was replaced by the scent of suntan lotion as she walked closer to the boardwalk, leading to the boat slips. She caught a glimpse of Pete heading in her direction and greeted him with a friendly wave.

"Hey, stranger, heading out for a ride with a client?" Pete teased as he jutted a thumb in the direction of the mooring yachts. "You wouldn't *believe* the size of the boat I was just on. I almost hid in the bathroom as a stowaway, just for the chance to ride on her. Have you been on *Gail's Second Wind*?"

Kinsley chuckled. "How I wish. No, truthfully, I was looking for you."

"Me?" Pete grinned, lighting his face in pure joy. He really did have a winning smile. "What gives me the lucky pleasure?"

"The other day, when Becca and I were at your restaurant, you mentioned that you'd share more about Daisy. I just thought I'd stop by to pick your brain and get the scoop."

"You're not gonna let this go, are you?" Pete asked with a raised brow.

"How can I? When—" Kinsley almost let the shoe slip from her lips, and she stopped herself by biting her lip instead.

"Did you *know* her? From the other day, I didn't get the impression that she was a friend of yours." He cocked his head to one side, as if waiting for an answer.

"No. That's not the point, it doesn't matter that I didn't know her. I can't let this go. And neither should you," Kinsley defended. "A young woman's life was snuffed out way too soon. And in the safety of our exclusive community, where she'd been invited to come and perform. It's literally unheard of."

With a large swing of his arm Pete gestured to the exclusive properties that lined the cliff walk. "You're naive if you think crime only hits in the ghetto. Crime can happen anywhere, chief." Kinsley often heard Pete address the male patrons who would step up to his bar as "chief." She'd heard him say on more than one occasion, *What can I get for ya, chief?*" However, this was the first time that he addressed her in that way.

"I know crime can happen anywhere, I'm very well aware of that." Kinsley rolled her eyes. "That's not what I meant."

Pete responded with a deep sigh and then summoned her to follow. "Walk with me."

Kinsley turned on her heel to follow the bar owner back in the direction of the Blue Lobstah. "I don't understand why you're so against trying to find the truth. And why you seem to be avoiding law enforcement if you might know something." There. She'd finally said it. Kinsley really wanted to know if Pete had any skeletons in his closet and why he seemed so skittish the other day.

"I'm not, I'm just minding my business," Pete defended, yet started to pick up his pace, as if wanting to avoid her, too.

Kinsley met his stride. "Okay . . ."

"Look, it's just that I don't want to get involved. My business is at stake. No way do I want patrons to connect my establishment to anything to do with a local murder. That's the last thing I want. I'm keeping my distance, and so should you."

"What about SeaScapes? I run a local business, too, ya know," Kinsley defended. "That has nothing to do with it."

"Look, I don't want any part of it. So keep my name out of your little investigation, okay?"

Pete slowed his stride and held out a pinky for her to shake.

"Really? We're doing this?" Kinsley teased as she linked pinky fingers with him.

"Swear," he said. "Or I won't share a thing."

"I swear." Kinsley crossed her heart after their pinky shake was over to double his confidence.

"I saw the girl, Daisy, with Luke, you know . . . the guy who's related to Edna Williamsburg. They were arguing at the bar. And then some girl came in, got in Daisy's face, and it got all heated between the three of them. I had to separate them and throw the one girl out of the restaurant."

"Who was she? I mean, the girl you kicked out of the restaurant?"

Pete shrugged. "Never saw her before, and I haven't seen her since. I told her to go somewhere else if she wanted to throw punches. Luckily for me, she took me seriously and hasn't walked through my doors since."

"Throw punches? That bad?"

"Yeah, that bad. But it gets worse . . ." Pete's voice trailed off.

"Worse than throwing punches? What the heck happened?"

The color drained from his face. "The girl who was attacking Daisy said, and I quote, 'You'll regret this.' That was the thing she kept saying, over and over. And then I heard that Daisy was found out there in that potato field!" His eyes widened.

Could this girl he was talking about be the one missing an earring? Maybe there was much more to this. Was Luke somehow involved, and did he have a coconspirator? Kinsley kept these musings to herself and waited for Pete to spill more. But she couldn't help but wonder if the note she'd found in Stacey's room regarding a meeting time at the Blue Lobstah had something to do with this. Had he summoned them both? Or was it a coincidence that Daisy was with Luke that night?

"I dunno, but I'm not helping to convict someone of murder and have them spend a lifetime in prison, over a word choice. Would you? It's none of my business." Pete ran a hand over the unshaven stubble on his cheek, and Kinsley couldn't help but think he was even more attractive with the five-o'clock shadow. But she didn't want to be thwarted from the business at hand. She needed to stay focused and not get caught up in the bar owner's magnetism.

"Whose side was Luke on? Did he seem to side with one of them over the other?"

"Look, that dude's an idiot, letting those girls fight like feral cats. It was probably his fault the argument escalated out of control; he could've stopped it. I hate it when that guy comes into my bar. It seems like drama follows him everywhere he goes."

"This is important information to share with the police, no? I know you don't want to get involved but—"

"Did I mention the flowers you planted in the whiskey barrels on the outer deck aren't looking very good?"

Kinsley hadn't noticed. "Really? That's your mode of deflecting the conversation. Hit up my flowers?" she teased.

"Kinsley, I'm serious. I know you're super busy with the Walk Inns event but if you don't have time, I'll just get rid of them. One of my customers commented on them." Pete then had a faraway look in his eyes and lowered his voice to a mere whisper, as if continuing the conversation with himself. "Maybe patrons are dumping liquor in them or something? Anyhoo, I should just drop the idea of having flowers out on the deck. I have enough on my plate."

This wasn't the first business in town where Kinsley's flowers weren't thriving. Something fishy was going on, and she needed to get to the bottom of it, and fast. If she found out that it was in fact Denny, she'd officially press charges. "I'll look into it. This is getting out of hand."

"What do you mean, out of hand?"

"Someone has been messing with my arrangements in front of Toby's Taffy, too," Kinsley admitted. "I have an idea who could be involved, or it could be someone else entirely, sending me a warning. I'm not going to say unless I can absolutely prove it. Didn't you just tell me you didn't want to convict an innocent person?" she added with a chuckle.

Pete stopped short, and alarm crossed his face. "Kinsley, this isn't good. What if someone knows you're poking around and investigating? You could be putting yourself in harm's way. What if they're sending you a message to back off, by way of your plants? You're gonna end up dead as a daisy. Let the cops handle this."

It's not exactly like she hadn't already thought the same thing, but she dismissed it entirely by saying, "Would you reconsider our pinky promise? I feel like you're just changing the subject, as usual."

Pete held up a hand in defense. "Look, I told you, I'm not getting involved. Edna sends all her theater groupies to converge over at my bar. I'm not getting on the woman's bad side by implicating her family members. Trust me, I know nothing." Pete put his hands over his ears, making himself look like a petulant child. "Besides the fact I don't *know* anything, anyway. People argue all the time at my bar."

"Yeah, they do. But people don't usually lose their life over it. That, my friend, is not coincidental."

Kinsley knew Pete's business was at stake, and she appreciated that. But something in his demeanor made Kinsley feel like there was more to it than that. She really hoped she was wrong, because it was the first time she'd questioned her feelings about the bar owner.

Chapter 17

It had been a long and backbreaking day when Kinsley had finally thrown in her trowel and called it quits. Finally, caught up and back on track in preparation for the Walk Inns, she decided to take a moment and meander to her favorite spot. The week had been so hectic that she hadn't even had time to have lunch out on the rocks facing the sea, per usual, and she'd missed it. She wondered if her coffee mug was still at her spot, abandoned the morning she'd met up with Edna, or if it had washed away with the tide. She was just about to step off the path and hop onto the rocks when she heard her name called out. Tilly must've followed closely on her heels, as she was at the top of the stairs and making her way down to the cliff walk to join her. When Kinsley turned to greet her, Tilly handed over a paper bag.

"What's this?"

"I brought you a brownie, fresh out of the oven. The one wrapped in a napkin is meant for you. I was hoping you could deliver the rest of them to Edna. I wanted her to know I was thinking of her. I just haven't had a moment to go over there myself to welcome Baxter back. If I stop over now, she'll keep me chatting for hours, but if you bring them, maybe you won't get as hung up? I need to sweep the porch, clean out the pantry, and the refrigerator needs an overhaul . . ." Tilly ticked off the to-do list on her fingers before Kinsley interrupted her.

"Oh yessss! I'd be happy to deliver them, and thanks for saving me one." Kinsley's mouth watered in anticipation because her aunt made the best brownies. They were perfectly chewy, filled with chocolate chips, and often were topped off with Heath bar bits. "Can you do me a favor, though? If you happen to see Becca, tell her I'll be right back? She mentioned she was planning to stop over after her six o'clock showing. I'm sure she'd love a brownie, too, and maybe some lemonade out on the deck? Did you happen to save some back at the inn?" Kinsley reached into the bag, unwrapped the brownie from the napkin, and took a large bite. "Heavens, this is divine, maybe you should make these for the Walk Inns."

Tilly smiled at the compliment. "Yes, I have more. There's a batch on the table for my guests, too, so there are plenty to go around, but they're not quite event-worthy, in my opinion. And yes, I will certainly keep my eyes open for Becca."

"Can you do me another favor? I left my mug out here the other day. Would you mind bringing it home for me?"

"Sure thing."

Kinsley hopped onto the rocks and found her coffee mug tucked inside the crevice of her hiding spot. She scooped it up and returned it to Tilly. "Thanks."

"No problem, and thank you again for delivering these to Edna! Much appreciated!" Tilly said with a wave good-bye before quickly making her way back up the path in the direction of the inn.

Kinsley was happy to oblige, as she wanted to check on their neighbor and see how Baxter was healing, too. After a quick bite of brownie, she licked the crumbs from her lips and made her way back to the path leading to Edna's. The Williamsburg estate also had a similar access to the cliff walk, however, at the top of the stairs, a grand fence surrounded the property, and the gate was always kept locked. Edna had shared the combination of the lock so that Tilly, or Kinsley, could enter anytime they wanted. Today, however, the gate was halfway open, causing Kinsley to hesitate. The sound of Luke's voice stopped her in her tracks.

"Why didn't you tell me this before?" Luke asked.

"Tell you! Why should I tell you?" A woman's voice rose an octave with each new syllable. "If it wasn't for you, none of this would've happened."

"Me? You're blaming me?" Luke's voice escalated to meet hers. "You're the one who wanted in on it, and you're making it my problem?"

Kinsley held her breath and crouched down beside the fence. She desperately wanted to see whom Luke was speaking with but didn't want to give herself away. The wind caused a faint scent of suntan lotion to float to Kinsley's nose. She wondered if the woman had just returned from the beach and caught Luke in front of the gate. From the sound of their voices, they were probably a few feet from her location, but the overgrown shrub roses blocked her. Kinsley crept deeper into the roses despite the thorns thrashing at her arms. Just then her cell phone chimed in her back pocket. She reached to silence it and a thorn tore through her flesh. A text from Becca stating she was on her way.

Kinsley grimaced when she heard the woman say, "What was that? Did you hear that? Was that your phone?"

"I don't know what you're talking about," Luke said. "I didn't hear a thing."

Kinsley gave a sigh of relief. A few moments passed before the woman continued, "I need to find it, and you need to help me."

"No way, I want no part of this. This is your problem."

"No!" she hissed. "It's *our* problem. If the police find out, they'll connect the dots. You need to find a way to fix this!"

Kinsley heard a rustling of footsteps on the other side of the gate and she squeezed deeper behind the roses, hoping she wouldn't be seen.

The gate swung open fully and the woman stomped down the stairs, oblivious to Kinsley. Long, angry strides led the woman to the cliff walk, and she kept pace without a backward glance.

Kinsley instantly recognized the highlighted hair color of the girl who was now tramping angrily down the cliff walk. It was the woman from the photo who had stood next to Daisy in front of the Salty Breeze Inn. The one whose picture had slipped from the *Playbill*.

Stacey.

After releasing herself from the rosebush, Kinsley noted blood trickling down her arm. She wasn't the only one who noticed.

"Kinsley?" Luke said, rounding the corner and about to shut the gate.

"Yeah, I'm okay," Kinsley answered before he even had a chance to ask.

"What happened, and what are you doing out here?" His eyes narrowed in on her accusingly.

Kinsley flung the paper bag toward him, and he snatched it with one hand. "What's this?"

"My aunt wanted me to deliver this. Unfortunately, I lost my footing," she stammered. "I tripped and fell into the rosebush," she added before stealing a glance at her arm, which looked as if she'd been attacked by an angry cat.

"Ouch. Let's get you inside and clean up those wounds." He led her by the elbow onto safer ground, and they began their long trek in the direction of Edna's house set far beyond the cliff walk.

"Thanks, I appreciate the help," Kinsley said genuinely. She was surprised at how accommodating Luke was acting. She hadn't experienced this side of him, though it had been only recently that he'd moved back to Harborside and spent more time with his grandmother. Tilly had said more than once that Luke was only after Edna's money. Kinsley thought it not fair to judge but couldn't help but side with her aunt on occasion. Maybe she hadn't given Luke a fair shot.

"I smell chocolate. What's in the bag?" Luke asked while they walked along the long, manicured path leading to the mansion that overlooked the sea. Edna's property was every bit as large as the Salty Breeze Inn, only it didn't house guests, just family members on occasion. Kinsley's favorite part of the buttery shingled home was the turret with its 180-degree view of the Atlantic. She'd been in the room only a handful of times but was in awe of the view every single time as if she were seeing it for the first time.

"Kinsley?" Luke said, interrupting her thoughts.

"Oh, I'm sorry, brownies. One of my aunt's many talents is in that bag. If I were you, I'd be sure and snag one before you hand them over to your grandmother."

"I've heard about her legendary brownies. I most certainly will," he said with a genuine smile, towering over her. He was so tall, Kinsley couldn't help but see how he could easily disarm a person with his imposing build.

"Did everything work out with your car? I mean, did you ever find out what caused the fire?"

"It sounds like the electric fuel pump shorted out; insurance will cover it. I was ready to trade it in anyway, the odometer just hit thirty thousand miles." He shrugged, but the undercurrent of his tone suggested . . . what exactly? Guilt?

"Yeah, I'm looking for something a little sportier," he continued. "Maybe even a Mercedes GTR. I really don't need all that trunk space."

Kinsley couldn't help but think that was an interesting statement. "Personally, I love my old truck and the space it affords me. But I use it for work, and as my personal ride." She chuckled. "I'm able to help Aunt Tilly haul things away in the back of it from time to time, too. So, it's really handy."

"I couldn't see myself ever driving a truck."

Kinsley winced, and Luke must've noticed, because he said, "You'd better take care and not injure yourself again. How would you keep your business thriving? Competition around here is fierce."

Kinsley thought that a very odd comment, too. So odd, in fact, that she completely stopped walking and flung her hands to her hips, causing the blood to trickle farther down her arm. "What do you know about it?"

Luke turned to face her. His eyes fixated on her face, and his unruffled demeanor started to rattle her.

"Mr. Davenport was over here earlier today, giving my grandmother a quote for her landscape. And may I add, it was hundreds of dollars less than yours. I heard you hire out the mowing and handle only the designs here. He's willing to do it all."

Anger coursed through Kinsley's veins. "Is that so?"

"Yep. You, fine lady, can't afford to get injured. That guy is certainly ready to pounce on your business," Luke said, turning on his heel and returning to a long stride.

Edna was on the oversized screened porch facing the ocean and rose from the wicker chair to open the door upon their arrival.

"Grandmother, your neighbor is injured. Will you sit with her while I go and grab a wet towel?" Luke dropped the paper bag full of goodies onto a side table that flanked the side of her chair.

Edna's eyes doubled in size. "My dear girl, what happened to you?"

"I fell in the rosebush." Kinsley was hoping the lies weren't beginning to show on her face. Were her cheeks the color of the roses she blamed? She never was a very good liar.

"Kinsley, please sit here, next to me." Edna gestured to the wicker chair covered with plumped navy cushions and ticking pillows, and when Kinsley obliged, she sank immediately into their comfort.

In an effort not to drip blood on the beautiful chairs, though, Kinsley forced herself to sit upright and lean forward. Edna handed her a tissue, and she dabbed at her wound. "Tilly sends her love in the form of brownies. She wanted you to know she's happy Baxter is returned home and all is well."

"That's so kind of her," Edna said, but her face didn't reflect gratitude, only sadness.

"What's wrong?"

"Baxter is inside sleeping. He never sleeps this much,

and his stomach hasn't been good. I'm hoping he really is on the mend." She folded her liver-spotted hands in her lap. "I'm a bit worried."

"He's sure been through a lot," Kinsley soothed. "He probably didn't sleep a wink while he was gone. And perhaps he got into something that upset his tummy. He'll be okay, Edna; he just needs a little more time."

"I suppose."

"The police didn't share if they found anything of value to propel the investigation further, did they? DNA, or anything like that?"

"I haven't heard a peep. But it's highly unlikely my Baxter had any involvement at that horrific crime scene," Edna said airily as if it were completely out of the realm of possibility. Something Kinsley did not agree with, given the blood on his fur.

"Can I ask you something?" Kinsley continued, leaning in closer to her neighbor.

"Sure. What is it, dear?"

"Was a girl named Stacey on the reunion committee? Or were Ginger and Luke the only ones who knew that Daisy was planning to perform?"

"As far as I know, only Luke, Ginger, and I were privy to that information. We didn't want to spoil the surprise, so we kept it to a minimum. Why do you ask?"

"No reason," Kinsley said when she noted Luke's expression when he returned with a washcloth. It was evident he'd overheard. And he did not look amused.

Chapter 18

"Everything okay here, ladies?" Luke asked as he tossed Kinsley the washcloth. He stood suddenly rigid and far less welcoming than when he'd initially shown concern for her injury.

Kinsley heard chimes of a grandfather clock tolling from inside the house, and silently counted them. She wrapped her arm with the wet cloth, thanked Luke profusely for the rag, and rose from the chair. "Is it seven o'clock already? I need to go. Becca is waiting for me at Tilly's and I shouldn't keep her. We had talked about heading over to the Blue Lobstah for a lobster roll."

"Would you rather come over here for dinner? You could invite Becca, too, if you'd like. I haven't seen your friend in eons. I'd love to have Tilly join us, too, but I'm sure she's tending to her guests and can't break away on short notice," Edna said, and then looked to Luke, who nodded absently in agreement. "I'd be happy to ask the cook, but I'm sure there is plenty of food to share," she added. "We'd love your company. Wouldn't we, Luke?"

"I'll go and speak to the staff to be sure they prepare extra for our guests," Luke said, disappearing into the house as if the decision had already been made. By his quick exit, Kinsley wasn't sure how he felt about Becca and her coming for dinner.

Kinsley desperately wanted to decline but wondered if she could gather more information about the investigation if she accepted the invite. She also wondered if Becca would forgive her, because if she didn't know any better, Edna had ulterior motives of setting Becca up with her grandson. Edna had shared on numerous occasions that she wanted the family name to continue. And for that to happen, Luke needed to provide offspring soon, as he was the last of the heirs. But the idea of Becca dating Luke didn't sit right with Kinsley, and she wasn't sure why. Was it because in her eyes, he seemed to be hiding something?

Edna must've sensed Kinsley's hesitation because she said, "I really would like you to join us, dear. After taking such good care of Baxter, please let me repay you. It's the least I can do," she pleaded.

Kinsley was ashamed then for thinking the invite might be more of a setup than simply Edna's way of showing gratitude. "If you're sure, on such late notice? We could do it another time . . ."

Edna beamed and clasped her hands together as she rose from the chair. "I'm tickled you'll both come. I love having guests for dinner, it gets lonely in this big ole house all alone."

"But you haven't been alone, you have Luke! He's here quite a bit recently—no?"

"Yes, I suppose." Edna's voice lowered. "But all he talks

about lately is how to get in my wallet. I need a diversion from that nonsense tonight." Her eyes twinkled with mischief, as if conspiring with Kinsley.

"Okay, well, I need to run home for a quick shower. I can't sit in your grand dining room looking like this." Kinsley glanced at her soiled work attire and then regarded the chair to be sure she didn't leave a mess in her wake. She brushed the cushion off with her hand, just to be sure.

"We look forward to seeing you both in a half hour or so?" Edna said, patting Kinsley on the back before her neighbor retreated into the house.

It wasn't hard to convince Becca to accept the invitation to dinner held at the mansion next door. After all, it was a chance for Becca to talk real estate and pick Edna's brain on whether any of her friends or business associates were in the market to sell. Kinsley left her friend happily sipping lemonade and chatting with Tilly on the outer deck while she rushed home to clean up. She decided to let her hair dry naturally as she slipped into her one and only sundress, which hung in her closet with the tag still attached, waiting for an occasion such as this. A quick glance in the mirror made her realize she'd need a light sweater, as her farmer's tan didn't quite match up to the spaghetti straps that now hung on her shoulders. Her bronzed skin did mean no need for makeup. Just a hint of lip gloss was required before slipping into a pair of jeweled flip-flops and quickly retreating out the door.

"You look marvelous!" Becca said as Kinsley made her way up the porch steps to greet her friend with a hug.

"You always look amazing coming from work. I guess I wanted to lose the gardening duds and try and look presentable this evening." Kinsley glanced down at her feet and dug her toes deeper into her flip-flops. "Sometimes, I feel like such a tomboy. I've never had much of an eye for fashion. Hopefully this works."

"Well, you certainly don't look like a tomboy to me." Becca whistled as if she were a construction worker with a model crossing his path.

Tilly stepped outside onto the porch and greeted her. "Well, look at you! My gorgeous niece!" she gushed. "Don't you look nice. Becca mentioned you were just going next door for dinner. What's the occasion?"

"You guys!" Kinsley swatted a hand to downplay the attention. "Thank you. I guess I need to clean up more often, with that kind of reaction," she added with a smile. It was nice to feel pretty for a change. She wondered if they would still stop off for a drink after dinner at the Blue Lobstah and hoped Pete would give her the same attention. She brushed the thought aside as she used her fingers to comb her damp hair, which was quickly drying from the heat. She was sure it would be completely dry after the trek next door.

"Ready?" Becca asked.

"After you," Kinsley replied, blowing her aunt a kiss before the two friends made their way down the steps and headed in the direction of the cliff walk.

"Have fun, you two. Give everyone my best," Tilly said behind them, and then Kinsley heard the screen door close behind her aunt.

"I wish your aunt could come with us. She deserves a night out."

"I know. It's a shame, really, she hardly ever gets a break. I've often told her I'd take over for her, but she refuses. And she would never willingly take a break during tourist season anyway. She's afraid I'll fall behind in my business, too. I wish she didn't always put everyone first, but that's my aunt Tilly," Kinsley said with a sigh.

"She really is a peach. You're so lucky to have her."

"I'd be lost without her," Kinsley agreed. "I don't even like to think of it."

"Thankfully, you don't have to," Becca encouraged.

The wind off the water blew Kinsley's hair like a blow-dryer. As expected, her hair was nearly dry, so she removed the hairband from her wrist and decided to put her hair in a ponytail as they walked along.

"You know, I don't think I've ever been inside Edna's house. I can't wait to see it," Becca said. "It's one of my favorite residential properties along the cliff walk."

"Really? I thought for sure you had. Well, you're in for a treat, it's a gorgeous home."

"Yeah, I can hardly wait," Becca squealed.

They made their way to the gate, and Kinsley pressed in the combination, but the lock didn't work, and the gate refused to open, even after three attempts.

"Huh. That's strange."

"We could walk around?" Becca suggested.

"I'm kinda lazy to go all the way back around. Do you have your phone? I'll just call Edna. I left mine back at the house."

"Sure," Becca said, digging into her oversized purse, plucking out her cell phone, and handing it over.

After making the call and waiting what seemed like forever, Luke met them at the back gate. He swung the door wide for them to enter.

"Sorry to make you come out here like that," Kinsley said. "For some reason the combination didn't work. I've never had an issue with it in the past."

"That's because I changed the combination today," Luke said. "With the recent events in Harborside, you can't be too safe. We won't be sharing the combination moving forward. I should've told you to come to the front entrance, via the security cameras. In fact, I'm having a camera brought out to the back gate, too."

Kinsley felt as if her hand had been slapped. The front entrance? She hadn't entered the front gate since she was a child and visiting with her parents. Was Luke isolating Edna? Or was the extra safety precaution really needed? And who was he to suddenly be making all of Edna's security decisions? Kinsley bit her tongue and let it slide.

"I wouldn't worry about it too much. I think the murder in Harborside was an isolated incident, don't you?" Becca said, and Kinsley wanted to give her friend a high five. Way to corner him, but Luke's demeanor seemed nonchalant.

"From what I gather, the police don't have any leads. I doubt they'll ever solve it," Luke said. "It'll probably end up as one of those cold case files, in the basement of the department we pay such high taxes to support," he added with a hint of sarcasm to his tone.

"Really, where did you hear that?" Kinsley asked.

"Just in talking with Rachel about the investigation, she pretty much alluded to the fact that no evidence was found at the crime scene, or anywhere else, for that matter. Sounds like a whole lot of dead-end leads."

"Hmm. You knew Daisy, yes? You were supposed to sing with her at the reunion?" Kinsley asked.

"Who told you that?"

"Your grandmother."

"Ah." Luke nodded.

"Since you were one of the few who had actually met Daisy, can you think of a reason why anyone would want to harm her?" Becca asked.

When he didn't answer, Kinsley pressed. "Yeah, did she share with you if she had any enemies? A bad breakup? Anything like that?"

Luke adjusted the collar around his neck. If Kinsley didn't know any better, she'd say he looked mildly uncomfortable, like he didn't appreciate the firing of questions. Or being in the hot seat.

"Can't say that she did. But maybe we should end this conversation before we go inside. I don't want to upset Grandmother any further about the matter. This tragedy in Harborside really has her feeling vulnerable. And I don't think any of us want that, now, do we?" He turned and waited for them to agree before opening the door.

"Yes, of course," Kinsley said with more feeling than she meant. Because she was pretty sure Luke was hiding something. She just didn't know what yet.

Chapter 19

As soon as the three entered the screened porch, Edna met them at the doorway. "Kinsley, don't you look lovely." She greeted her with a kiss on both cheeks and then moved to greet Becca in the same manner. "Dinner is not quite ready yet. We can start with a glass of merlot in the library. How does that sound?"

They followed Edna into the house and stopped in the expansive entryway. High coffered ceilings and rooms poked out in all directions like a wagon wheel with an oversized grand staircase directly in front of them.

"You have a library?" Becca gushed. "Oh, that's an absolute dream of mine!" She clasped her hands in delight and her face lit with pure admiration.

Edna smiled. "We sure do, and it's filled with generations of collected books. My family has a long history of readers, so our shelves are filled to the top. It's fun to pick up some of their private diaries, too." She lowered her voice to a whisper, as if sharing something taboo. "We've learned all kinds of family secrets that way. Haven't we, Luke?"

"I prefer the classics, myself," Luke answered flatly.

"I love the classics, too. Hemingway is my one of favorites," Becca chimed in.

"Well, we have something in common then, don't we?" Luke looked at Becca with a new light in his eyes, and the two shared a smile.

Kinsley held back an eye roll while watching the two swoon over each other.

"Speaking of classics, I'm not sure I mentioned it, but Becca is a local real estate agent. She's just building her client list here in Harborside. I'm sure she'd like to hear more about your lovely home, Edna. Not that you'd ever be willing to sell, but touring homes is right up her alley," Kinsley added, correcting herself. "What year was this built?"

"Oh, how wonderful, Becca! This home has been in my family for countless generations. I believe it was built in the late 1800s, although you'd never know it to be true, as so many renovations have come over the years."

"How many bedrooms?" Becca asked.

"It boasts many bedrooms and bathrooms. We have five fireplaces, if you can imagine, one of them in the formal dining room. We also have a breakfast room, walk-in pantry . . . Oh, my dear." Edna laid a hand to her cheek as if exhausted. "The rooms are endless. Thankfully we have a team of housekeepers, otherwise I'd never be able to keep up. We also have a keeper's quarters on our property for the staff, which is quite handy."

"Don't forget the extensive wine collection in the wine cellar, and you'd be amiss, Grandmother, if you didn't share the most special place in your home, which is the turret, yes? It most certainly is the favorite room of the house, according to everyone who pays a visit," Luke added.

"I hope I'm not being too presumptuous, but Becca would love a peek inside the turret if you don't mind? It's such a special room, and since real estate is her absolute world, she'd love the opportunity," Kinsley said. "Wouldn't you, Bec?"

Becca reached for Kinsley's arm and sent her an agreeable smile. "If it isn't too much to ask. Oh, I'd love a peek at it," she squealed. "Very few people along the cliff walk have one of those! A visit to the turret would be such a treat."

"Of course! Luke, would you mind taking them on a tour? My sciatica has been acting up a bit the last few weeks, so if you don't mind I'll wait downstairs." Edna looked up at her grandson with a slight cringe regarding her pain. Luke acknowledged with a furrow of his brow.

"How about this—why don't you all meet me in the formal dining room when you're through? Dinner should be on the table by then," Edna said. "We'll save the library for another visit." Edna tapped Becca on the arm to see if this would be agreeable, and Becca agreed with a wide grin. It was obvious she was dying to see the space that Kinsley had bragged about earlier.

"Yes, Grandmother, and if your back is bothering you, be sure and get off your feet," Luke said as he gestured a hand for Kinsley and Becca to follow. "Right this way."

Kinsley knew the route like the back of her hand, as she'd been inside Edna's home countless times. She never wearied of a visit to the turret and followed dutifully as they made their way up the wide oak staircase leading from the back of the stately home to an upper floor.

When they reached the second floor, they followed the

carpet runner that covered the polished oak floors down a long hallway until they reached the solid, burgundy-stained door. Luke swung it open, and a rounded staircase led them to the octagonal room facing the Atlantic. The windows flooded the room with natural light and Becca gasped the minute she stepped inside the space.

"This is breathtaking!" Becca gushed.

"My favorite room of the house," Luke admitted. "The best view of Harborside is right here. You can see for miles. I always feel like I'm on the top of the world when I'm in this room."

The high coffered ceiling made the room feel more expansive than its square footage. Curved nooks of plump royal blue seats lined the back walls.

"It's amazing," Kinsley added. "Every time I come up here, I'm awestruck. It really is stunning!"

The three moved closer to the windows and Kinsley took in the sun, not quite ready to set, its rays dancing across the ocean. The jagged coastal rocks along the cliff walk were pounded by the waves that rolled gently onto the private beach beyond that. Breakwater Lighthouse, boats bobbing along the sea, and the marina and private beach were all in the panoramic view. She also could pick out the Blue Lobstah off in the distance but couldn't make out specific patrons or Pete. They all looked like flies, scattered across the outer deck.

"Listen to this." Luke reached to crack open a window, and they all took in the rhythmic sound of the sea.

Kinsley breathed deeply, letting the sound soothe her.

"The sound of the waves is so peaceful," Becca said finally. "That symphony certainly would lull me to sleep! It's amazing!"

"I used to camp up here as a child when Grandmother

would allow it. A rare treat indeed," Luke admitted. "Speaking of the symphony, if you ever want to travel down to Boston, I have season tickets to the Boston Pops, if that's something of interest to you."

Kinsley didn't get the impression she was part of the invite but piped up just the same. "Have you always had an interest in music, Luke? I didn't know you were a singer until I heard you were planning to perform at the reunion." She intentionally left out Daisy's name in hopes she could prod him without making him feel like he was getting the third degree once again. Hopefully, he'd crack open like a shell.

"Yes, I've had singing and piano lessons all my life. Since I was a young child my parents expected me to be cultured."

"Oh, you play, too?" Becca asked. "I've always wanted to learn how to play the piano," she said wistfully. "My aunt had a piano when I was growing up, and I only learned how to play 'Chopsticks,'" she added with a chuckle. "A far cry from Beethoven."

Kinsley was starting to feel like she was a third wheel on a first date. Luke and Becca seemed to be swimming around each other like two fish checking out shiny new scales, and she was a measly sea urchin at the bottom of the sea. She let the feeling pass and decided to take the opportunity they were given to allow Becca to get to know Luke more. Knowledge, after all, was power. She strode over to the telescope in the far corner of the room while the two kept up with their small talk.

Kinsley leaned in to the telescope to chance a peek and was shocked to see the image in front of her. The telescope was zoomed in, not on the south side of the ocean, but on the potato field. Most of the view was blocked by a clump of maple trees and thick wooded pines, but it was evident just the same. The question was . . . Why was the telescope focused on that location in the first place? If Edna's sciatica was acting up, it was certainly not the homeowner who had made the climb and pointed the telescope in that direction. In Kinsley's mind, it meant that Luke had been the one in the turret checking out the crime scene. The question was—*why?*

Chapter 20

Kinsley and Becca strolled along the cliff walk, walking off their four-course meal and enjoying the evening breeze. The orangey-pink sun, the color of a blooming hibiscus, was slowly sinking in the horizon, leaving a glittery path along the waveless sea.

"Was it me? Or did you notice how much Luke seems to be distancing himself from the murder investigation?" Kinsley said as she hugged the sweater tighter around herself. Despite the calm weather, the wind seemed to have a bite to it, as if a hint of things to come.

"I didn't notice. I was too mesmerized by the gazpacho soup. That was the best meal I think I've ever had."

"It was delicious, wasn't it?"

"Divine. Remind me to hire a cook when I become rich and famous," Becca said with a chuckle, shoulder-bumping Kinsley. "Or when I become the top agent this side of Harborside."

"And one day, you will," Kinsley answered confidently. "Just remember who your friends are," she added lightly. "And don't forget to hire SeaScapes to landscape all of your properties."

"You know, if it wasn't rude, I would've asked for a doggie bag," Becca said. "But I didn't want to push my luck."

"Edna probably would've made sure you left with a hefty portion. She's a real sweet lady, isn't she?"

Despite their banter around the meal they'd recently devoured, Kinsley couldn't keep thoughts of the murder investigation at bay. "The fact that Luke's saying he only met Daisy on a few occasions, to practice for the reunion, is the opposite of Edna's account. His grandmother made it sound like he was falling in love with the girl."

"Maybe so, but wouldn't you try to distance yourself if you'd been around Daisy, too? Would you want to insert yourself smack-dab in the middle of a murder investigation? I don't think so."

"Oh boy," Kinsley mumbled.

"What?"

"You enjoyed his company tonight, didn't you?"

"He is rather charming," Becca admitted with a smile.

Kinsley couldn't argue the fact. True to Luke's word, he'd kept all talk of Daisy entirely out of the formal dining room. And he'd also promised Becca a few introductions to prominent members of Harborside who might help with her real estate career. Was he being nice? Or was he just trying to keep their minds off the crime and concentrated on dinner conversation? Was it guilt? Or was he really that protective of his grandmother? All these questions tugged at her mind before Kinsley continued.

"I forgot to tell you; Luke also had a bit of an argument with Stacey. She's the one I told you about who left the reunion because someone had spilled wine on her dress. Remember, she's also the one who had her photo taken with Daisy. Do you think there's a connection? Perhaps she's in on it?"

"Are you *actually* saying you think Edna's grandson is responsible for murder? I'm sorry, but I can't imagine he'd be so calm after killing someone, like, a week ago. In my opinion, he seemed very relaxed tonight."

"Maybe it was the wine?" Kinsley suggested. She, too, was feeling a bit tipsy despite the four-course meal. Well, maybe not tipsy, but she was definitely . . . relaxed. Apparently, there was more of an uptick in the alcohol content in those expensive wine bottles that she'd never had the chance to sample until now.

"Could be. Speaking of that, I wish I hadn't declined the glass of wine, but I really thought I would hear back from a potential listing client. It's getting late, though, so I guess I should've toasted, 'cause it doesn't look like they're planning on getting back to me tonight." Becca frowned. "They promised they'd call with their final decision after discussing the pros and cons of moving over dinner."

"We could still walk over to the Blue Lobstah for a drink. I'm up for that."

Just as the words were out of Kinsley's mouth, Becca's phone rang in her purse. Her friend never missed a phone call, as every call was an opportunity to show, or list, a home. She picked it up on the second ring. Kinsley crossed her fingers and held them in the air in hopes this was the call Becca had been anticipating.

"Yeah, we'll be right there," Becca said. Instead of happiness, concern riddled her friend's face and her tone sent alarm bells ringing through Kinsley.

"That didn't sound like a client ready to list their house

for sale. Everything okay?" Kinsley asked when Becca slipped her phone back into her purse.

"No, it's not. That was your aunt. Toby called. He said all the flowers outside the candy shop are dead, and some of the businesses in town are starting to grumble because theirs aren't looking so good, either. They're afraid you won't be able to fix this before the Walk Inns. Someone called an emergency town council meeting."

Hearing that news sobered Kinsley immediately. "You're kidding. I probably shouldn't get behind the wheel. Can you give me a ride over there? I need to see what's going on, firsthand."

"Absolutely."

The drive to town was quiet between them, both lost in thought. Kinsley finally broke the silence as they headed down the road leading directly onto Main Street. "Remember that incident with Denny, at the Blue Lobstah?"

"Yeah?"

"I can't help but think he's purposefully killing my plants."

"Really, Kins? You think he'd stoop that low?"

"Am I wrong to think that after our run-in at the bar? Who else would do this? I've heard he's also been running around town handing out quotes like candy bars on Halloween. Including quotes to *my* clients." Kinsley's voice rose an octave, and she evened her breath to settle herself. The anger was beginning to churn in her stomach, too.

"Who told you that?"

"Luke said he'd given Edna a quote. My own neighbor, for Pete's sake! I've been taking care of her property since my gardening business began!"

She clenched her fists and held them tightly atop her legs.

"The nerve!" Becca's tone mimicked her own.

Kinsley loved that her friend always had her back. She reached for Becca's hand across the console, to give it a squeeze in gratitude.

"I can't help but think he's sabotaging my business."

"I guess I can understand why you would feel that way."

"Do you know how expensive it's going to be to replace all of this? Not to mention the time I have invested?" Kinsley said when she saw firsthand the wilted flowers outside of Toby's Taffy. As soon as the car came to a complete stop, she threw open the passenger door and went directly to the whiskey barrels. Anger coursed through her veins; the war was officially on.

Toby was outside the taffy shop, cleaning the front window, and turned to Kinsley as soon as he heard an expletive fly from her lips. He dropped his cleaning supplies and came to her side.

"I'm so sorry, Bumpkins. I don't know what could be causing this problem. Is it possible you got yourself a sour batch of soil or something? Sure is bad timing with the event coming up. You must be swamped." Toby threw his meaty arm around Kinsley's shoulder and enveloped her in a comforting half hug. His oversized apron smelled of caramel corn, strawberries, and marshmallows. Kinsley didn't want to let him go, instead she wanted to stay in the comfort of his fatherly arms and hide.

"No, it's not that. A few flowers looked a little sad the other day, but I thought it was an isolated incident and limited to one or two plants. Now they're all dead! This is definitely not a soil problem; this problem is man-made," Kinsley said flatly.

"I promise you, I didn't touch your flowers. I wouldn't dare," he said, finally releasing her. "And I hate to be the bearer of bad news, but we're not the only ones." His glance traveled down the sidewalk to the nearby seasonal gift shop, and Kinsley's eyes followed. She couldn't believe the carnage of dead flowers, now in full view. They seemed to journey all the way down Main Street, like a line of funeral cars.

"No, you're not the bearer of bad news—I already heard. Aunt Tilly sent the forewarning." Kinsley sighed heavily.

After parking the car Becca arrived at her side, and gasped. "Oh, Kinsley, this is awful!"

Jenna stepped outside the taffy shop and beckoned to her husband. "I need a hand, hon; we're backing up in here! Hi, ladies," Jenna acknowledged with a friendly wave before disappearing back into the shop.

"If you don't have time to replace them, don't worry yourself about it," Toby said, retrieving his cleaning supplies. "I'm sure you have enough on your plate right now. But you'd better go and have a chat with Chris, he's gathering a special town council meeting for early next week, so you might want to touch base."

"Chris?" Kinsley groaned. Chris was an alderman with a booming voice. The one most often causing discord within the common council, instead of making peace. She'd much rather go directly to the mayor, but figured she best stick to the chain of command, if that's what Toby suggested. If she got Chris on her side, it would be best anyhow.

"I'd better get back inside before Jenna has my hide. You catch that rhyme?" Toby laughed, as if desperate to lighten Kinsley's mood. When she didn't oblige, he tried taffy instead. "Free samples! Come on in, ladies," he threw over his shoulder before rushing inside.

"I don't think all the taffy in the world is gonna make you feel better, is it?" Becca asked timidly. Her friend knew her weakness for sugar, and quite often Toby's was the place

Kinsley ran to for comfort. The only thing that would make her feel better now, though, would be wringing Denny Davenport by the neck, but she kept mute about that. Kinsley sighed heavily.

"This is so wrong," Becca said.

"You're certainly right about that. Something is *definitely* wrong here, Becca." Kinsley cocked her head and studied the floral carnage in front of her. She reached out and plucked the ivy to take a sniff and prove her own point—that her plants most definitely had been tampered with. And she was pretty darn sure by whom. When she did so, something else caught her eye, and she moved the plant to see what was poking out of the soil. It was a pink Barbie doll shoe. A shiver ran down her spine.

Kinsley knew instantly what the toy meant.

The person who did this knew she'd hidden Daisy's shoe!

It was a warning . . .

To back off.

Either way, she got the message—crystal clear. And it wasn't a good one.

Chapter 21

An emergency meeting was called between those in the know about the Cinderella shoe. Those present were Kinsley, Becca, Tilly, and Rachel. They held their gathering in Kinsley's secret spot, concealed within the rocks facing the Atlantic. Hidden from onlookers and their conversation dulled by the lapping waves, it felt like the safest place on earth. Darkness was upon them, too; only the beams of their respective cell phones lit the private discussion.

Kinsley reached into the pocket of her hooded sweatshirt and plucked out the evidence and then held the Barbie doll shoe in her palm for all to see.

"Whoever planted this outside Toby's Taffy knows about the murder—and is clearly sending me a warning. And the only person I know who would want to destroy my work is Denny Davenport," Kinsley said firmly. "He's been quite vocal about it."

"But what connection does he have to the crime? Did he even know Daisy? Was he even interviewed?" Becca asked.

They all looked to Rachel for confirmation.

"No, he wasn't questioned," Rachel confirmed. "This is the first I'm hearing his name mentioned with regard to the murder. But clearly, if he's the one responsible for burying the Barbie shoe, he has some involvement."

"There has to be a connection. The toy was definitely planted specifically for me." Kinsley tucked the Barbie shoe back into her pocket for safekeeping, then thought twice about it. "You can't extract DNA off that, can you?"

"The mere size of it won't allow for a fingerprint, and the fact it was buried in your flowers leads me to believe it's highly unlikely. To get a sample someone would have to transfer biological material and it would've been disrupted by the dirt," Rachel answered.

"Besides, the person who planted it was probably smart enough to wear gloves, I'd imagine," Kinsley added. "Wouldn't they?"

Nodding heads settled that question among them.

"What about my niece's safety?" Tilly asked, her voice riddled with concern. "Sending out a warning like that. This person is obviously disturbed."

"I'm fine." Kinsley reached out and patted her aunt on the arm to console her. "No need to worry about me, I can take care of myself," she confirmed, but Tilly didn't look overly convinced.

With an encouraging nod Rachel looked to Tilly. "Kins, if you ever feel unsafe, you call me right away. Put my number on speed dial."

"Already done," Kinsley said firmly.

"Does anyone else know about Daisy's shoe except the four of us? If so, spill it now, so we can get to the bottom of it. There's obviously a leak somewhere," Tilly said, now growing visibly frustrated.

"I didn't say a thing." Becca zipped her lips with her fingers, confirming the fact she wasn't the leak.

"Nor did I," Tilly said.

"I'm sure no one saw me; I mean, I buried it right away. And Rachel, when you took it that day for evidence, it's not like anyone was around us watching. I hate to say it, but could it be that someone in law enforcement is the leak?" Kinsley asked, hesitantly. "Do you know if Denny is friends with anyone at the police station?"

"I understand that you want to cover all our bases, so I won't take offense that you asked. Rest assured that only a few in the department know, and those who do are involved in the testing of the shoe for DNA. As far as Denny being friends with an employee, that I'm unsure of, but I'll look into it. Since I've been there, I haven't heard a peep about dirty policing, so I think the mere idea is highly unlikely," Rachel said, closing her eyes as if searching for something that would make sense. When she opened her eyes again, she added, "We need more leads." She blew out a breath of frustration. "This case is becoming the bane of my existence."

"Any results on the real shoe? If you're saying the Barbie shoe can't provide any DNA because of being buried in the dirt, can Daisy's? Or is that a shot in the dark, too?" Becca asked.

"Great question," Kinsley said. "Rachel?"

"Nothing conclusive, yet. Yes, it's true that Daisy's shoe being buried is a bit of a glitch. But DNA is not outside the realm of possibility. We found a single hair inside the toe of the shoe. And it's not Daisy's. They're extracting the hair follicle to see if there's a match in the system. And there were bite marks to the shoe, evidence that an animal had it in its mouth at one time," Rachel confirmed.

"The bite marks from Baxter?" Kinsley asked.

"Possibly. We're testing that sample as well, thanks to Kinsley."

Kinsley smiled weakly at the compliment. She was happy to know her gut call had provided at least some help in the investigation.

"Anyhow," Rachel continued, "we're still waiting on the blood DNA from the lab. These things take time. Besides, our department hasn't had to handle anything like this in many, many years. We're overworked, understaffed . . . ah . . . never mind." Her lips came together in a firm line.

Kinsley secretly wondered if Rachel was wishing Kyle was working at the police department, too. Her old partner in crime. She wasn't the only one missing her brother, especially now. Kyle was always so protective of the women in his life. And seemingly now, more than ever, she needed protection, according to her aunt.

Tilly turned her head in the direction of the cliff walk and then back toward the group. "I hate to break this up, but I really need to get back to the inn. It's time for me to serve up the nightcap-tea-and-cookie hour. My guests really love that part of their visit. It would be a shame if I didn't meet their expectations."

"Yeah, I have work to finish up tonight, too," Becca chimed in with a yawn.

"Would you mind walking Aunt Tilly back?" Kinsley turned to Becca, sure of the response she would receive. "I don't think any of us should be alone right now. But I have a few things I'd like to talk to Rachel about privately before we head back."

"Sure," Becca said, maneuvering off the rock to a standing position and raising her hands over her head in a long stretch. Tilly rose to join her.

Tilly directed a pleading look to Rachel. "And *you*. Please make sure Kinsley makes it safely to her door, too. Promise me?"

"You have my word," Rachel said, lifting her fingers in Scout's honor. "Don't worry, I'm packing protection, too." She leaned to her side and patted her gun to drive the point home.

Becca shone the flashlight on her phone in the direction of the cliff walk and looped Tilly by the arm. "Come on, Miss Tilly, let's get you back to your guests."

"Weapon or no weapon, don't be long out here in the dark, you hear?" Tilly said over her shoulder before the two disappeared into the darkness.

Rachel turned to Kinsley once the lapping waves were the only sound left between them. "What is it that you wanted to talk about that you weren't comfortable saying in front of them?"

Kinsley toyed with the right words before speaking her mind. The last thing she wanted was to get anyone into trouble, especially if she was wrong. But the nagging just wouldn't end.

Rachel wagged a finger between them. "Go ahead, you have my complete confidence this will be kept only between us. Spill it, Kins."

"Edna is my aunt's closest friend. I don't want to implicate her grandson any further if it's nothing, but I can't help but feel he's hiding something about Daisy." Kinsley went on to share everything she knew, including the argument she'd overheard between Stacey and Luke. And his SUV, which had erupted into flames (Was he hiding critical evidence, moving a body?), as well as the telescope interestingly pointed in the direction of the crime scene. He also might have been the last person to see the victim alive. When she had spilled everything on her mind and reiterated to Rachel information the detective probably already knew, she ended with a pointed question.

"Did Stacey tell you that she knew Daisy?"

"What do you mean, knew her? That she'd met Daisy prior to the reunion, you mean?"

"Yeah. Did she mention that?"

"No, but several at the reunion corroborated Stacey's story that her dress was covered in wine and that she had returned to the reunion rather quickly after changing. Based on the timeline, there's no way she could've committed the murder. Daisy's body was found early the next morning, after the night of the reunion, when they were all back at the inn. It just doesn't fit."

"Right. But if she had an accomplice, say . . . like . . . Luke?"

"Luke wasn't at the reunion. He was waiting for Daisy, and they were to ride together to perform, yet she never showed."

"That's what he claims." Kinsley gnawed at her cheek and then went for it. "Edna is his only alibi, right?"

"Yes, that's true. Why? Do you think there's reason not to believe her? Why would Edna lie?"

"To protect her grandson. To protect her namesake. He's the last heir, you know . . . He's one day going to inherit all of this." Kinsley gestured a sweeping hand behind her. "Even if he *was* guilty, Edna would refuse to believe it. Wouldn't you? Could you believe a crime as shocking as this being committed by someone you knew? Never mind a close relative of yours?"

"I suppose not," Rachel answered.

Kinsley looked out toward the dark sky. The full moon peeked from behind a cloud and lit the water. The Atlantic blinked back, as if in a cinematic moment. The world, it seemed, was in perfect, sparkly calm.

Only, inside Kinsley's gut a big storm was brewing. Because someone she knew might be involved somehow. And that didn't sit well.

Chapter 22

Kinsley thrust her shovel into the dirt with such vigor, she wondered if the trowel could handle the pressure. She, too, was feeling the pressure. Someone—she was 99 percent sure it was *Denny*—was sabotaging her business. And the more she replanted, the more frustrated at the situation she became. The financial loss alone was enough of a pinch to SeaScapes, but ruining her good name on top of it was enough to send her over the edge in the aggravation department. She was fuming about this when Alderman Chris Chesterfield rounded the corner and nearly bumped into her.

"Kinsley! Lovely to see you," Chris said genuinely. His full head of gray hair shone in the midday sun like a mass of silvery seaweed atop a clump of kelp. He tucked his meaty hands into his pockets, leaned in closer, and said out of the side of his mouth, "Looks like you're having a hard time keeping up. We've all noticed some of your planters didn't make it this year." He cringed. "Of all times, eh?"

Kinsley dropped the trowel and turned to face him.

"The Walk Inns event, I'm sure, has you busier than ever," he continued. "You know, we talked about this at the last town council meeting, and some of us thought it might be a good idea to form a committee to handle the downtown florals moving forward. In fact, it's high on the agenda for our next meeting. Instead of leaving the heavy work for you to carry on your shoulders alone. We understand it's a lot for you to take on. Or maybe you could partner with another company? I hear Mr. Davenport is willing to step in and help."

Kinsley wiped her brow and bit her tongue to defend herself. "I'm really sorry this happened, but I assure you, my shoulders are strong and capable. And all of this will be fixed in no time." She smiled as wide as she could muster. "Don't you worry about it, Chris; I've got it all under control. I promise," she added confidently.

"Just keep that idea brewing in the back of your mind, okay? It's something to consider. You don't need to handle this all on your own. Adam's a good kid, but maybe not as reliable as you'd hoped?"

"Adam's doing just fine, and I assure you, this isn't his fault. There will be no need to form a committee. Didn't you notice? It's all back to the way it's supposed to look and dare I say it's even better." She squared her shoulders and gestured for him to follow her lead in looking down Main Street to confirm. "Beautiful, isn't it?"

Chris clucked his tongue. "I'll admit, Kinsley, you do a wonderful job. A wonderful job indeed," Chris said, rocking back and forth on the balls of his feet and nodding vigorously.

"Thank you. So if you don't mind canceling the emergency meeting that is planned for next week, I would really appreciate that. I promise you, and everyone involved with the town council, I've got this," Kinsley said. And she meant it. She turned from him then and thrust the trowel back into the planter as a way of hopefully squelching this conversation. Chris took the subtle cue.

"Yes, I'll cancel it and let everyone know you've got this handled. You have yourself a very nice day," he said as he moved to disappear into the confines of the bank.

"You, too," she called out after him. But wondered if he'd even heard as the door closed softly behind him.

Kinsley started to feel herself fume once again. Heck if she was going to see her life's work turned over to a committee and handed over to the town. Denny *had* to be behind this. She pounded her fist into her thigh.

No, she wouldn't have it. It was her job to keep Harborside in living color, and she wasn't going to let this little snafu stop her.

However, Kinsley realized, she had to keep the sabotage to herself. If she shared her thoughts that someone was purposely killing her plants, they'd think she was out of her mind. So she swallowed her pride and continued to replant. She had just finished up Main Street when Adam, with the watering can dangling from one hand, came to join her.

"I think that about does it," the teen said proudly. "I can't believe we got it all done. I really didn't think we'd finish it today. I thought we'd have to come back later."

"Thank you so much, Adam. There's no way I would've been able to accomplish this alone, and I have you to thank for that. Be sure and stop in at Toby's on the way home. I bought you a box of cupcakes. Jenna has it behind the counter for you to pick up. I wanted to buy you taffy, but I thought your mom would have my hide if it caused trouble with your braces. She doesn't need that additional orthodontist expense."

"Seriously?" Adam grinned. "You didn't have to do that; you already pay me to work for you."

"Yeah, but neither of us was expecting this extra load. I really appreciate you, kiddo. Just make sure you share them with your sister." Kinsley removed her glove and gave the teen a light squeeze to his shoulder. "Now, go get your treats and get outta here." She grinned. "Enough work for today."

Adam turned on his heel and galloped in the direction of Toby's. "Yes, ma'am!" he said without a backward glance.

Kinsley looked to the various security cameras that dotted Main Street. The person responsible for destroying her flowers was cunning. The prominent places in town with cameras pointed at them had flowers that were still alive and flourishing. Including the ones in front of the mayor's office. So there was no way of trying to catch the perpetrator in the act via CCTV.

But noting the security cameras triggered something in her mind. She needed to catch Denny in the act—that would surely help. Then maybe the police could charge him with something and he'd be forced to answer pointed questions about the murder investigation, too. He was obviously the one messing with her flowers, and who else would think to put a threat like the Barbie shoe in the flowerpot in front of Toby's Taffy? She could only conclude that Denny had to somehow be involved with both things. If Denny was the one to bury Daisy's shoe on her aunt's property, was he indeed the murderer, covering his tracks while simultaneously trying to ruin her career? *Why?* What motive would he have to do all that? Kinsley needed to put these pieces of the puzzle together once and for all. She called Becca so they could meet for drinks, as an idea was forming in her mind.

The two gathered on the outer deck of the Blue Lobstah, in their new favorite location, outside of earshot. It seemed Pete was avoiding them, as Kinsley caught him looking over on occasion, but making a point not to visit their table. Very unusual. Kinsley suspected it was because they were seated outside, and Pete knew what that meant. They were looking for privacy to discuss Daisy.

Becca noticed it, too, because she said, "Pete's hiding from us today. I guess he doesn't want to talk about the murder investigation, huh?" She took a sip of her iced tea from a straw and then sat back in the chair.

"I was just thinking the same thing. I know a way we can get him over here. Let's order something to eat. I'm starving anyway, aren't you? A plate of fish and chips to share sounds about perfect."

Becca waved her hand to get Pete's attention, but he seemed to purposely turn on his heel and ignore her. "Either he's really busy or he doesn't want *any* part of this conversation."

"I suspect the latter," Kinsley said. "Anyhow, you up for a little spy work tonight?"

"Spying on Denny?"

"Yup. It's time we start following Denny around for a bit to see what he's up to. In a perfect world, we'll catch him in the act of destroying my flowers and record it on our cell phones. Then we'll take the proof to Rachel, and then she can scoop him up on a misdemeanor charge. Maybe she can get more out of him and find a connection to Daisy during the interrogation. A swab of DNA wouldn't hurt, either."

"Won't he recognize you?"

"Yeah, I was wondering that, too. Which is why we'll do it together. I'll hide somewhere in the background. What do you say?"

"You don't think he'll remember me from standing with you at the bar?"

Kinsley scratched her head. "You're right. Who am I kidding? You're a knockout, of course he'll recognize you." Kinsley leaned her elbows on the table and put her head in her hands to think it through.

"Do you still have those wigs from that Halloween party?"

Kinsley looked up to see Becca's lips curl upward.

The suggestion made Kinsley sit upright in the chair. "Yeah, as a matter of fact, I do."

"Well, then, it's settled. We'll wear a disguise." Becca twirled the straw with her fingers before taking another sip of her iced tea.

Kinsley pushed aside her empty glass of tea. Her stomach rolled, reminding her of a missed lunch. "You know, that's not a bad idea. We could actually pull this off."

"Darn right, we will."

"How will we find out where he lives?"

Becca shook her head in disapproval. "Seriously? I'm the best real estate agent in town, that's how. I sold the house across the street from him. Don't you know I do my homework? I encourage all my clients to get to know their neighbors before they move in," she teased. "Actually, I saw him out mowing the lawn the day of closing when I was dropping off a housewarming gift to one of my buyers," she admitted.

"He could've been working. Maybe it was just a client's house?"

"Does he check the client's mailbox, too? I'm pretty sure it was his place, but we can see if his work van is in the driveway, to verify. He drives that hideous van with the flowers all over it. It's so gaudy." Becca rolled her eyes. "I swear, even with his van, he's trying to one-up you. But it's nothing compared to the beauty of your SeaScapes truck."

"Have I told you lately how much I love you?"

Becca winked. "Back at ya. But I'm not really feeling the love from our other friend tonight. I guess we'll have to see if your aunt Tilly has any leftovers for dinner." She stole a look at Pete, who was over at another table, throwing his head back in laughter.

Kinsley couldn't help but agree. And it bothered her. Why was Pete suddenly avoiding them?

Chapter 23

After heading to the inn and donning their Cagney and Lacey wigs, Kinsley and Becca ducked into Becca's black Acura. There was no way the SeaScapes truck could provide their hideout, as it was a dead giveaway with Kinsley's business logo plastered on the side of it.

"I loved watching those reruns with your aunt Tilly when we were kids," Becca said as she navigated her car out of the Salty Breeze Inn parking lot. "Some of my best memories are sipping cocoa and eating those to-die-for fresh-baked cookies while we binged *Cagney & Lacey* all winter long."

"Do you think we look like them?" Kinsley laughed as she tucked the wig beneath a baseball cap to further disguise herself and then adjusted it on her head using the passenger-seat mirror. She added dark sunglasses, even though the sun was slipping into the horizon.

"All I can remember is last Halloween, Pete calling us

Thelma and Louise all night long." Becca threw her head back and laughed. "Remember that?"

"Yeah, he might be too young for *Cagney & Lacey*, too. If it weren't for Aunt Tilly, we never would have watched the show, either, I imagine." Kinsley giggled.

As they headed down the road, Kinsley plucked her oversized purse from the floor at her feet and laid it across her lap.

"What's in there? You packin' a weapon?" Becca teased. "Or is there a huge rock in your purse and you're planning to disarm our adversary with it if we get in a pickle?" She chuckled.

Kinsley opened the oversized purse and began removing items. "Popcorn, M&M's, Fritos . . ."

"Seriously, did you raid the junk food aisle?" Becca laughed. "Remember how you'd stuff a backpack purse to take to the movies when we were kids? I was always afraid we'd get caught with all that candy and thrown out of the theater."

"No movies tonight, but we may be sitting beside the road for a while. I just wanted to be prepared. I skipped lunch, and Pete avoiding us didn't help, either." Kinsley patted her stomach and it growled in response.

Becca smirked as she adjusted her wig in the rearview mirror and then returned her focus back to the windshield. "I hope you have your cell phone in there—that's what we really need. In case one of us misses something. Hopefully, with the two of us recording, we'll get something of value tonight."

Kinsley removed her phone and held it up for verification. "Of course, and I have a full battery to boot. I'm so ready. Bring it on!" She pumped her fist in the air.

The remainder of the ride was quiet between them until

Becca slowed the car and parked it along the side of the road, down the street from Denny's house. Kinsley had to remove her sunglasses because now it was officially dark, and she could barely see her own hand in front of her face. She looked across the street after Becca pointed out the house.

The blinds were fully open, and a floor lamp was lit. Easily, they could view Denny sitting in front of his television set.

"It looks like he's alone. And it certainly doesn't look like he's going anywhere." Becca slouched into the seat, and they watched Denny kick back in a recliner. His feet were now comfortably raised in the chair.

"Popcorn?" Kinsley asked, slowly opening the bag as if not to make a noise. She wasn't sure why she was being so careful. She doubted anyone could hear anything outside the Acura. A set of headlights came from behind and they both ducked in their seats. They noticed as a neighbor pulled into the garage and then shut the door. Kinsley didn't realize she'd been holding her breath, and finally inhaled when the car disappeared.

"Oh no, that's Bob. I hope he didn't recognize my car." Becca winced.

Kinsley sat upright in her seat. There wasn't much they could do to prevent that.

It seemed like hours had passed when Kinsley looked at the dashboard and realized it had been only forty-five minutes. "Boy, this seems so much more exciting on cop shows," she uttered before popping an M&M into her mouth. She held the bag open for Becca to take a handful and instead poured a few into her palm.

"No kidding," Becca said with a yawn. "This kinda

sucks," she added, gesturing to dig into the M&M's bag for more.

"Yeah, it does."

"I can't believe you haven't noticed."

"Noticed what?"

"I silenced my phone tonight, because I didn't want the constant sound to be a dead giveaway." Becca took what was left of the M&M's in her hand and stuffed the lot into her mouth.

Kinsley was impressed because Becca never silenced her phone. She knew her friend was making huge exceptions on her behalf, and she was grateful.

"I have a few missed calls and one voice mail," Becca said, scrolling.

"Go ahead and listen to it. Nobody can hear us out here."

The subdivision was eerily quiet. Except for two cars, hardly anyone had come down the road since their arrival.

"Hey, Becca, it's Larry. Any word on those buyers? Call me." He quickly ended the message.

"I'll call Larry back later." Becca slid the phone into her lap. "He's waiting for an answer that I don't have yet, anyway. My buyers can't commit to a decision, and I don't blame them. The property has a railroad practically in the backyard, but the inside has been renovated to the nines. You should see the kitchen—" she began, and then stopped.

The rolling sound of a garage door caught their attention, and Becca squealed, "Uh-oh! It's Bob! And he's coming this way." She ripped off her wig and fluffed her hair with her hands. She then reached into the back seat for a folder and dropped it in Kinsley's lap. "Here, flip through these pages!"

Within moments they were greeted by a tap on the window. Becca pressed the button to roll it down. "Hey, Bob. Nice to see you."

The man leaned his arm on the window casing and said, "Everything okay out here? Did your car break down or something? I can give you a ride if you need." His gaze then traveled to Kinsley, and she flipped the pages of house listings in front of her as directed.

Becca chuckled. "Oh no, we're fine." She gestured a hand to the passenger seat. "This is my client Thelma . . ."

Kinsley coughed, holding back the giggles.

"She's just trying to decide which house she wants to see next. Isn't that right?" Becca shifted in the seat. "Have you decided yet, *Thelma*?"

Kinsley held up a paper and smiled.

"Ah, finally," Becca said. "These decisions are sometimes hard, as you know," she said, chatting with Bob. "How many houses did we look at before you picked this one, do you remember?" Becca flicked a finger in the direction of his house and then cocked her head, waiting for an answer.

"Quite a few." He grinned. "This is a great neighborhood if you're in the market. But I'm not sure if there's anything available, is there?" Bob asked, and Kinsley just smiled sweetly.

"I'll never tell if something's coming on the market." Becca held her finger in front of her lips as if it were a grand secret between them. "I think one of your neighbors is considering."

"Really? Who?" Bob asked.

"You'll know it if the sign goes up," Becca answered in

a whisper, and then continued, "Thanks for checking on us, though."

"You bet. Have a nice evening, ladies, and good luck with your house hunt," Bob said, leaning in again to regard Kinsley. He then backed away from the car and headed for home.

"Whoops." Becca grimaced.

"Busted!"

And then the two broke out in laughter. Kinsley nearly spilled the remainder of the popcorn on the console between them. She then rolled the bag and tucked it back into her oversized purse for safekeeping.

"I guess he recognized your car, so we better get outta here," Kinsley said with a sigh.

"We should've borrowed Tilly's. What were we thinking?"

"Yeah, that would've gone over well. She would've asked what we were up to, which in her mind, would've been no good. I suck at lying to her."

"That's true."

Just as Becca started the engine, a car passed them, pulled into Denny's driveway, and immediately turned off the headlights.

"Wait." Kinsley reached out to have Becca stop the car from rolling, and then ducked down into the seat. "Who is it?"

"I have no idea."

Kinsley slowly lifted her head from beneath the dashboard and watched as a motion light shone on Stacey, who then entered Denny's house. "It's Stacey!"

Becca slowly rolled the car back to their original position and left the headlights off but kept the engine running. "What do we do now?"

Kinsley laid a soft arm across the console to quiet Becca while she watched Stacey go into Denny's living room. Stacey looked animated as her hands flailed in the air and she leaned forward as if she were giving Denny a tongue-lashing. She then crossed her arms across her broad chest and waited while Denny left the room. She walked closer to the window, and Kinsley wasn't sure, but it seemed as if she were gazing out at them.

"Duck! Duck!" Kinsley tapped Becca on the arm before dropping her head in her lap.

"Goose!" Becca whispered, and they both laughed as they ducked deeper within the confines of the Acura.

"Do you think she saw us?" Kinsley said.

"Doubtful. I think she was just looking outside—it's dark in here. I don't think she noticed."

"Man, I wish I was a fly on the wall! I wanna hear what she said to him!" Kinsley whispered. "First, she gives Luke a tongue-lashing and now Denny. Interesting, to say the least."

"No kidding."

When Stacey left the window, they peeked over the dashboard and waited.

Denny returned to the room and handed Stacey a small paper bag. She took it and then dug into her purse and held a wallet in her hand.

"Is she paying him?" Becca asked.

"It sure looks like it." Kinsley squinted her eyes for a better look. "And I doubt she's paying him for landscaping services, in cash, on a random weeknight."

"Definitely fishy," Becca agreed.

"Stacey certainly gets around. She seems to be the common denominator in our list of suspects. First, I find her in a photo with Daisy, then I find her arguing with Luke, now Denny? I think we need to find out the connection between all of them," Kinsley said.

A common denominator couldn't be coincidental in a murder investigation. At least not in Kinsley's mind.

Chapter 24

Kinsley rolled in her bed and stared at the ceiling. She wasn't looking at the rustic barn beams, though, she was looking for answers. Answers that simply evaded her and caused a fidgety night of sleep. She felt like a squirrel on the hunt for food, harboring little nuggets anywhere she could but nowhere near ready for winter.

Any motive surrounding the people closest to Daisy still remained unclear. Where did Denny fit in the equation? If he fit at all. The more Kinsley tried, the more she failed to piece the people, and a potential motive, together in her mind. It was like a thousand-piece jigsaw puzzle with half the pieces missing. She needed more information.

It suddenly occurred to her that one person she hadn't spoken with was Ginger. Didn't Edna say that she was the only other person privy to Daisy's surprise performance at the reunion? And didn't Gabby mention that the police had questioned Ginger heavily? Perhaps Ginger could fill in a few gaps in her mind regarding Stacey, Luke, and Denny, to see if she knew how these people all fit together. At some point, one of these suspects needed to be eliminated from the list so Kinsley could get closer to finding the truth. And finding out, once and for all, who had buried that shoe at the Salty Breeze Inn.

Kinsley threw off the covers and rose from the bed. She decided to make it her mission to seek out the missing link, and get to the bottom of it, today.

After taking a quick shower and donning her SeaScapes attire, Kinsley headed out the door. A cool morning mist rolled off the water and sent goose bumps along her arms as she walked to her truck. She knew by midmorning the sun would burn it off, but the cool air hung like a dewy early-spring day instead of mid-June.

As she opened the driver's-side door and climbed into the driver's seat Kinsley had the unnerving sense that someone was watching her again. Just to be sure, she locked the doors. The guests were still asleep and the parking lot side of the inn was eerily quiet except for the wind chime that occasionally sent out a charming tune. After looking around within the safety of the truck, she shook off the feeling and chalked it up to paranoia as she pulled out of the driveway.

While en route to start her workday, Kinsley purposely drove down Main Street and was happy to see her plants were in the condition she'd last left them—alive. This realization sent a smile to her lips. She then decided she would stop off at all the properties that were taking part in the Walk Inns, to see if they needed any last-minute adjustments, or if anyone had tampered with them, before the fast-approaching opening day of the event.

Toward the end of the workday, Kinsley finally landed at the Rolling Tides Inn, which belonged to Douglas Stapleton. This was the last property on her checklist. As she perused the property to inspect her design, she was pleased with the result. The gardens were flourishing. She had brought her clippers along, and a paper bag to remove spent flowers along her journey. Petals danced in their spots, as if showing off their costumes in a dance recital, right on cue.

Douglas stepped out onto the lawn and greeted Kinsley with a friendly wave. His golden retriever, Rudder, met her legs-first.

"Hey, Rudder. Hey, boy," Kinsley cooed as she stroked the freshly groomed golden. His beautiful coat was as soft as silk and shone in the sunlight. Kinsley dropped the paper bag and clippers to the ground to give Rudder more attention, and he sniffed around the bag before disregarding it and instead handed her a paw to shake.

"Good to see you, Ms. Clark," Douglas said.

"Good to see you, too. All set for the big event?"

"Indeed, we are." He nodded as Rudder moved to sit obediently by his feet. "The long-range forecast, so far, looks like we'll have sun then, too."

"That's great news. My aunt certainly has been busy like a bee preparing for the event. I'm sure you've had much to do around here, too. The flowers are looking well, though, I'm pleased to say." Kinsley glanced around the yard, in approval.

"Speaking of that, I just wanted to let you know, a fella by the name of Mr. Davenport stopped over with a proposal. He said he was planning to take over for you. You're not planning on leaving us, are you, Ms. Clark?" His thick brows, which reminded Kinsley of woolly caterpillars, furrowed together in deep concern.

Kinsley cleared her throat. "No, I'll be taking care of your property as long as you'll let me," she added with as much grace as she could muster, but with a tone of finality.

"You're happy with my services, yes?" Kinsley asked with a hint of trepidation. She hoped it didn't show, but it must have, because Douglas reached out a hand in concern.

He immediately gushed, "Absolutely, we're pleased. It's just that Mr. Davenport said you wouldn't be with us much longer. So, I was unsure."

"He did, did he?" Kinsley could feel her anger rising and fought to tame it.

"I thought you might be moving somewhere . . . away from Harborside." His voice trailed off as he looked approvingly around his yard, and then continued, "We sure would miss you around here. Our guests have nothing but compliments on your floral designs."

A trickle of dread came over her. Kinsley really hoped Douglas misunderstood, and Denny wasn't suggesting she *"wouldn't be with us"* for another reason other than a move.

"I have no plans of moving out of Harborside," Kinsley encouraged. "Don't you worry about that."

"Wonderful news, indeed." He tipped his cap. "Well, then. I won't keep you any longer," Douglas said, turning on his heel. "Have a wonderful day, and give my best to Matilda." He waved a backward hand over his shoulder, and Rudder obediently followed, after Douglas tapped his leg to come.

Kinsley really hoped what she heard was an oversight and not a death threat. She gathered her tools and headed off to her next appointment, knowing that as soon as her workday was finished, she would get to the bottom of things.

As Kinsley stood in front of the Harborside Playhouse, she stopped to take it in and inhaled deeply. The granite building had stood the test of time. To her, it looked as if hardly any renovations had taken place on the old schoolhouse since she'd lived in Maine. The large building had a slew of old windows in the front of it that were positioned in a way that made it look like they were making a face. Suddenly, it was as if she were catapulted back to her twelve-year-old body. The flooding memories came on like a tidal wave but she pushed them down and swung open the heavy entrance door.

The stale smell of light mildew greeted her, and even that held a place in her memory. The red carpet had aged with time, but still looked clean despite the many patrons who Kinsley imagined had traipsed across the rug since the last time she'd entered.

Aunt Tilly had taken her to see a live performance of *The Wizard of Oz* soon after her parents had died, on the cusp of her thirteenth birthday. During the intermission, her aunt had explained that, like Dorothy, she'd always have a place to call home. Kinsley knew, even at a young age, that the gesture was meant to comfort. But instead, she found herself suspended in the tornado of grief.

To deal with it, Kinsley had pretended that her parents were just on another deployment, and she'd see them again on their next leave. But as soon as the words were uttered from her aunt Tilly's mouth, the realization came swiftly that her parents were never coming back. Her mother would never again braid her hair or pick out a special Easter dress to wear to church, and her father would never sing "You Are My Sunshine" on her soon-to-be thirteenth birthday. She would never travel with them to a new airbase. Never walk down the aisle with her father, arm in arm, or have her mother to dote over her future children. Never. She'd *never, ever* see them again.

Ever since that day, Kinsley had avoided the Harborside Playhouse. She had even avoided driving down the road that took her there, as the sting came back to bite whenever she attempted to enter the building again. When a friend from high school had invited her to *Peter Pan*, she'd fled the performance in tears and never looked back. Until today. She knew it was silly. But even now, she was catapulted like a boomerang back to heartache.

Kinsley uttered a silent prayer for her parents and moved in the direction of the ticket office. A woman was standing by the window and greeted her with a friendly smile. Her hair was dyed the color of a burning bush in autumn and her eyes, the color of English ivy, greeted her enthusiastically.

"Can I help you?"

Kinsley immediately looked to the name tag pinned on the woman's blouse and gave a silent sigh of relief. The tag read GINGER, which meant Kinsley wouldn't have to hang around this building a moment longer than she needed to. The office was quiet, and after Kinsley checked again to verify, she said, "I wonder if you have a moment to talk with me? I'm Kinsley Clark, my aunt owns the Salty Breeze Inn. Are you familiar with it? We're located right next door to Edna Williamsburg's estate."

A look of knowing washed across Ginger's face before she said, "Oh yes, we're very familiar with Ms. Edna, she's on our board of directors, you know. If it weren't for her, we might not still be here." She admitted easily, "She has donated so much of her time and money for our benefit."

"Yes, I do recall Edna mentioned on several occasions that she's a member here. She's very proud of all the work you've all done for our community."

Ginger cocked her head in question. "Is there something I can help you with? Did you want to make a donation?"

"Um, not today. As I'm sure you're aware, many who

attended the reunion stayed at my aunt's inn, and we've discovered an earring, but it seems we can't find its rightful owner." Kinsley shrugged and then leaned closer to the counter that divided them and pressed her fingers into the granite slab. "Do you happen to know if anyone from your class is missing one?"

"Oh." Ginger frowned. "The earring? The police asked me about that, but I hadn't heard anyone was missing one. I'm guessing this has something to do with the girl who was murdered out in that field. Wasn't it Daisy who was missing one?"

The way Ginger described it made Kinsley believe that she had no direct connection with Daisy's murder. Kinsley was secretly relieved, because the last thing she wanted was to add more suspects to the growing list. First of all, Ginger mentioned the earring had come from Daisy, which it did not, and secondly, she stated that Daisy was murdered in the field, but that wasn't the case. Rachel had said that Daisy's body was *moved* there. Kinsley believed Ginger's choice of words meant she couldn't have been involved.

"It looks like I lost you." Ginger chuckled. "Still with me?"

Kinsley shook her head of the cobwebs. "Sorry, I have so much on my mind," she said airily, twirling her finger around her head as if she were losing it. Which she agreed was quite possible. This investigation had her reeling, for sure.

"Happens to the best of us." Ginger mirrored her smile.

Kinsley lowered her voice. "Rather shocking to have a murder happen right here in Harborside. I can't get over it. It seems to be the only thing people around town want to talk about. Which I totally understand—this stuff just doesn't happen in our community."

"Yeah, it's been awful, especially with it being tied to

the reunion. Did you know that the victim was planning to perform for us? It wasn't supposed to go like that, it was supposed to be a wonderful surprise and a reminder of how talented our thespian group was, back in the day." Ginger rolled her eyes. "It's not exactly what you want to remember after a gathering like that. But many of my classmates said that unfortunately, they won't remember the fun we had that night. Instead, they'll forever remember the interrogation by the police department. It was rough," she admitted, dropping her hands to a stack of folders and pushing papers around aimlessly.

"I can't imagine. Was Denny part of your class?"

"Denny?" She stopped shuffling and looked up.

"Yeah."

"I don't remember a Denny. Unless you mean Dennis Height? But I didn't think anyone ever called him Denny."

"No, that's not the one."

Ginger shrugged. "Anyhow, I need to get back to work. Did you want to buy any tickets? Our opening night of *Cinderella* is this weekend. Or did you just stop in to ask about the earring?"

"*Cinderella*?" Kinsley gasped, and then covered her mouth.

"Yeah, I know, bad timing, huh?" Ginger said.

"How did I not know about this?"

"We're not marketing as much as we normally do, because of the situation. So, we're sort of keeping it on the down-low, inviting friends and family. I know it probably seems in bad taste, but honestly, if it wasn't for the local news dubbing Daisy the Cinderella murder, we wouldn't be faced with this. We have so much time and money invested. The show must go on! I feel bad for Stacey, though," Ginger murmured.

"Stacey?"

"Yeah, she has the leading role. She's been studying those lines for weeks, and now this." Ginger snorted. "Why? Do you know Stacey?" Ginger leaned in closer and studied her.

Stacey again! Kinsley hurried to recover. "Sure, you know what? Let me help you out. I'll take two tickets," she answered, rummaging in her pockets and hoping she had enough cash to cover it.

She handed over the money, and in return, Ginger gave her the tickets with a smile. "You'll love this show."

"I bet I will. Enjoy the rest of your day," Kinsley said before turning on her heel and heading quickly out the door.

What Kinsley wanted to do upon exiting the playhouse was toss the tickets to *Cinderella* in the trash can. However, she couldn't help but think someone involved in the production just might be a murderer. What were the chances that Stacey was playing the leading role in *Cinderella*, and suddenly a real Cinderella was found murdered?

Chapter 25

The night of the performance held at the Harborside Playhouse, Kinsley and Becca sat arm in arm, waiting for the curtain to open and the show to begin. Kinsley tried to focus on why they were there, and not her past, as she glanced at the very seats where she'd had her life-altering realization. It was amazing how grief worked. Life could cruise along and then, wham! Suddenly pain, sharp as a tack, would rear its ugly head. She breathed in deeply and let it out slow. Becca must've caught on, because she leaned in and whispered, "It must be important for you to be here tonight. You've said, on numerous occasions, that you wouldn't be caught dead in this place."

"Yeah, that's a fact," Kinsley said adamantly. "And according to Mr. Stapleton, if Denny has anything to do with it, soon I'll be six feet under. Won't I?"

Becca shook her head vigorously in a blatant attempt to argue the fact. "Come on. I'm sure Mr. Stapleton misunderstood what he'd meant. I realize Denny was undermining your work, but if he wanted to kill you, surely he'd have done it already." Becca chuckled, elbow-bumping Kinsley and then fluttering her arm like an injured chicken with its wings flapping. Her attempt at lightening the load, however, fell flat.

"Oh, that's nice," Kinsley defended sarcastically.

Becca reached down between the seats for her bag that was tucked beneath them and plucked out her cell. Kinsley noticed her checking for messages and then silencing her phone. "Hey, you got any of those M&M's left in your purse?" she asked, tossing her bag back into position and then kicking it beneath her feet.

"No, Thelma, I don't," Kinsley said. "We finished the bag the other night."

"You're Thelma, I'm Louise," Becca corrected with a sly grin. "And anyway, we were *supposed* to be Cagney and Lacey." Becca shifted in her seat. "You really don't have anything? I was hoping you had another bag of them."

"Oh sure, now you want my snacks." Kinsley chuckled.

"I'm so hungry I could eat a cow. My day was jam-packed, I didn't get a chance to eat." Becca laid her hands on her stomach and rubbed like she was caring for a sick child. "Listing appointments, showing appointments, one right after the other. I just hope one of these pops and my day wasn't a complete waste of time."

"Maybe we can stop by the Blue Lobstah and see if our Boston friend will feed us this time and not completely ignore our existence." Kinsley lowered her voice to a whisper. "I can't get over how weird he was the other day."

"I'm up for that. A lobster roll sounds really good about now."

"It's a plan then," Kinsley said, settling it between them.

"Anyway, if you're that concerned about Denny, why didn't you call Rachel and tell her what's been going on?" Becca asked. "I kinda feel like he's all brawn yet no brain, if you know what I mean. Do you really think he's that much of a threat to you? Because, seriously, if you think he's dangerous, you probably should file a police report, at least, get something in writing."

"As a matter of fact, I did call her before I picked you up."

"Really? And you neglected to fill me in on any new intel? For shame!" Becca grinned.

"There's not much to tell, really." Kinsley looked around and confirmed they were away from hungry ears looking for gossip. Those around them seemed deep in their own conversations. Just in case, she lowered her voice to a whisper again. "Rachel did mention that the hair follicle inside the shoe didn't match any DNA in their system. She also said there was an unidentified makeup stain on Daisy's dress that they think was rubbed off during the altercation when she was strangled. That DNA didn't match anything, either. Both are inconclusive."

"Huh."

"What? I can see your brain is churning like butter. Spill it."

"Stage makeup, perhaps?"

"My thoughts exactly, my dear. Which is why we're here. Did you catch my rhyme?" Kinsley chuckled.

"Yeah, you sound like Toby."

Suddenly the lights flickered, off and on, three times, signaling the show was soon to begin.

Becca held her finger to her lips, silencing them.

Although Stacey did an amazing job at her performance, Kinsley had a hard time focusing on the show. Between her past hurts within the confines of the Harbor Playhouse and the ongoing murder investigation, she was relieved when the curtain fell and the lights came on for the fifteen-minute intermission.

"I need to get some air," Kinsley said.

"I'm right behind you," Becca encouraged, nudging her on the arm and then rising from her seat to follow.

The two joined the crowd, like a train of cars, slowly making their way up the aisle. Becca shook Kinsley's arm to gain her attention and directed her across the aisle to a parallel line on the other side of the theater, heading out the door.

"There's your buddy from channel four news," Becca whispered in her ear.

"Roy's here?" Kinsley looked for him, but he must've just slipped out the door, because she didn't lock on a visual.

"Ahh, on a first-name basis, are we?" Becca teased, batting her eyes. "I'm guessing there's more you're not telling me about lover boy!"

"I promise you, he's not my type," Kinsley said rather gruffly. She hadn't meant to be so abrupt, but sometimes her friend just wouldn't give up. The last thing she wanted right now was a more complicated life. And in her mind, men were complicated. Just look at her brother and Rachel. A perfect relationship ruined for no reason other than his reenlistment and geography. Which in her mind was no reason to end it—they were perfect for each other.

Kinsley's gruffness led Becca to respond with a shrug and a dismissive wave of her hand.

The crowd gathered in the open corridor, and the sounds of multiple ongoing conversations rumbled over the room like a cadence of running bulls. A long table with refreshments lined the wall, and ticket holders made a beeline for cupcakes and cookies. Kinsley was just about to send Becca and her hungry stomach in that direction when she felt a tap to her shoulder.

"Well, look who it is. We meet again!" Roy said, and then took a dramatic step backward. "We don't want to crash into each other again, now, do we?" he jeered. Kinsley couldn't help but think Ginger wouldn't be happy to see anyone from the press at this performance after what she had mentioned about keeping the show on the down-low. Kinsley protectively wondered if she should try and locate her and give a heads-up.

Roy continued, "I just bought these shoes at Mallards, and I'd rather avoid them getting nicked." He held out a foot for display.

Kinsley looked down at his shiny new black dress shoes and then met his eyes with a forced smile. "You remember my friend Becca." She gestured to her friend, who blushed in response.

"Hello, nice to see you again," Becca gushed. "I was so starstruck the other day, I don't even think I spoke a word. I'm a huge fan, by the way. It's great to officially meet you in person. What an honor." Becca held out a hand to shake. Instead, Roy took Becca's hand in his and brought it to his lips, softly kissing her hand.

"The pleasure is most certainly mine," he said, giving Becca the once-over.

Kinsley wanted to gag. But she thought Becca seemed charmed by it, so she let it go.

"Are you enjoying the show?" Kinsley asked.

"It's wonderful! That main lead, well, she's something! Isn't she?" Roy said, his eyes darting between them. "Quite an actress!"

"I'm always in awe of how they can remember all those lines. Yeah, she is amazing," Becca added.

"Indeed," Kinsley said.

"Though, I'm a bit surprised they went on with the show." Roy lowered his voice. "After the murder and all, you'd think they would've avoided anything that referenced Cinderella." His face squeezed as if he'd just tasted a sour lemon.

Kinsley held off blaming the man. If it wasn't for him dubbing the recent crime the Cinderella murder, the Harborside Playhouse wouldn't be in that position in the first place. Instead, she said, "Can you two excuse me? I think I need to use the facilities before the curtain goes up; I'll be right back."

Becca didn't seem like she needed a wingman, so Kinsley quickly moved away from them and navigated herself through the crowded corridor into the bathroom. She was shocked to see Stacey standing at the sink and not using the restrooms located in the back of the building, strictly used by performers.

"Wonderful show," Kinsley said, meeting her at the sink. "You're doing great out there," she added, and she meant it. Stacey was definitely the highlight of the show.

"Thank you." Stacey beamed. "Would you mind holding that door? I want to sneak out, but I just need a moment. The bathrooms closer to backstage are broken." Stacey rolled her eyes after the explanation. Kinsley moved to stand by the door and held it closed.

"Sure, no problem." Kinsley was desperate to corner Stacey and barrage her with questions, but she fumbled and didn't know what to ask. Should she ask about Denny? Or about the argument with Luke? She hadn't prepared herself for this chance meeting. And now that it was here, she was suddenly struck mute.

Stacey dug her hand into her costume and removed a pill from her bra. She stuck her head under the sink, to wash the pill down. Kinsley couldn't believe what she was witnessing.

"ADHD meds, I can't perform without them. Don't tell anyone my secret." Stacey held her finger in front of her lips, as if they were in cahoots, after wiping her mouth with the back of her hand. "Thanks for holding the door." She slipped past Kinsley and out into the crowd.

Chapter 26

Relief came when Kinsley threw open the exit door of the Harborside Playhouse and took a clean breath of fresh Maine air, finally escaping the reminder of the loss of her parents and the memories she'd held so tight. The sun was slipping into the horizon, and even though it was nearing nine P.M., it was still light enough to see across the parking lot. One of the many blessings of the summer season was long, warm nights. Kinsley removed the sunglasses from the top of her head that she'd worn as a headband and slid them into her purse, allowing her hair to fly freely and frame her face.

"I'm so proud of you," Becca said as they made their way across the sidewalk that led to the parking lot.

"For what?"

"For going back in there, after all those years, and facing your deep loss. I shouldn't have made light of it earlier. I know that couldn't have been easy for you." Becca threw her arm around Kinsley's shoulder and gave a light squeeze of encouragement. "You okay, my friend?"

"I guess I just need to get over it and grow up sometime, huh?"

"I don't think it's something you ever get over," Becca said tenderly, slowing her pace to face her. "I think it's something you learn to live with."

"Ain't that the truth, Becs. Despite the passing years, certain things just trigger the loss on a deep level. As dumb as it sounds, sometimes it feels like it just happened yesterday. I often wonder what would've happened to my parents had they survived. Where would they live? Would they be in Harborside? Would they have taken early retirement from the Air Force? Where would we have spent our Christmases? On an airbase or with Aunt Tilly? That sort of thing."

"I can't even imagine."

Just as Kinsley was sliding into the passenger seat of Becca's Acura, she noticed Denny step out the back door of the theater. He looked conspicuously over both shoulders before ducking into his car, which was parked by the entrance.

"Follow that vehicle!" Kinsley said, pointing out Denny's hideous work van.

"No problem, hard to miss." Becca chuckled. "Wonder what he's doing here? I didn't see him in the audience, did you?"

"Probably pushing more ADHD meds on Stacey. After what we witnessed at his house, I wouldn't be surprised."

"Say what?"

Kinsley pointed a finger in the direction of the van. "Remember the other night on the stakeout it looked like Stacey was buying something shady from him? I think I just found out what it was. Keep on him!" she added before explaining more of her encounter with Stacey during the intermission. Because they'd used up the bulk of the intermission chatting with Roy, Kinsley had missed her opportunity to share what had transpired.

Becca one-handedly rolled the steering wheel in the direction of downtown Harborside, in hot pursuit. She'd even flown through a yellow light to stay on him. They followed Denny for a few miles until he officially reached Main Street and pulled in front of Toby's Taffy and came to a complete stop.

"What's he doing? Toby's is closed for the night. Get your phone, see if you can catch him on video." Becca had tossed her bag deep into the back seat, out of reach. She waved a hand for Kinsley to hurry.

Kinsley scrambled for her phone, and it tumbled from her grasp, landing on the floor of the car with a thud. She struggled to retrieve it, but the more she reached around her feet, the more she pushed it deeper beneath the seat, instead of getting a firm grip.

"Look! He's out of the van!" Becca squealed, dragging Kinsley's attention away from retrieving her phone.

Kinsley watched as Denny rushed away from the vehicle, plucked the geraniums from the whiskey barrel, and chucked them onto the ground before squealing off in the van.

"I knew it!" Kinsley said, pounding a fist on her leg. "I knew it was him! He has some nerve sabotaging my plants once again!"

"Do you think he knows we were following him? And just did that for spite?"

"He wouldn't know your Acura, would he? And besides, how would he know I'm onto him? Unless Pete said something, but I don't think he would break a confidence like that. Do you?"

"Good point."

"No, Denny's just being hateful. I wish I hadn't dropped my phone and had caught him in the act. But we're both officially considered eyewitnesses, I would think." She thought about it a minute longer as she finally grasped ahold of her phone. "I'm calling Rachel."

"Good idea." Becca nodded, but they were no longer following Denny, as his car had ducked down a side road, and it would be obvious if they continued. It was futile at this point anyway; they got the confirmation they needed. No sense confronting the man and letting it further escalate, because Kinsley's hot button was officially pushed.

After phoning Rachel to share the incident in front of Toby's Taffy, and then a quick Google search for a phone number, Kinsley noted they were finally pulling into the parking lot of the Blue Lobstah.

"Grab us a table and go ahead and order. I know you're hungry, but I have one more quick phone call to make and then I'll be right behind you. I promise."

Becca didn't argue, which meant she was beyond starving. "Should I order a lobster roll for you, too?"

"That would be great, thanks."

As soon as Becca shut the driver's-side door, Kinsley dialed Denny. She tried her best to level her tone before she spoke. "Hey, Denny. It's Kinsley from SeaScapes."

"Kinsley Clark?"

"Yeah, it's me," Kinsley said lightly. "Are you still up for that drink? I think you're right; we should call a truce. Maybe we could even partner on a few landscape deals. What do you say? Blue Lobstah tonight?" She wondered if that little white lie might have been over the top. She bit her lip nervously and waited.

Kinsley could hear a pin drop. "Are you still there?"

"Yeah, I'm thinking about it. I'm not sure if tonight works for me," he muttered.

Kinsley wondered if the man felt any guilt at all for what he'd done, and now hearing her offer had made him apologetic.

"Hey, it was your idea," Kinsley said, reminding him. "I'm here at the Blue Lobstah if you're up for it. Bye." She quickly ended the call before he had a chance to respond. Hoping Denny would have a need for the last word, he'd either call her back or show his face. Kinsley hoped for the latter as she left the car and made her way to join Becca at their table inside the restaurant. She slid into the booth across from her friend and must've looked concerned, as Becca immediately asked, "Everything okay? Did you call Tilly? Or . . ."

"No, I didn't. I called Denny. I think I have a plan."

"A plan for what? You gonna nail this Jell-O to the wall, once and for all?" Becca grinned. "I want in on this."

"Exactly. I'm hoping Denny shows up here, and we can extract his DNA. Because honestly, it will either implicate him or exonerate him. I think he was involved with Daisy in a drug deal somehow. Maybe she found out he was dealing to other thespians and called him on it. And he was fearing arrest. Either way, I need to know if he's involved. I'm expecting Rachel will show, too. She said she would." Kinsley moved the menu that was atop the place setting to the opposite side of the table. She took a sip of the ice water that was set in front of her.

"How exactly will we do it? I mean, the extracting part?" Becca leaned in closer and folded her hands on the table between them.

"I'll buy him a beer."

"Good luck getting a beer outta that man's hands." Becca laughed sarcastically.

"I'm hoping at some point we'll distract him and I'll sneak the empty bottle from the bar."

"How are we going to distract him?"

"You're gonna come on to him," Kinsley stated matter-of-factly. "That'll work."

Becca sat upright. "Excuse me? I'm going to do what, now?" She tucked a hand by her ear, as if she hadn't heard correctly.

Kinsley confirmed it. "You heard me, put on your sexy charms. A little more lipstick on those pouty lips might help," she added, pointing to Becca's purse, where she knew her friend housed her lipstick.

Becca just sat across from her with the biggest frown Kinsley thought she'd ever witnessed splattered across her face.

"Come on, Becca, you're a knockout. Trust me when I say, you'll *easily* distract him," Kinsley said with supreme confidence that Becca could handle the job.

Becca's glance darted to the bar. "Speaking of knockouts, Pete seems to be avoiding us again. He sent Raven over to take my order before you came in. Something's definitely fishy."

Kinsley's gaze left her friend and scoured the restaurant in search of the bar owner. She finally caught Pete coming from the back room with a case of clean glasses in his hands, which he set down behind the bar. She waited what seemed an eternity before catching any acknowledgment of her presence. He finally acquiesced with a curt nod of his head. Not his usual friendly wave, firework smile, and walk over to the table, but Kinsley defended him anyway. "He's busy."

"He's never been so busy that he didn't make it a point to say hello. Anyhoo . . . we have a bigger fish to fry at the moment. Back to nailing what's his face . . ." Becca's voice trailed off.

Kinsley leaned into the table and lowered her voice to a whisper. "You're right, we need to strategize our plan."

"Yeah, so I seduce him, and then what?" Becca asked with a raised brow.

"Then I'll take one of my garden gloves out of my purse, steal the bottle, and *voilà*! DNA!"

"Ooh, this could work. I was worried you didn't carry gloves with you. I should've known better." Becca grinned. "Once a gardener, always a gardener. I suppose you dead-headed Pete's plants before coming in here, too, eh?" she teased with a wink.

"Not only do I have gloves but I have a large plastic bag in my purse to put the bottle in. The other day I shoved it in there just in case we had extra M&M's. Thankfully, we didn't." Kinsley grinned.

"Brilliant."

"Yep, and then hopefully Rachel will be here and we can do the handoff, so she can have it tested."

"Sounds like a slam dunk. And by the way, your rival just walked in," Becca said after a slight lift of her head in the direction of the entrance.

Kinsley turned to see Denny walk into the Blue Lobstah and head immediately for the bar.

Chapter 27

"S howtime. You ready?" Kinsley asked as she rose from the booth and then navigated around patrons to make her way over to the bar to execute their plan. Becca followed like an obedient puppy, close at her heels and waiting to pounce.

By the time they arrived, Denny was already nursing a beer and turned when she said his name.

"Glad you came," Kinsley said. And she meant it. Only not for the way she imagined Denny perceived it.

"Yeah?" He leaned an elbow against the bar and ran his hand through his thick hair before kicking back another sip. "So, you wanna call a truce, eh? Ready to share a piece of the Harborside pie with me?" He studied Kinsley so closely she wondered if he was onto her motives. "I didn't think you'd ever share any of your clients. Don't tell me you're too busy to handle it. You could just hire someone, whaddya need me for?" he said, confirming it.

Kinsley reached for Becca's arm and shoved her friend between them.

"You remember my friend Becca, don't you?"

"Hey," Becca cooed. She generously gave Denny her most radiant smile and a gentle touch to the arm. The man immediately took notice and stood up straighter.

"You'll have to forgive me, I actually don't remember you," he stammered as he gave Becca another once-over. "I certainly should have."

"That's okay . . . I remember you . . ." Becca batted her eyelashes and leaned in closer to Denny as if vying for a shield from the others that began to crowd the bar. Denny took this all in like a thirsty sponge and corralled her in protectively with his arm.

"You do?" He feigned a shocked look. "How do you remember me?"

"How could I forget a face like yours?" Becca looked up at him innocently. "You remind me of that football player—oh, I wish I could remember his name, the one who plays for the Patriots." She tapped a finger to her freshly lip-sticked lips. Kinsley wondered then if her friend had taken her advice and reapplied while en route to the bar.

"Can I buy you a drink?" he asked, already waving over Pete to take the order. And apparently not at all worried about the "truce" that he had been called to discuss, because suddenly Kinsley was completely invisible. Her plan was working.

Kinsley turned away from the bar momentarily and was relieved to notice Rachel enter the restaurant. It would be good to have her here in case anything went sour. But Kinsley didn't want to blow it. She made a discreet *cut across the throat* gesture and Rachel must've understood, as she ducked into a corner booth and took a seat.

Becca was now clinking amber bottles with Denny. She and Becca inconspicuously shared a glance of affirmation. And then Becca homed back in on their target as planned, like Roundup to a thorny weed.

It didn't take long for Denny to gesture Pete over again for a second beer. Kinsley slipped in closer to remove the empty bottle. Becca noticed and purposely tripped into Denny's arms. He caught her with one hand. "Whoops. You okay?" He held her by the arm and leaned in to check Becca over.

"Yeah, I think someone stepped on my foot," Becca answered, looking down at her feet, and Denny's glance followed as if for verification.

Kinsley took the cue. She slipped on her garden glove and went in to reach for the bottle, but Pete was too fast and removed it before she had a chance.

"There you go, chief," Pete said to Denny, replacing the empty bottle with a full one, and then helping the next person down the line who was waiting for a drink.

"Ah, thanks, man!" Denny said as he reached for the new bottle and held it tight.

Kinsley gritted her teeth and quickly shoved the glove into her pocket. If she asked Pete for the empty bottle, it would be totally obvious what she was up to. Plus, now Pete's fingerprints most likely contaminated it. Maybe she needed to let Pete in on their little plan.

"I'll be right back," Kinsley said.

Becca clearly understood, as she barely acknowledged Kinsley's departure and instead kept tight on their target. She had never been prouder of her friend's performance.

It wasn't easy for Kinsley to maneuver her way through the growing crowd. The restaurant was packed like an overplanted flowerpot high on Miracle-Gro. As soon as she left the bar, the hole was filled, swallowing her visual of Becca. Rachel caught her attention and waved to join her over at the table. Instead, Kinsley held up a finger, giving the detective a *one moment* signal, and hurried to seek out Pete. She wasn't ready to fill her in yet.

"Can I have a sec?" Kinsley traveled around behind the bar, which she had never done before as she pretty much assumed doing so was sort of off-limits. She tugged at Pete's arm until he had no choice other than to follow her to a private corner of the restaurant.

"This really isn't a good time, Kins. Can't you see how busy we are tonight?" He reached to hold her back, but she shook him off and continued walking.

"It'll just take a second, I promise," she said over her shoulder. She dodged and weaved through the crowd as if trying to reach center stage in a rock concert.

Pete seemed as if he was annoyed with her but she had little choice. As soon as they were out of earshot and in a private space, she said, "I'm sorry, I know you're swamped. I wouldn't have pulled you away if it wasn't totally necessary."

Pete just stared back at her. A baffled expression washed over his face as he waited for an explanation.

"Don't be so quick to clean up after Denny next time, okay?" Kinsley whispered. "I'm on a stakeout."

"You're *what*?"

"Just trust me, will you?" Kinsley leaned in closer. "I need the man's DNA."

"You actually think he's the one who committed the murder? If that's the case, shouldn't you just leave this up to the authorities? Why would you lure him here?"

"Lure him? What makes you think *that*?" Kinsley defended, folding her arms protectively across her chest.

"I watched you leave the booth as soon as the guy ordered a beer from the bar. It doesn't take a rocket scientist to see you two are up to something," Pete stated, and then scrutinized her, waiting to see how she would respond.

"You noticed that?" Kinsley was surprised he had been watching them that closely and she hadn't noticed. To her it seemed Pete couldn't have cared less that they were even inside his establishment. "Look, we need to either nail the guy or exclude him, because he's definitely involved somehow. It's that simple. The police need his DNA in order for that to happen. And I'm going to get it," she added resolutely.

"Oh, okay. Let me get this straight. You're planning on extracting DNA from everyone who pays a visit to my bar until you get a match. Is that it?" Pete folded his arms across his chest and looked at her as if she'd just fallen off her rocker. "That's just brilliant," he added with a huff.

"I can't *believe* you don't want to help!" Kinsley said between gritted teeth. "What's wrong with you?"

Pete jutted a thumb to his chest. "What's wrong with me? You mean, what's wrong with *you*?" He flung a hand in her direction. "You're the one who keeps trying to get me involved in this, and I told you I want no part of it. Seriously, Kinsley, you should let this go and let the police handle it."

Kinsley stood stunned as Pete turned on his heel and moved away from her.

The walk back to the bar was intense for Kinsley, as she fought the argument growing inside her head. On one hand, she thought she was helping. On the other hand, was Pete right? Was she just barking up the wrong tree? Was she secretly hoping to pin the murder on Denny so she'd have reason to get the man off her own back? Suddenly, she was having second thoughts about her motives but decided to continue along with their plan. Becca would never forgive her for taking it this far and not finishing the mission.

Kinsley looked up to see Rachel calling her to the table once again. And once again, she held up the *one more minute* signal. She was afraid Denny had finished his beer by now, and she'd lose her chance yet again. Becca had thrown her head back in laughter and had kept up such a superior acting gig that Kinsley wondered if her friend shouldn't join the Harborside Playhouse for a part in *Cinderella*.

When Kinsley reached Becca's side and Denny looked up at the TV that hung above the bar, she mouthed, "You got this? You ready?"

Becca nodded her head inconspicuously, so Kinsley knew it was go time for a second attempt at the prize. She reached into her pocket once again and plucked out her garden glove and discreetly laced it on her fingers. Becca suddenly threw her arms around Denny's neck and brought him in for an excited embrace. Kinsley swiped Denny's empty bottle from the bar. Just as she was about to slip it into her purse, a rowdy drunk banged into her, hitting her elbow.

"Watch it, lady," the drunk slurred.

She watched with horror as the bottle flew from her gloved hand and crashed to the floor.

Chapter 28

It was as if the entire restaurant had turned their attention on her in slow motion. The bottle had catapulted from her hand like a live grenade. And now her glance fell once again to the ground, to witness the bottle's destruction.

The rumble of the crowd stopped momentarily, and an eerie quiet settled in the room, as though it were the corridor at a funeral director's office.

The patrons seemed to wait for a reaction from Kinsley. When no reaction came, they looked to the broken glass, realized there was nothing left to see, and then returned to their friends. And then the rumble of conversations ensued, louder than before, finally providing some relief. Kinsley looked over and noticed Pete standing behind the bar and shaking his head slowly, as if in frustration and disbelief.

Kinsley's glance dropped once again, this time to her hand, and she noted how ridiculous she looked wearing her garden glove inside the restaurant. Had anyone understood why? She slipped it off and jammed it into her back pocket.

"Are you okay?" Becca asked, waking her from her reverie. "I noticed some idiot banged into you, causing you to hit the bottle off the bar." Becca's eyes drilled into Kinsley so she would follow along. "Good grief, some people just can't handle their liquor," she added with an eye roll, and then took a swig of beer.

Denny interrupted a chance for Kinsley to answer when he pointed out her hand. "Why did you just put garden gloves in your pocket?" he asked with a frown. "Were you actually wearing them in here?"

"Oh, don't mind her." Becca threw her head back in mock laughter. "Kins does this all the time; she deadheads her container plants at local businesses while we're supposed to be 'out having a good time,'" she added as she threw her manicured fingers up in air quotes. "Workaholic, I say. She doesn't know when to quit."

"Yeah," Kinsley said, recovering. "I was just heading outside to check how my plants are doing out on the deck. I've been so busy preparing for the Walk Inns I haven't had a chance to stop by here and clean them up. Pete mentioned they've been looking lanky." Everything in her wanted to scream, *And I'm sure it's your doing*, but she refrained.

"You really don't get out much, do you?" Denny said, and then turned his attention back to the large TV behind the bar, as if checking the baseball score before returning his attention to Becca.

Kinsley and Becca shared an inconspicuous sigh of relief before Pete entered the scene with a whisk broom to remove the broken glass. Kinsley knelt to lend a hand and gave Pete a weak smile and mouthed, "Sorry."

After the bar owner threw the mess in the trash can, he

returned to Kinsley's side. He looped her by the arm and gave a tug. "You're coming with me."

"Are you throwing me out?" Kinsley asked, horrified, as she tried to keep up with his long stride. The crowd parted like the Red Sea for them to easily walk through, arm in arm. It was amazing how Pete could command a room. Just minutes before it had been like squeezing through an empty tube of toothpaste to get through.

"I should throw you out, shouldn't I? Give me one good reason to let you stay," Pete answered when the two were standing outdoors in the far corner of the deck, where he had turned to face her squarely.

Before another word was uttered from his lips, Rachel rushed over to her side.

"What is going on here, Kinsley? I thought you asked me to dinner, and I've been sitting at the booth all this time waiting. What gives?" Rachel looked from Kinsley to Pete and then her eyes narrowed in and rested back on her.

"Yeah, I was just about to . . ."

Rachel didn't let her finish. Instead, she said, "I noticed you and Becca were chatting it up with Denny at the bar. Is this one of those keep-your-enemies-closer moments? Why didn't you want me to join you two? What exactly are you up to?"

"She's all yours. Keep her safe, will you? I'm done trying . . ." Pete said, throwing up his hands in defeat before turning on his heel and going back inside the restaurant. He didn't turn once to look back. Kinsley had never crossed Pete, and silently she wondered if the bar owner would ever forgive her. Her shoulders dropped in disappointment, and she let out a long sigh.

Kinsley turned and leaned on the railing overlooking the sea. The wind had picked up, and a few crashing waves could be heard in the distance. She took in the sound and matched her breathing to its cadence. The moon lit a glittering path in front of them, and she wished she could walk out to never-never land and join it. Sometimes she wondered if her parents could see the beauty of it, too. More than ever, she missed them.

"Kins?" Rachel lightly hip-bumped her, to get her to open like a flower. But as of now, Kinsley was as closed as a spent day lily.

"Look, I was only trying to help," Kinsley defended. "You mentioned you have a DNA sample of a hair follicle you found inside Daisy's shoe. I only thought if I could match it to Denny, it would be case closed. Or at the very least he would be eliminated, and we could move on to the next suspect on the list."

"Ahh, I see," Rachel said. "You definitely are watching too many cop shows," she teased. "I do recall Kyle warning me about this."

"You talked to my brother?" Kinsley turned to face Rachel directly and folded her arms protectively around her chest.

"Yeah, he's doing well, Kins. Germany is good for him," Rachel said with a hint of what sounded like defeat. "He asked me to look after you," she added, her tone turning resolute.

"You didn't tell him about the murder, did you?" Kinsley already knew the answer, but she had to confirm.

"Of course I did," Rachel admitted. "That's the reason I called him."

"Oh no." Kinsley wearily wiped her hand across her face. She thought this was a very bad idea. She knew her brother, and he would take emergency leave in order to protect his sister and his aunt. Which was totally unnecessary.

"You told him we were fine, yes?" she pleaded, holding praying hands in front of her. "He really doesn't need that added stress. His job is stressful enough."

"I told him not to worry about either of you, that I'm keeping you both safe. He's familiar with my work."

"Thank goodness, Rachel, because I know my brother. And he would be on the next plane off the base. I kinda wish you hadn't told him."

"I understand that," Rachel said.

Kinsley wondered if she did. Otherwise, why did Rachel tell him? Was this her ploy to get Kyle to come home? She turned her attention back to the ocean and allowed her thoughts to be washed away with the tide. She didn't have the time, nor the energy, to travel down that rabbit hole. The deed was done, anyhow, not much she could do to change it. Except maybe put in a call to her brother and reassure him that they were fine. Which is exactly what she would do just as soon as she was back at her aunt's place and Kyle could have the added bonus of hearing Tilly's voice, too. Hopefully that would be enough to convince him they really were fine.

"Hey, if you're willing to give a statement, we can arrest Denny right now. Is that what you want to do? Keep in mind, though, he might not ever forgive you for this."

"You can? On what grounds?"

"Destruction of property. Didn't you tell me on the phone that he ripped your flowers out in front of Toby's?"

"Oh yeah, that. I thought about that, but that still doesn't allow you to get his DNA . . . and I don't want you to arrest him on something petty that I can handle myself."

"Petty? Seems to me he's upping his game. First the Barbie shoe warning, and now he's ripping your flowers out on Main Street. Where he could easily get caught. If he *is* the one responsible for Daisy's murder, you could be in grave danger."

"Can you take him in on drug charges?"

"What are you talking about?"

Kinsley explained how she thought that Denny was the one who had been supplying Stacey's ADHD medication and how she saw her in the bathroom taking drugs at *Cinderella*.

"We'll get into the fact that you shouldn't be doing stakeouts later. Right now, I still don't have probable cause for that charge," Rachel admitted. "Unless Stacey actually told you that she received the drugs directly from Denny, I have little to go on."

Kinsley scratched her head and deliberated. If she had the man arrested on destruction of property, he'd haunt her business for the rest of her life. On the other hand, she really wanted this to end. She was desperate to protect her aunt as the Walk Inns event was right around the corner. She also wanted to make peace with Pete and let everyone in Harborside get on with their lives. Not to mention, and most important, get justice for a woman's life that had been snuffed out way too soon. "Is there any way to keep my name out of this? I'm reluctant because of the backlash I might receive."

"Kins, I'll ask Denny for a sample when I take him in. And if he denies a swab, trust me when I say, I'll get it another way."

"How, though?" Kinsley asked.

"I have my ways. It's as simple as offering him a can of soda or a water bottle. Trust me, this isn't my first rodeo, I can get the job done," Rachel taunted with an elbow bump. "You need to trust me, Kins. I'm good at my job. Are you ready to provide a statement? I'll have uniforms here to arrest him before you can say . . ."

"Lickety-split," Kinsley finished.

"Exactly."

"Let's do it," Kinsley confirmed. She just hoped she was making the right decision. Because something in her gut was telling her otherwise.

Chapter 29

The minor incident of the bottle crashing to the floor inside of the Blue Lobstah seemed trivial now, in comparison. Because the crowd had vacated the bar and assembled outside of the restaurant to watch the arrest of Danny Davenport unfold. Kinsley and Becca followed it, too, as Denny ducked his head while a uniformed officer helped him get safely into the back seat of the police car.

"I didn't do it! I didn't do it!" Denny kept defending at the top of his lungs until the squad car door officially closed him in and only the rumblings of his hopeless defense remained.

The crowd just looked on with shock pasted on their faces and murmurs between friends. Everyone assumed Harborside had their killer, even though the man had been arrested only for destruction of property.

Becca leaned into Kinsley's ear and said, "Do you think

he's just saying that to save face, or do you think he's innocent?"

"I don't know what to think. Rachel told me they were just arresting him on a destruction-of-property charge," Kinsley said honestly. "We never tied a motive to him. I don't exactly want to pin a murder on someone who is innocent. They can't be arresting him on just hearsay, can they?"

"I doubt it. My guess is that Rachel didn't share with you everything they had on the guy. There must be more. Or when she called it in, other information was disclosed."

"Well, either way, it's her job to clear him, or hold him, based on the DNA sample. For now, I guess it's out of our hands."

"Have you seen Pete?" Becca asked as she rose on her tiptoes and scanned the crowd in search of the bar owner.

Kinsley shook her head. "Nope. I have a feeling he's still avoiding me. I'm sure he's not happy that Denny's arrest happened in his establishment." Kinsley winced. "To be honest, I'm not sure he'll ever forgive me for this."

"Yeah, half his patrons left the bar—this can't be good for business. And the other half are standing out here with us."

"You think I should go in and apologize?" Kinsley asked.

"Nah, you did the right thing, and he'll understand down the road. Just give him time to cool off." Becca threw an encouraging arm around Kinsley's shoulder and gave a light squeeze. "He'll be fine and this will all eventually blow over once Denny is put away for good. You'll see."

Kinsley lowered her voice and whispered, "I just don't understand Pete's hesitation."

Becca frowned. "I think he just doesn't want his restaurant to have any part in it. Maybe he sees it as a stain on his reputation?"

"I suppose," Kinsley admitted with a shrug. "To me, I would want this case solved, no matter what. I think he's hiding something," Kinsley finally admitted out loud. She looked to see Becca's reaction, but her friend seemed unbothered as she continued to watch the events in front of them unfold.

"Some people just don't like getting overinvolved. He's trying to build his business and put his stamp on Harborside. And so far, he has a strong reputation here. I say we cut our friend Pete some slack."

"Then that's what we do. Wanna get out of here?"

Becca nodded her assent.

The two began to walk slowly in the direction of the parking lot. Kinsley turned on her heel and looked back one more time and continued to walk backward. She noticed Rachel chatting with coworkers and completely focused on her work and in her element. Kinsley wondered if she should approach her and ask what additional information had come to light, and then thought the better of it. She'd learn in time. For a moment, Kinsley wished Kyle were standing with her. Becca gave her arm a tug, to redirect them toward the parking lot.

Beneath the streetlight, Kinsley noticed Edna's car pull into the parking lot, but her neighbor was not behind the wheel. Instead, she pointed out Luke. "Hey, look who's here."

Becca stopped short and the two came to a halt as Edna's vehicle narrowly avoided hitting a woman walking to her car.

It seemed as if Luke had taken notice of the police presence, because Edna's vehicle pulled a U-turn and peeled out of the parking lot, leaving them wondering.

A few days had passed, and without an update from Rachel, Kinsley couldn't help but feel fidgety. She took her nervous energy out on the flower beds in front of the Salty Breeze Inn, where she deadheaded the hot-pink geraniums that flanked the front steps. She had already pulled any weeds in the front yard that had peeked through the soil. And the flower beds by the curb were flawless. Purple salvia strategically looked like waves among the pink and red begonias and made a further statement among the vanilla white marigolds. Kinsley was pleased and ready for the visitors who would soon view her handiwork firsthand, at the upcoming Walk Inns event.

The heat of the day bore down on her, though, almost as heavy as her heart. She hadn't talked to Pete and she wondered if she'd messed up their friendship over their differences of opinion. Or if in time he'd forgive her. She thought about bringing him a gift to win back his affections but abandoned the idea when she realized a gift probably wouldn't cut it. Then she toyed with the idea of asking Tilly if she would be willing to set up a table with craft beers from the Blue Lobstah, possibly a menu, and business cards to entice visitors to the inn to make a stop at the restaurant after the event.

After tossing the spent geranium stems into her wheelbarrow and wiping her brow, Kinsley looked up to see Roy from channel four news approach. She held her breath. What did he want?

"Good afternoon," he sang out merrily as soon as they were within earshot of each other.

Kinsley stretched her back and then stood upright. She massaged the back of her neck with her fingers and pasted on a weak smile as soon as he reached her side.

"Hey, what are you doing here?" Kinsley asked.

There must've been a slight harshness to her tone, as the newscaster looked taken aback, but he wasn't afraid to cut to the chase. "I thought I'd come by and ask you a few questions regarding the arrest of Denny Davenport."

"Really, why me?"

"I'm an investigative reporter, soon to be promoted to news anchor," he said with a hint of pride in his tone while he rocked on the balls of his feet. Kinsley thought if the man had suspenders, he'd be pulling on them, too. Luckily, he didn't.

"Congratulations on your promotion," Kinsley said, this time giving the man a genuine smile.

"A little birdie told me that you were the one who led to Denny's arrest," Roy added. "I applaud you!"

"Is that right? The gossip wheel is already turning, I see," Kinsley said, stepping behind her wheelbarrow and wheeling it to the other side of the yard. The last thing she wanted was to be quoted about the murder or to be cornered to involve herself even further than she'd already been. Suddenly, she understood why Pete might feel the way he did.

"You must be relieved to have that monkey off your back. I remember you telling me at the taffy shop that he was a thorn in your side."

Kinsley needed the ocean, needed to hear the waves crashing to shore. She wished to flee the entire ordeal and leave it all behind. And she really hoped that Roy wouldn't try to make this about the fact that she and Denny were competitors in a highly coveted landscape business location. She never should've slipped and said Denny's name in front of him.

The newscaster followed her.

"Hey, slow down. Are you going to ignore me?" Roy asked, keeping up with her stride.

Kinsley now realized she was pushing the wheelbarrow so fast, it was as if she were a NASCAR driver, advancing on the winning lap. "Look, the Walk Inns is tomorrow and I'm not trying to be rude. I honestly don't have time for this," she said over her shoulder. "Nor do I want anything to do with reporters at this time."

"Are you kidding? This is the biggest story that's ever hit Harborside, and you're not talking to me?" Roy challenged. "After what I did for you by giving you an exclusive interview?"

She reached the porch facing the sea and stopped abruptly, turning to face the man squarely. "I'm not really sure what you want from me. Denny Davenport was arrested, that's it. There's my statement."

"How about another interview? Let's get you on the record in front of the cameras."

Kinsley held up a hand in defense. "No thank you. I don't want to go on any record stating anything I can't take back or that might misrepresent the situation. Because what if I'm dead wrong?"

The screen door opened, and then Tilly sang out, "Kinsley, darlin', time for your—"

Kinsley turned her head in the direction of her name, to witness her aunt beckoning. A look of surprise washed across Tilly's face when she noted who was standing next to her. Her aunt made her way quickly down the steps.

"Hello, Mr. Maxton, lovely to see you." Tilly reached out to pump Roy's hand in a handshake, and then said encouragingly, with a generous wave of her hand, "Please join us for some lemonade out on the porch, won't you? I just brought some out for my niece, but there's plenty to go around." Tilly had a wide smile on her face.

"I still have a bit of work to do," Kinsley said, scanning the property and hoping for a large invasive weed to grab her attention. Instead, the property looked immaculate, which was good and bad all at once. She gritted her teeth.

Tilly gave her a stern look. "You need a break. Come." She gave Kinsley an encouraging pat on the backside with a flick of the towel from her shoulder and then a slight push toward the stairs when Kinsley still hadn't budged.

Roy started up the stairs. "I'd love a glass," he said as he took a seat in one of the many rocking chairs facing the sea. "What a view you have here! I certainly will be in the running to start looking for a piece of property like this soon. Whew, I can imagine waking up to this every morning. Now this is the life, I tell you!"

Tilly smiled proudly. "Yes, we're very blessed indeed, aren't we, Kinsley?" Her aunt looked at her rather sharply, with pursed lips, and waited for an answer.

"Not a day goes by that I take it for granted," Kinsley said genuinely. She then took a seat beside her aunt and looked toward the Atlantic. The sun was jumping across the water like a glittery ball, and a soft breeze blew, cooling her off beneath the shade of the porch.

"So, what brings you to visit the Salty Breeze Inn today?" Tilly asked as she poured the newscaster a tall glass of lemonade and then handed it to him.

"Thank you, this looks so refreshing!" Roy said enthusiastically, causing Tilly to smile proudly. Roy raised his glass, took a long sip, and then rocked slowly back and forth in the chair.

Tilly poured Kinsley a glass and handed it over.

"Thanks," Kinsley said, and she, too, immediately took a large sip of the refreshing beverage.

"Are you planning on doing a live feed of the Walk Inns event tomorrow? And thought to include us?" Tilly asked excitedly. "Is that why you're paying us a visit?"

"No, I'm not here about the event tomorrow. I actually stopped by to see if Kinsley would be willing to go live, beforehand, and break the story behind the arrest of Denny Davenport."

"Oh." Tilly seemed taken aback. She put her hand to her heart and sank into the chair. "I'm not sure that would be such a good idea, with so many visitors here for the event." She frowned. "I don't think the timing would be good."

"I was actually thinking first thing in the morning, for our early risers broadcast," he pushed.

Kinsley piped up. "Although we appreciate your visit to the inn today, I really don't want to get involved. And besides, I'm not even sure if the police are going to hold Denny or not. I just don't feel comfortable—"

Roy leaned forward in the chair and set his lemonade on a nearby side table. "You mean, you haven't heard?"

Kinsley and Tilly shared a look of confusion before waiting for Roy to continue.

"The hair follicle inside the Cinderella shoe belonged to Denny Davenport. The DNA is a match. At least in the preliminary testing. That's the word on the street."

Chapter 30

A match?" Kinsley sat upright in her chair, stunned. Although she'd participated in Denny's arrest, for some reason she'd just assumed the charges wouldn't stick. And he'd be let go on a misdemeanor and remain a thorn in her side.

"That's right! The Cinderella murder has been solved, thanks to you. You're a hero!" Roy nodded vigorously and raised his lemonade as if they should clink glasses to celebrate this momentous occasion.

"Wow," Kinsley said, trying to allow this information to sink in.

"So, will you do the interview? I thought we could do it right out there." He pointed just beyond the porch. "Where you planted the daisies in her honor. You did plant them in her honor, didn't you?"

Kinsley nodded her head numbly.

Roy continued, "We could do a live feed right where you found the Cinderella shoe and cracked the case. Right over there! Where the shoe was found!" He wagged his finger up and down, as if Kinsley didn't remember the location that would be burned in her memory for a lifetime.

Kinsley knew she should feel a sense of relief, but instead she was left rather speechless. "Roy, thanks for stopping by, but I really need to get back to work. I know you're looking for a big story to catapult your career; I'm just not your gal," Kinsley said, officially removing herself from the situation and rising from the chair. "It sounds like you already have the anchor position solidified anyway, right? You don't need me."

"Yes, I already have the new anchor position sealed tight. Truth is, I just thought you'd like to be the hero in this story." Roy stood and handed Kinsley a business card. "Give me a call when you change your mind."

Kinsley took the card and then looked to her aunt for help, and Tilly provided it. "We really do have a lot to do before the event. Thanks for stopping by, though." Tilly encouraged his exit by rising from her chair and gathering the empty glasses onto the tray, marking the conversation officially over. Tilly didn't even offer him a second glass of lemonade, which her aunt would normally trip over herself to do. Kinsley wanted to give her a high five.

Roy finally took the cue and headed for the stairs. "Call me, day or night, if you change your mind," he said over his shoulder, and the two remained quiet until the newscaster disappeared from view.

Tilly set the full tray of drinking glasses back on the table and sank back into the rocking chair. "That's not at all what I was expecting. You?" she asked. "I really thought he was here to suggest a follow-up story or include the Salty Breeze for the Walk Inns event tomorrow. What a disappointment." She sighed.

"No, I knew he wasn't here for that, but—" Kinsley said, taking a seat beside her aunt. "I have to admit, I'm shocked. I wonder why Rachel didn't call me to share the news. I have to hear all of this secondhand, from a reporter?"

"She's busy. Rachel has a lot on her plate, too. We all do," Tilly added, with a cluck of her tongue. "In fact, I probably shouldn't be sitting right now. I have beds to strip, wash, and remake before morning. The to-do list is long before the big event. I need to get a move on."

"I suppose," Kinsley agreed. "Honestly, I'm a little relieved. I thought Luke might somehow be involved, so I'm glad to know at least Edna won't have to deal with that."

"Luke?" Tilly gasped.

"Oh, Aunt Tilly, it's a long story . . . and you said you have beds to strip." Kinsley chuckled, and then pressed her fingers to her forehead. "We'll save it for another time."

"Better for me not to know anyhow." Tilly chortled, patting her leg. "But yes, I would hate for Edna's grandson to have any involvement at all. That would break my dear friend, for sure." Tilly rocked slowly back and forth in the chair, as if pondering.

"What?" Kinsley finally asked.

"Did you tell Roy that you planted those Shasta daisies in the victim's honor?"

"No. I didn't," Kinsley admitted.

"How'd he learn that, then? I could understand if the Cinderella shoe being found there was leaked now that Denny's DNA is a match, but the flowers?"

"That's a very good question." Kinsley gnawed at her cheek and pondered. "Maybe he just assumed?"

"Huh, I find it strange. A bit of a leap, in my opinion. I guess he's just astute, is all. Well, I better get back to it," Tilly said with a groan, rising from the chair. "These old bones," she added with a chuckle. "This might be my last event for a while. Dare I admit, I think I'll be glad when it's over. Maybe I need to retire after all."

This was the first time Kinsley had heard her aunt Tilly complain. She wasn't one to talk about her ailments, but she knew preparing for the Walk Inns and all that had transpired had been taxing on her aging relative.

"Anything I can do to help?" Kinsley asked.

"Nah, you have your own work to keep up with." Tilly rolled her shoulders to seemingly work out the kinks, then scanned the property and turned to her with a proud smile. "You did a great job out here; the yard is absolutely perfect. Not a blade of grass is out of place. Thank you, Kinsley." She beamed. "You always do a nice job, but the new planters and the living garland along the railing really make the place shine. I love you, my sweet," she added warmly.

"Thanks, you're the best," Kinsley said, and she meant it. "And thanks for the lemonade, Aunt Tilly. I love you, too. You care for me like no one else in the world."

Tilly patted her lightly on the cheek before gathering the tray of glasses and disappearing into the inn.

Kinsley rocked slowly back and forth in the chair as she contemplated what her aunt had said. The breeze picked up, causing the nearby purple fountain grass to sing and dance in the wind. How *did* Roy know she'd planted the flowers in Daisy's honor? She chalked it up to the reporter just being perceptive. After all, he paid attention to details.

The problem was, so did she.

Chapter 31

Ever since Kinsley learned that Denny was on the hook for murder, a nagging feeling wouldn't escape her until she could meet with Rachel to fill in the gaps. She'd asked the detective to meet at her favorite hiding place tucked within the rocks along the cliff walk. The sun was sinking in the western sky, and the puffy pink clouds had transformed the water into an iridescent lavender color. Waves gently rocked against the shore, as if in a lullaby. In the distance, sailboats slowly danced across the horizon line in the direction of the marina. Summertime in southern Maine was mostly warm, but often the breeze off the water in the evening kept the air at a comfortable temperature. Kinsley zipped her hoodie to avoid the chill that would soon come after the sun made its final exit.

While she waited, Kinsley enjoyed a Reese's Peanut Butter Cup and was just licking the peanut butter from her fingers when she heard someone calling out her name.

She turned and smiled when she saw Rachel maneuvering her way across the rocks.

"You know, very few people know about this spot, and you're one of them. I only share this hidden gem with people I love," Kinsley admitted easily, patting the rock beside her for Rachel to take a seat.

"Tilly mentioned that to me the last time the four of us met out here. She said she was surprised you'd shared it," Rachel said, making the final jump across a large tidepool to reach her.

"It's the only place I know of where I can have complete privacy. When I was a kid, this was my hidden fortress. For years, Kyle didn't even know about it. I'd see a plane overhead and imagine my parents were coming home on leave. But we both know that was delusional. I guess that's how I coped back then." Kinsley brought her legs up and hugged her knees tighter.

"Thank you for sharing that with me." Rachel gave her shoulder a light squeeze before taking a seat beside her. "I'm sure you still miss them."

"Every. Single. Day."

"I'm so sorry, Kins."

"It's a beautiful night," Kinsley said, changing the subject. She wasn't sure why, but her parents were on her mind more than ever recently, and they seemed to be on the tip of her tongue, too. She wasn't sure if it was from her recent visit to the Harbor Playhouse or just the vulnerability of life that had propelled her memory like a slingshot. In any event, that wasn't why they were here now.

"It's gorgeous. Look at that sky!" Rachel said.

"I know, right? I love nights like this. You might wanna tuck your legs up or you'll get your feet wet, though."

"It's warm enough." Rachel shrugged. "I don't mind,"

she added before removing her tennis shoes and socks and allowing her feet to fall freely again.

"Yeah, until the sun dips. As soon as it's gone, it's amazing how cool summer nights in Maine can be. Right?"

"I love it here," Rachel admitted. "You might come out to your spot sometime and find me in your hidden fort," she teased.

"Just as long as you keep it our little secret." Kinsley winked. "By the way, I invited Becca to join us. She had a showing across town and said she'd text when she was on her way. So far, I haven't heard anything." Kinsley lifted her cell off the rock beside her to verify. She'd kept it on vibrate to keep their private hideaway undisclosed from the tourists who might be traipsing along the cliff walk.

"Do you want to wait for Becca, then, to discuss the case?"

"No, I'd rather not. I can fill her in. I'm surprised you didn't call me, though. I kinda thought you would've as soon as you were sure you had the right guy."

"Kins, this is the biggest case our department has seen in decades. It's been a little overwhelming, to say the least. But I'd be remiss if I didn't take the time to thank you, though, so I'm here now, sitting next to you, after a very long shift," she added with a light shoulder bump. "And I brought you this." Rachel reached into her pocket and tossed over a handful of Reese's Peanut Butter Cups.

Kinsley gasped with delight and caught them expertly. She set them aside on a nearby rock and pulled the empty wrapper from her pocket, to show the detective. "You know me so well," she said, grinning.

"I am in law enforcement, remember?" Rachel chuckled. "Don't eat them all in one sitting."

"Yes, Mom," Kinsley teased, and then held one out to share. "Want one?"

"Oh, trust me, I had a few on the way over." Rachel laughed. "I'm good." She waved her hands as if she were an umpire, calling the baseball player safe.

Kinsley couldn't wait another moment to get the details. "The DNA was a match, huh? For some reason, I wasn't expecting that. I don't know why, but it surprised me."

"Yep, it sure was. The hair follicle found inside Daisy's shoe sealed the case. Think about that for a minute. One little hair, found in the toe of a shoe, can literally put you away for life. Denny is going away for a very long time."

"Wow, isn't that crazy? I mean, yeah, the guy was a thorn in my side, but a murderer!" Kinsley opened a Reese's wrapper slowly and then took a nibble before adding, "I mean, it's weird when you find out someone you know, or at least thought you knew, is capable of that kind of crime. It's just a disturbing feeling, is all. I never would've put Becca in that position had I really thought it through." Kinsley shuddered after licking the peanut butter crumbs from her lips. "I guess that's why I'm having a hard time digesting the facts."

"I hear you. You don't expect anyone with a pumping heartbeat to be capable of such terrible things. Unfortunately, that's what keeps me in business," Rachel said somberly.

"Did you get a confession out of him? Why'd he do it, you think?"

"Daisy's toxicology reports showed large amounts of unprescribed methamphetamine in her system. It's the chemical found in some ADHD medications, which are often used for weight loss, or maybe in Daisy's case, to help her focus and memorize her lines, because nothing in Daisy's medical records showed she was diagnosed with ADHD. Not sure why she took it. After you gave me the go-ahead to arrest Denny on destruction of property, I then obtained a search warrant for his house, to confirm what you'd shared about Stacey, and all of this came to light. We've had our eye on him for a while for Schedule II drugs. Your tip-off only led them to dig further. Denny was dealing that, along with other drugs we obtained in his possession, such as marijuana, speed, et cetera. Of course, Denny won't admit to any of this, but we think maybe Daisy was planning to out him or something."

"But why would she do that? If she was willingly taking the medication and he was supplying it? Wouldn't that just cut off her own supply? I'm not sure it makes sense." Kinsley leaned her weight atop her fists and looked out to sea, pondering. A gust of wind caused one of the sailboats to lean treacherously to one side, and Kinsley was thankful when the captain righted it.

"Well, we have his DNA tying him to the shoe. I ran that as soon as we obtained the swab. It's pretty much a slam dunk. Truth is that most perps won't share their motives with police. It's just something we learn to live with. Sometimes people are just not in their right head. It's not my job to figure out the mind of a killer. It's my job to put the pieces together so that we have a solid case to present to the district attorney." Rachel picked up a handful of loose stones and seashells and began tossing them into the sea, as if she were making wishes in a wishing well.

"I suppose," Kinsley said, turning her attention away

from the Atlantic and aiming it squarely at Rachel. "What about the shoe—how did it get buried on my aunt's property? That's a huge question mark, in my mind."

"Given the teeth marks and the blood, we think Baxter took it from the crime scene. We're still trying to connect how it ended up in Denny's hands, but we'll get there. Maybe his motive was to bury it for good, away from his jobs, or put the onus on you?" Rachel suggested.

"You mean Denny didn't admit to burying it there?"

"No." Rachel chuckled. "He lawyered up pretty quickly."

"Oh."

"Anyhow, for me, it's a job well done," Rachel continued. "And I have you to thank for that," she said, patting Kinsley's leg.

"Glad I could help."

"Well, my dear, it's been a long week. I best be on my way; my bedroom is calling and I'm more than ready to answer," Rachel said with a groan. She donned her socks and shoes and then got to her feet. "I want to thank you again for keeping me in the loop and helping me with this case," she added, giving Kinsley a shoulder squeeze before turning to navigate off the rocks.

"No problem."

"Don't be a stranger," Rachel said over her shoulder, and then turned for a second to add, "Let's stay in touch, okay? Maybe lunch sometime?"

"Sure, I'd like that," Kinsley said before the detective disappeared from her view.

Kinsley returned her attention to the sea and took a cleansing breath. The sun had officially set and a cool breeze tickled her neck and sent a shiver down her spine.

The murder investigation was over. It was finally over.

Daisy's perpetrator had been brought to justice and they could now look forward to the Walk Inns event tomorrow.

Why, then, did Kinsley still feel uncertain? Why couldn't she let it go?

Chapter 32

Kinsley walked slowly back to the caretaker's cottage to settle in for the night. She thought about checking in on Tilly but figured any interruption the night before the big event would probably just be a distraction. Her aunt would want to dote on her, feed her supper, and chat endlessly about what Rachel had shared. Tilly would be up half the night to make up for it, finishing up all her last-minute details. Kinsley couldn't do that to her. She would wait until after the Walk Inns, when they would have all the time in the world to discuss it over a tall glass of lemonade.

After checking her cell phone for missed messages and coming up with none, Kinsley tucked her phone back into her sweatshirt pocket. She slipped the key into the lock, opened the door, and closed it behind her. Suddenly, she was exhausted and it was good to be home. The cottage seemed to wrap its arms around her like a comforting hug and wink at her when she flicked on the lights.

Kinsley shrugged off her sweatshirt and tossed it onto a nearby chair. She decided to open the windows and let the ocean breeze blow through while she listened to the lull of the waves. Instead of turning on the television, reading a good book with the sound of the waves as a backdrop sounded perfect. She had opened one window and was on the second when she was interrupted by a sharp knock on the door. She smiled, quickly moved for the door, and opened it wide.

"Bec-ca," she said, and then took a surprise step backward when it wasn't her best friend, but the reporter for channel four news, standing at her doorstep.

"Roy? What are you doing here?" Kinsley looked around his shoulder, as if the cameraman might be close at his heels and they were about to corner her, live on the air, but the newscaster was alone.

"Hello, Kinsley," he said. Something about his tone gave her pause. Kinsley reached for the door, to hold it protectively between them, but he held it back with his shiny new shoe.

"It's late, Roy, I'm sorry, I'm just not interested—"

Before Kinsley had a chance to continue, the reporter shoved his way inside the cottage and closed the door behind him. She heard the eerie sound of the dead bolt clicking shut, leaving no way of escape between them. It had all happened so fast, her mind couldn't comprehend it.

"What are you doing in my house? You need to leave," Kinsley said in the most demanding tone she could muster.

"We need to talk."

"I don't—"

Roy interrupted her by covering her mouth with his hand. His physical touch made her stomach lurch.

"Why are you still digging into the murder investigation? You should leave the digging to SeaScapes and keep your nose out of other people's business." He moved his hand and tapped her on the nose with his finger. "Don't you think?"

"I don't know what you're talking about." Kinsley tried to play it cool, but she could feel her face flush red-hot, and a trickle of sweat poured down her back. She glanced at her sweatshirt, which was draped atop the chair and held her cell phone inside the pocket. If only she could get to it.

"I knew when you declined my interview, we might have a problem." He patted his fingers to his lips and scrutinized her before continuing. "No one denies me. No one!" Roy's voice rose an octave, almost shrill. "And then when you said you thought they had the wrong guy, I knew you'd get in my way."

Trying to defuse the situation, Kinsley said, "Honestly, I—"

"Don't you know, the right person has been arrested for the crime? You need to leave it alone now," he said, slowly shaking his head and wagging a finger at her as if she were a petulant child.

"Yes, I'm glad—"

"Tell me why you called that detective over here," Roy said, his breath hot on her. His eyes turned dark and demanding.

"Oh, Rachel? She dated my brother. In fact, I thought one day they would marry . . . but the distance . . . Anyway, she and I are friends. That had nothing to do with—" Kinsley stuttered.

"Really? You expect me to believe that?" he said, interrupting her.

"Are you stalking me?" Kinsley heard the vibration of fear trickle from her own voice but didn't want to give Roy the satisfaction. "You've been following me, haven't you?" Kinsley squared her shoulders then in a defensive stance. The reporter was taller than her by more than a foot. There was no way she could overcome him. And he stood between her and the exit, and he had locked the dead bolt.

Roy laughed pitifully. "You wouldn't leave it alone; you still won't." He combed his hand through his hair, causing his ear to show. His left ear, where Kinsley now noticed the lobe was covered in a crusty scab. "This might be a problem," he said under his breath.

"I notice you have an injury on your ear. I'm pretty sure I know what happened, unless you'd care to explain it to me." Kinsley couldn't help but sound accusatory.

His face turned ashen as he raised his fingers to his ear. "Daisy ripped my earring out," he spat. Then he looked at her in shock about what he'd just revealed.

Kinsley then knew, with absolute certainty, that the earring found on the ground beside Daisy's lifeless body had belonged to Roy. She realized the makeup found on Daisy's dress wasn't stage makeup, either. It didn't belong to a woman—it belonged to the wannabe news anchor. The sordid details were all coming together and forming a perfect picture in her mind. "You wanted the big story, is that it?" Kinsley uttered. "Nothing happens in Harborside, nothing big enough anyway, to catapult you to the anchor chair. So, you created it."

A sly smile crossed Roy's face and Kinsley knew she was in serious trouble.

"Becca is on her way over," Kinsley explained. "We were planning on celebrating the closed case over a glass of wine . . ." She took a step backward, and he reached for her wrist and held it tight.

"Are you going to leave it alone, case closed? Or are you

going to be the model citizen you think everybody wants you to be? No one will ever believe you." His eyes bore down on her.

Kinsley decided to play to his ego. "Rachel said they had their guy. The case is officially closed, based on the DNA. Don't worry, I'll keep your secret. Brilliant for you, it worked. Now let go of my arm, you're hurting me."

Roy nodded assent. "Yeah, pretty lucky on my part that your adversary found that dog running with the shoe and left his DNA inside it. He created the perfect alibi for me! That's all it takes, you know, one little hair." His lip curled upward, but he gripped her wrist even tighter. "But you had to keep talking to that detective, asking too many questions. Didn't you? You shouldn't have done that. I won't let you ruin this for me."

"That Internet troll, that one you claimed was saying nasty things about me? You lied about that, didn't you? You were trying to make me believe my nemesis had something to do with this, because I mentioned Denny's name to you that day at Toby's Taffy. You wanted me to believe it was him?" Kinsley demanded.

"You mean, anonymous 455?" Roy shook his head innocently. "I can't take credit for that. Nope, you can't pin that on me. You really do have some haters out there." A creepy-sounding laugh spewed from his lips, and he gripped her wrist tighter.

Kinsley didn't believe a word he said at this point. "Stop. You're hurting me." She winced as she fought to have him release her. Surprisingly, Roy let her go. She vigorously rubbed where he'd held tight to her, and then she folded her arms protectively around her chest. "Did you hide the shoe on purpose, then? So you could break the story and call it Cinderella? I bet your intention was to thwart the investigation and lead authorities by the nose to the Harborside Playhouse, was that it? People would remember Cinderella for decades to come. At least that's what you'd hoped." Kinsley figured if the man was going to kill her, she could at least get the details that were still unclear.

"A dog came and swiped it when Daisy fell to the ground after I pulled her out of the trunk of my car. I finished her off at the farm field. You know, I'm not stupid enough to murder someone in broad daylight! I ran after the dog, but the nasty little furball got away. Having your nemesis get ahold of the shoe worked perfectly for me," Roy admitted, and then ran his hands nervously through his hair, as if reliving the ordeal in real time. "As for Cinderella, Daisy wouldn't let me interview her, either. She was too good for local television," he sneered. Roy then looked at her and said, "You realize I'd be a fool to let you get away at this point."

An uncomfortable pause ensued between them. But Kinsley held her stance. They were like two raging bulls, ready to knock horns, yet neither ready to make the first move.

Kinsley's phone vibrated, inside her sweatshirt, breaking the silence between them.

"I need to get that. It's probably Becca on her way over here, and it's not a good time for her to visit. Unless of course, you want to keep lining up dead bodies. You'll have to think smart, some evidence might slip if you're careless." Kinsley chewed the inside of her cheek nervously. She hated talking about her best friend in this way, but she thought only of Becca's protection. The idea of dragging Becca into this mess made her breathless.

"Get it," Roy demanded. "But put the phone on speaker. I'm listening," he warned.

Kinsley rushed to her cell phone while Roy followed

tight at her heels. She held it between them after hitting the speaker button.

"Hey, Kins," Becca's voice sang out. "I'm on my way, sorry I'm late. I had to write up an offer for my buyers. Fingers crossed the sellers will accept. I'm hoping not to negotiate this all night long. Is Rachel still with you?"

Kinsley cleared her voice. "No, she had to go."

"Oh. I still wanna hear all the details about the murder investigation. I'll pick you up and we'll head over to the Blue Lobstah for a bite. Whaddya say? I'm starving."

"Um, no," Kinsley stammered. "I'm tired, I think I'm gonna head for bed."

"Now? It's only eight thirty."

"Yeah, I'm tired."

"Are you avoiding Pete? Is that what this is all about? We can grab a pizza instead . . ."

"No, not tonight."

Roy nodded his head and lasered his focus in on her. His eyes refused to leave Kinsley for even a millisecond.

"Oh. All right . . . I suppose I understand that, after the week you had . . ." Becca paused. "I wanted to hear what Rachel had to say. Can you at least fill me in?"

"Not now. Maybe tomorrow? We can go to the beach and talk. Bring the water wings."

"Okay?" Becca's tone was one of confusion. "Isn't tomorrow the Walk Inns—"

"Yeah, I might need a lifesaver," Kinsley added, and knew she took it too far, as Roy took a step closer and snatched the phone from her hand. He mouthed the words, "Say good-bye."

Kinsley couldn't help but think he meant forever.

Chapter 33

Kinsley knew her options were limited but she needed to get away from this crazed man. The wind blew the gauzy curtain away from the open window, sending an eerie whistling sound into the room. Roy paced in front of her as if planning her execution, while she could do nothing but hopelessly wait. Her life suddenly flashed before her eyes, rapid-fire.

Continuing to play to his ego, Kinsley decided, would be her only chance for survival. "I won't tell a soul." She held up her hand, as if taking an oath. "You have worked so hard to get that anchor position. I, for one, understand competition in the workplace. Harborside's elite clientele . . . well . . . Believe me, I was happy when Denny was arrested; the man has been a thorn in my business—"

"Stop talking," Roy said calmly. His demeanor was terrifying. The newscaster didn't seem nervous—he seemed calculating.

This scared Kinsley to the core.

"You're right, though," he muttered. A sly smile crept up his lips.

"Right? What do you mean, I'm right?"

"I can make this a story . . ." His eyes wandered, as if looking to connect the dots.

"No, hang on," Kinsley stammered. "I don't understand."

"You." He looked down at her with what Kinsley could describe only as *If looks could kill.*

Kinsley swallowed.

"*You* can be my next big story," he added, rubbing his hands together as if in anticipation of something great. "Local woman found . . ." Roy nodded eagerly. "Wait, give me a minute to think of a good tagline."

Suddenly, Kinsley's mouth went dry. She attempted to swallow again but instead a lump formed in her throat. "No, no, no . . . wait." She shook her head violently in dissent, to sway his mind. "Think about it. Denny's in custody. If you kill again, the police will look for someone else. Right now, you have the perfect escape. Don't blow the alibi that's been handed to you on a silver platter," she pleaded. Her voice sounded more desperate than she would've liked.

Roy's eyes met hers. He frowned and then returned his focus to the ceiling.

Kinsley took this chance to lift her leg high off the ground and stomp on the man's shoe as hard as she could, causing him to reach for his foot in pain.

"You stupid girl!" he spat, swinging a long arm out to grab her.

Kinsley ran for the door and unlatched the dead bolt, only to have Roy follow and crush her body up against the door in a body slam. Her face scraped along the wood panel, and she lifted her hand to her face to feel for blood. There was none, but she was sure her cheek would bruise.

"You're not going anywhere." His eyes blazed, and Kinsley cowered from his touch. It was clear she'd angered Roy, and she was desperately afraid of what he'd do next. She needed to act quickly. Her eyes pinballed around the room, landing on the fireplace, where the fireplace poker leaned against the wall.

"I need to sit down and put my head between my legs," she said weakly. "I don't feel so good. I think you knocked the wind out of me." She clutched her heart dramatically.

In one fell swoop, Roy dragged her by the arm and tossed her, like a rag doll, to the denim sofa. Kinsley bowed her head and waited for what seemed an eternity for her adversary to take a single step backward. When he did so, she leaped for the pruning shears that she suddenly remembered she'd tucked beneath the couch, now thankful she hadn't had time to properly put them away. She swung the shears wildly at his head. After hearing a crack and seeing the man fall to the floor, she ran for the window, as it was closer than the door. She knew she hadn't hit Roy hard enough to knock him cold, only enough to momentarily stun him. Kinsley looked back quickly and noticed him shake his head and then attempt to follow her after a stumble.

After a karate kick to the screen, Kinsley flung herself through the open hole and fell from the window, thankful for once that she hadn't planted the red rosebushes beneath it that she'd originally planned. She rolled from the fall and then caught her stride.

She must've hurt her leg in the fall, but the adrenaline pumping through her veins worked like Novocain and she was able to keep going. Kinsley ran as fast as her injured leg would carry her. Instead of heading for the inn and bringing the trouble to Tilly's doorstep, she ran for the cliff walk. The sound of footsteps running behind her kept her moving. The flagstone steps were lit by the moon and Kinsley was thankful for it.

"Get back here!" Roy hissed.

This made Kinsley take the flagstone steps even faster. She expertly sprang across the cliff walk. A sharp pain ripped through her leg, causing her to fall to her knees. She quickly picked herself back up and limped across the rocks to escape to her hidden fortress. A quick peek over her shoulder revealed Roy in hot pursuit, blood running down the side of his face as he crossed the cliff walk.

After reaching her destination, Kinsley ducked into her hideout, held her breath, and waited. Roy followed her across the rocks, stood above her, looked out to the Atlantic, and called her name.

"Kinsley . . . Clark . . . You know I'm going to find you! You may as well give up, sweetheart," he sang out.

"Don't call me sweetheart!" Kinsley cried as she reached up for her assailant's leg and gave a hard tug to disarm him. Instead, this caused Roy to lose his balance and slip atop the rocks. Kinsley looked on in horror as his fall sent him tumbling into the depths of the sea. And then a wave came and swallowed him.

Kinsley shook violently as she held tight to her knees and watched as the Atlantic grew more and more forceful. The wind had picked up, and the roar of the waves filled her ears thunderously. She tried to steady her breath in its cadence.

"Kinsley!"

The sound of her name caused her head to turn. Becca and Rachel joined her atop the rocks and came immediately to her side. "Are you okay?" Becca sat beside her and gathered Kinsley into her arms and held her close.

Kinsley continued to shiver, but not from the cold.

Rachel took a seat on her other side, so Kinsley was sandwiched protectively between them.

"We saw the broken window," Rachel explained.

"And I called Rachel right away because you said you needed a lifesaver. The water wings, I finally understood what you'd meant . . . I never heard you so desperate!" Becca cried, tucking her face into Kinsley's arm. "You had me worried sick!"

Kinsley pointed a shaky finger out toward the Atlantic. "Roy—"

"Roy?" Rachel asked.

"The reporter . . . from channel four news. He . . . killed her," Kinsley stammered.

"What?" Becca gasped. "What about Denny?"

"No, it wasn't him," Kinsley confirmed with a vigorous shake of her head.

Rachel followed Kinsley's pointed finger and stood atop the rock to look over the cliff. She immediately called the precinct to send an ambulance.

"He's down there?" Kinsley gulped, surprised. She'd assumed Roy's body had been washed out to sea.

"He's caught up on the rocks. I need to go and see if he's alive," Rachel said.

"No!" Kinsley said in horror. "No! It's not safe!" She reached out a hand to hold her back.

"It's my job, Kins," Rachel said, meaning to comfort, but it made Kinsley tremble more.

Kinsley laid her head on her knees and rocked back and forth to stop the trembling that had overtaken her body. But it did little to help.

"Take her back to the house," Rachel ordered Becca. "I've got it from here." She turned her focus back on Kinsley. "And don't worry, Kins, backup is on the way."

Becca scrambled to her feet and obediently reached out a hand to help Kinsley to her feet. Kinsley winced when they finally reached a standing position.

"You okay to walk?" Becca asked.

Kinsley threw her arm around her friend's shoulder. "Only if I have my water wings with me," she said, trying to lighten the mood.

"Come on, let's get you out of here," Becca said as they slowly made their way back to the safety of the inn.

Chapter 34

The sun shone brightly on the Salty Breeze Inn, as if encouraging the residence to show off its grandeur. The morning of the Walk Inns event had finally arrived, and the picture-perfect summer day was the ideal backdrop for the individuals who would be lucky enough to pass through its welcoming doors.

Kinsley wanted to be sure her aunt Tilly didn't dote on her and instead focused her attention on the many guests that were sure to enjoy a tour of the property. Becca had resurrected a set of crutches from when she'd sprained her ankle during a volleyball game back in her high school days. And Kinsley willingly accepted the crutches, to make everyone around her happy. The ER nurse had cleared her the previous night and said she'd only strained a muscle. Nothing was torn, thankfully. Her body would heal in time.

Regardless, Becca had spent the night at the caretaker's cottage, not leaving her sight for a millisecond.

"I hope you get a chance to mingle today. Maybe you'll find a few new clients out of this event," Kinsley said, encouraging her friend. "You never know who might cross your path."

"Honestly, I couldn't care less about that. I just want to be sure you're okay," Becca said as they slowly made their way from the caretaker's cottage to the wide porch of the inn. "You've been through quite an ordeal."

"I appreciate that, but really, I'm fine. Aunt Tilly has worked so hard to prepare for this event, let's just try and let it go for today, okay?"

"You bet."

Luke, carrying a bouquet of flowers, had just topped the cliff walk staircase and was headed in their direction across the lawn. When within earshot he said, "Grandmother wanted me to deliver these to your cottage, but I see you're up and about. Happy to see you're on your feet!"

"Oh, that's so kind of Edna." Kinsley leaned forward on her crutches and took a deep sniff of the pink and orange roses while Luke held the bouquet in his hand. "Can you carry them for me, Becca?"

"You bet." Becca took the bouquet from Luke and the two waited an awkward moment before Kinsley said, "Look, I think I owe you an apology."

Luke tilted his head sideways and waited.

"I sort of thought maybe you were involved somehow . . . when I overheard you and Stacey talking out by the cliff walk the other day. Anyhow, I'm sorry. I should've never jumped to conclusions about you."

"Oh, you heard that?" Luke's face suddenly flushed red.

Kinsley bit her lip. "Yeah, kinda. I wasn't meaning to eavesdrop, I only meant to deliver the brownies. But I heard what I heard . . ."

"Oh."

"You mind if I ask you something personal?"

"I guess not?" Luke's gaze dropped to the ground as if in avoidance.

"Why did you have the telescope pointed at the crime scene up in your grandmother's turret?" Kinsley asked.

"The police were out there digging around, looking for clues. Guess I'm one of those citizens who are just curious about the investigation." He shrugged.

Kinsley held her breath, but then went for it. For her own peace of mind, she just had to know. "What was Stacey worried about that might implicate you both with the police?"

"It's over now, you don't have to say anything," Becca defended. And suddenly Kinsley wondered if her bestie really did have eyes for Luke. Or at the very least, she was protecting potential clients that Luke could provide for her real estate business.

Luke paused a minute before lowering his voice. "Daisy was taking drugs. And Stacey was providing them."

Luke didn't add anything that would implicate himself in the situation, and they didn't have a chance to dig further because they were interrupted by the sound of Kinsley's name being called.

"Kins!"

"Look, I need to run. Catch you both later." Luke turned quickly on his heel and retreated in the direction of the cliff walk, as if happy for the interruption and a quick escape.

"Kinsley!"

Kinsley turned to see Rachel round the corner and catch them before she hit the bottom step. She then understood why Luke seemed to do a disappearing act.

"Mornin', Rachel! Coming to check up on me? I promise I'm fine. Everyone needs to stop doting on me," Kinsley teased after greeting the detective with a half hug. "It's just a bruise."

"Well, for one . . . yes, I wanted to check on your physical wounds, but your psychological wounds might take a bit longer," Rachel admitted. "I needed to pay a visit before I head off to work." She studied her before asking, "How you holding up?"

"I'm good, really. I appreciate everyone's concern, but I'll be fine. I just want to focus on the event today and make sure Aunt Tilly enjoys it. I really think—" Kinsley was about to continue when she stopped, as she was suddenly confused by the wide smile that crept across Rachel's face.

"What?" Kinsley asked.

"I have a surprise for you back at the car," Rachel said. "Wait here."

Kinsley looked down at her crutches and then back at the detective. "No worries, I'm not going very far." She chuckled.

Rachel jogged back in the direction of the parking lot, and Kinsley and Becca shared a look of confusion.

"A surprise?" Kinsley said. And as soon as the words were out of her mouth, she saw her brother, dressed in his Air Force fatigues, round the corner. She blinked as she thought she might be seeing a mirage. "*Kyle?*" Her brother's blunt blond hair was tucked beneath his military cap.

And his eyes, the color of blooming blue hydrangea globes, creased in a smile.

Kyle greeted her with a wave of his hand, and Kinsley dropped the crutches to the ground. Despite her injured leg, Kinsley ran into the arms of her brother.

"Hey, sis," he said, smoothing her hair while she broke down in tears.

"What are you doing here?" Kinsley blubbered into his shoulder. She held her brother tight before holding him at arm's length. She refused to let him go. Tears flooded down her cheeks, and she couldn't have cared less.

Kyle wiped her tears with his thumbs. "I needed to see you for myself and make sure you're okay. The phone conversation just didn't cut it for me," he said tenderly. "I'm sorry I wasn't here, and you had to go through all of this alone."

"I was never alone. I felt Mom and Dad with me the whole time," Kinsley admitted. A new wave of tears washed down her cheeks. "I swear, they protected me . . . I've been feeling them so close!"

"I'm sure they did. I love you, Kins," Kyle said, taking her into his arms once again.

"I love you, too." Suddenly, Kinsley remembered they weren't standing alone. "My brother's home!" Kinsley squealed. "I can't believe it!" she cried.

Becca was just as elated. "Kyle!" She threw her arms out, almost dropping the bouquet of roses to the ground.

Kinsley backed away so her best friend could greet her brother with a hug. And then Rachel lifted the crutches from the ground and made sure Kinsley was resituated with them.

"Thank you for your service," Becca said. "But it sure is good to have you home."

"No problem, it's my pleasure," Kyle answered. "What a good day to be home on leave!" he said, looking toward the sun shining over the Atlantic. He raised his hands in gratitude.

"The sun sure is shining on us today," Kinsley said with a wide grin. "I can't believe you're here in the flesh!" She shook her head in disbelief.

After the four of them shared a few more pleasantries, Rachel said, "Kins, I know you have a few questions for me before I head back to my shift. Now's your chance. I have to go soon, so fire away."

Kinsley gulped. "Is he . . . alive?" She wasn't sure if she could live with herself if someone had died by her own hand. She wondered how her brother and Rachel had joined the Air Force, knowing one day they might have to take matters into their own hands in order to serve and protect. "Can I just say, I have so much respect for what you two do for a living. I wanna thank you *both* for the services you selflessly do each and every day." Kinsley's eyes bounced from her brother to Rachel and back again. "I just don't know how—"

"Roy's going to make it," Rachel confirmed.

Kinsley heaved a huge sigh of relief. "Ohhh . . . Thank you, Lord." Kinsley sank deeper into her crutches and let them hold her weight. "As strange as it sounds, that does make me feel so much better."

Kyle patted his sister on the shoulder approvingly, and she looked up at her brother and beamed.

Kinsley then looked to the Shasta daisies fluttering in the wind and asked, "I need to know for sure. How did the shoe get there, was it really Denny? I know it couldn't have been Baxter. The reason I say that is because after some thought, I remembered the soil was a different color. And the soil covering the shoe certainly wasn't native to Maine, so someone buried it there," Kinsley said.

Becca piped in, "Trust our amateur sleuth here, she knows her soils!" She grinned.

The four of them broke out in laughter.

"Hey!" Kinsley defended. "It's the truth, a good gardener knows these things," she added with a grin.

"Yes, our amateur-sleuth-slash-garden-expert is correct!" Rachel said. "Denny finally admitted to burying the shoe. After he knew the murder charges were dropped, the guy's mouth opened and it all came tumbling out like a waterfall. Unfortunately, because of the hair gel he so freely applies, his hair stuck inside the toe of the shoe. He's still getting charged on the drug possession, but it's up to you, Kinsley, how you want to proceed with destruction of property. And we will get him on impeding an ongoing investigation . . . so there's that, too."

"So did he also admit to burying the Barbie shoe in front of the taffy shop to scare me?" Kinsley asked.

"Yup."

Kinsley continued, "How did Denny get the Cinderella shoe in the first place?"

"The dog was running down the road with the shoe in his mouth and Denny attempted to rescue the dog for Edna but instead, the shoe was dropped, and Baxter took off. Denny then decided to make it your problem and not his. His plan was to bring trouble to your doorstep, but you found the shoe before he had perfected his plan."

"What about Roy's earring? Did it tie him to the crime?"

"No, but testing was done beneath Daisy's fingernails. We assume we're going to find Roy's DNA there from when she ripped it from his ear. Plus, we found Roy's makeup smeared on her dress. That was a match, too."

Kinsley brushed her hands together as if wiping herself free of the investigation. "I'd say Daisy's murder investigation is officially solved. Now, hopefully, she can rest in peace."

Chapter 35

Becca helped Kinsley up the wide steps of the inn, and they were met by Jenna and Toby at the top of the stairs. Jenna rushed to greet Kinsley with a hug, while Becca held her crutches.

"Oh, my girl! I heard what happened to you! How are you holdin' up?" Jenna held her at arm's length and inspected every inch of her. "Oh, look at your face. Does your cheek hurt?"

"I'm good." Kinsley smiled. She knew that body slam against the door would bruise, and makeup did little to cover it. "Thanks for coming. I bet Aunt Tilly is thrilled you're both here. What a beautiful day for the event." Kinsley tented her eyes with her hand and looked out toward the sparkling sea.

Toby plucked a piece of taffy from his pocket and handed

it to Kinsley. "We made a special flavor for the Walk Inns; we're calling it the Salty Breeze special. It's got a hint of blueberry to represent the state of Maine, and a bit of other flavors I'm not gonna disclose. You'll just have to try it and see if you can figure out what I added." He winked and then reached into his pocket for another and tossed it to Becca, who caught it in one hand.

Kinsley popped the candy into her mouth and tried to discover the flavors. She couldn't, but it was delicious just the same. "It's amazing, and surely it'll be a hit with the tour guests!" she said between chews.

Toby beamed.

"We were just about to set up inside. Your aunt has been gracious enough to lend us a pub table to display our candy and treats. She has such a heart, that Tilly." Jenna turned her focus to her husband. "But we need to hurry so we can get back to the shop before opening," she said. "Neither one of us was willing to stay back and miss checking up on you," she added with a smile.

Kinsley was glad her aunt had taken her idea to heart. Tilly had not only invited Toby's Taffy, but also extended a hand to several of the local businesses to display their wares. This would encourage those who walked through the doors to explore more of their unique seaside community before leaving Harborside.

"But not before we tour a few rooms," Toby warned his wife. "It's been years since we've been inside any of the guest rooms—they're usually occupied. And I wanted to see some of Tilly's renovations," he added.

"We must be on our way then." Jenna encouraged her husband with a tug of his arm before turning her attention back to Kinsley. "If you need anything, you just give us a call, you hear?" Jenna patted Kinsley's arm before the two disappeared into the inn.

"I love those people. Aren't they just the sweetest couple?" Kinsley said.

"They're as sweet as the saltwater taffy they create, that's for sure!" Becca agreed with a nod. "Here, let's set you up over here on one of the chairs." Becca leaned the crutches up against the house, and then helped Kinsley into one of the rocking chairs. "I'm gonna run inside and fetch us some coffee. And drop these roses in a vase of water. I'll leave the flowers inside for now until you're ready to take them home."

"Thanks, Bec, that sounds wonderful. And, if you wouldn't mind, put the vase at the check-in table where everyone can enjoy the scent of them—they're just gorgeous," Kinsley said as she adjusted herself in the chair. "I bet Aunt Tilly has some banana bread or blueberry muffins in there, too, so be sure and help yourself before Kyle steals them all. I noticed he already followed Aunt Tilly into the kitchen. Oh, and she promised we could finally try that chocolate ooey-gooey recipe that she had talked about, which she made special for the event. She found an Oreo truffle recipe that looks amazing. You'll have to snag a few of those, too. Unless she's waiting until later today to set out the good stuff."

"Do you want something to put your leg up on? A stool, perhaps?"

"You're so sweet, my friend, but really, I'm good. I took some ibuprofen before we left the cottage," Kinsley said with a weak smile. "Once it kicks in, I'll get back on my feet."

"Okay, I'll be right back," Becca said before disappearing into the house.

Kinsley looked out toward the Atlantic and noticed the glitter from the sun dancing across the sea, as if in a ballroom. The squawking of gulls overhead could be heard in the far distance. She inhaled the salty breeze and let it soothe her to her core. Nothing quieted Kinsley better than the sea. She must've closed her eyes momentarily because the sound of the screen door closing caught her attention. But it wasn't Becca, Tilly, or her brother who walked over the threshold. It was Pete.

"Hey," Kinsley said, tenting her eyes. "What are you doing up? Kinda early for a bar owner, no? I guess I assumed you slept until noon to make it till closing."

"Nah, I don't sleep much," he teased, then his tone turned serious. "Your aunt said I could display a menu and a few items from the bar for the event. I have a few T-shirts to give away, too. I can save you one, if you'd like." He motioned a thumb toward the door and grinned.

"Oh, nice. I'd love a T-shirt from my favorite restaurant." Kinsley smiled.

"Yeah, they turned out pretty cool. They're light blue with a navy blue lobstah on the front." He circled his belly animatedly as if demonstrating where the lobster would be shown on the shirt. "I bet it'd make those blue eyes of yours pop." His eyebrows danced up and down, teasingly. "You could be my walking billboard."

"I'll wear it proudly," Kinsley said with a grin.

"Do you mind if I join you?" Pete gestured to the chair beside her.

"Why would I mind?" Kinsley asked with a chuckle.

"You looked like you were sleeping. Wicked long night, huh? I heard you had a rough one. You hanging in there okay?"

Kinsley rocked slowly, using her uninjured leg to give her a push. "All good, my friend."

Pete looked over each shoulder as if checking to see if they were alone before he said, "Can we talk?"

Pete's tone gave Kinsley pause. "Sure. What's up?" She stopped rocking and adjusted in the chair to face him directly and give him her full attention.

"I feel like I owe you an apology."

"Me? For what? If anything, I think it's the other way around," Kinsley admitted.

"For getting upset instead of helping you with the whole Denny thing. Even though it turns out he wasn't the guy, that's not the point. I'm sorry I let you down." Pete hung his head.

"I appreciate it, but seriously, no need to worry about any of that. It's all over now anyway." Kinsley waved a hand of dismissal, and he took her hand in his, surprising her.

"I don't like the feeling of disappointing you," he admitted, stroking her hand with his thumb. "Or having this thing . . . between us."

"Really, it's fine—"

"It's not," Pete said, squeezing her hand before letting it go.

Something inside of her wished Pete still held on to her hand.

"I feel like I need to explain," Pete continued. "Why I didn't want to get involved in any of this."

"I'm listening." Kinsley folded her hands together and held them in her lap to prevent herself from reaching for his hand again. Pete hadn't ever touched her so tenderly, and she was surprised at how much she liked it. She secretly wondered what it would be like to be held by him. To feel the comfort of resting in his arms.

"My younger brother was in this fight at a bar one time. Anyhow, he got blamed for something he didn't do, and it got way out of hand. There was this girl, and her boyfriend was physically abusing her, so my brother got involved. The cop jumped on my brother's back to stop him from clocking the guy, but my brother took a swing at him. He actually did some time for it." Pete's face flushed red, as if embarrassed. "I never really trusted the authorities after that," he admitted, scratching the back of his neck. "I should have helped you. Look, I'm sorry, okay?" His eyes pleaded with her. "You forgive me?"

"Pete, it's okay," Kinsley said. "I'm sorry that happened to your brother—"

Pete interrupted, "Please, let me finish." He reached for her hand again, and she willingly let him hold it.

"I should have protected you and I didn't. And I'm mad about that, too," he said as if unburdening himself.

"I appreciate that, but I don't need your protection."

"Maybe if I had gotten involved, you wouldn't have gotten hurt—and none of this would have happened."

The screen door opened, and Pete quickly pulled back his hand.

Becca came through with a tray while Tilly held the door. Instead of following her out, Tilly disappeared back inside, the sound of her laughter floating all the way outdoors.

"Your aunt is in rare form today. Can't you hear the hooting and hollering going on in there with Toby?" Becca teased. "Tilly's definitely in her element."

"I'm so glad. I was afraid with everything that happened, that she'd be exhausted. I'm relieved that's not the case and that she seems to be rallying."

Becca set the tray beside Kinsley, and the smell of coffee floated to her nose. She couldn't wait to have a cup. "That smells so good," she admitted aloud.

"Good morning, Pete. How are you doing this fine day?" Becca asked. "Care to join us for a cup of joe and a fresh blueberry muffin? Tilly just took a batch out of the oven— they're still warm."

Pete rose from the chair. "I appreciate that, but I really gotta run. I have a ton of stuff going on today. How 'bout you two stop over at the bar later? Dinner's on me, it's the least I can do."

"You don't need to do that." Kinsley rolled her eyes.

"What? For the two heroes of Harborside?" He threw his arms out dramatically with a wide smile that could light the porch. "I insist."

Pete was officially back to his old self.

Kinsley and Becca shared a glance before both saying, "Sure," at the same time, which made the three share a laugh.

"I got a T-shirt for both of you, back at the bar. Remind me when you get there," he said before rushing down the steps.

"T-shirts?" Becca asked.

"Later, ladies," Pete said over his shoulder before disappearing around the corner.

"You didn't catch his display inside? I guess he had T-shirts made for the bar and he's giving them away. Good marketing plug on his part. I'm surprised he didn't do it sooner."

"Ah, great idea. Good for him." Becca said.

"What a gorgeous day. It doesn't get much better than this," Kinsley said as her eyes grazed the backdrop of the sparkling Atlantic and then the foreground, where her flowers were beginning to flourish in a cadence of miraculous hues and showing so much promise.

After handing Kinsley a mug, Becca raised hers in cheers.

"To Harborside, and a peaceful life by the sea," Becca said, clinking her mug against Kinsley's.

"To Harborside, I'll drink to that." Kinsley grinned. "I'd never live anywhere else."

TIPS ON HYDRANGEA CARE AND HOW TO CHOOSE THE BEST ONE FOR YOUR GARDEN

DID YOU KNOW?

There are many varieties of hydrangeas. Pruning and care may differ, depending on the variety you choose for your garden. Be sure to do your homework before taking out the shears or underwatering, because failure to do so will affect the number of blooms the following year!

A FEW OF THE MANY VARIETIES THAT YOU CAN CHOOSE FROM:

MOPHEAD VARIETY, OR BIGLEAF (*H. MACROPHYLLA*)—The most common hydrangea, this is the one with showy, large, globe-shaped flowers. These showy globes can vary from deep blue to pinkish purple, based on the pH of your soil.

> *Note: You can play with the color by raising or lowering the pH of the soil, using products found at your local garden center.*

Here's how you can adjust your soil to change the bloom color:

Soil pH 5.0 to 5.5 = Blue

Soil pH 6.0 to 6.5 = Pink/purple

Soil pH 5.5 to 6.5 = Purple, or both blue and pink

Note: To make sepals bluer, add aluminum sulfate to the soil and maintain low levels of phosphorous, moderate levels of nitrogen, and high levels of potassium.

PRUNING—Best in late summer, however, hydrangeas technically don't ever need to be pruned back unless they're old and you want to reshape them. Removing dead stems is the only requirement to keep the health of the plant. Dead blooms can be removed at any time. This variety blooms on *old growth*, so too much pruning can result in no flowers the following year. Use caution!

Morning sun and afternoon shade are where this beauty will thrive in your yard, and this variety loves to stay moist.

Yes, I repeat, this variety requires a lot of water—these mopheads are thirsty!

OAKLEAF HYDRANGEA (*H. QUERCIFOLIA*)—Beautiful fall color, but provides year-round interest. Tolerates drier conditions.

This one differs from the mophead hydrangea in that it thrives in a sunny location but can handle shade, and usually blooms later in the summer.

PRUNING—Best in early spring or summer after flowering. This variety blooms on *old growth*, too, so don't get overzealous with those snippers!

PEE GEE (*H. PANICULATA*)—Provides white flowers that turn a pinkish hue.

PRUNING—Best to deadhead, also cut back in late winter/early spring before frost.

These flowers dry in a lovely way for fall/winter arrangements, as they start out creamy white and turn a rosy pink as they age.

Note: Different varieties of Pee Gee hydrangea can provide different hues. Pinky Winky has long, cone-shaped white and pink flowers, and Vanilla Strawberry is white to the tip and a darker reddish hue at the base. The Limelight variety provides chartreuse flowers that morph pinkish in autumn.

GRANDIFLORA, OR HILLS OF SNOW HYDRANGEA, SMOOTH HYDRANGEA (*H. ARBORESCENS*)—Habitat of five feet tall and domes of creamy white flowers beginning in early summer.

PRUNING—Prune to the ground each winter/early spring. (This is one hardy hydrangea!) Blooms on *new growth*. Tolerates light shade and will bless you with blooms from June to the fall.

White globe blooms can reach twelve inches in diameter!

CLIMBING HYDRANGEA (*H. ANOMALA*)—A vigorous, sprawling woody vine, midsummer white flowers with rich green foliage.

PRUNING—No pruning required but you can, to keep shoots under control, in the summer after flowering, as this hydrangea flowers on *old growth* as well.

RECIPES

AUNT TILLY'S OREO TRUFFLES FOR THE WALK INNS EVENT

1 14-ounce package Oreos
1 8-ounce block cream cheese, softened
Pinch of kosher salt
1 12-ounce package semi-sweet chocolate chips

Use food processor to crush cookies into fine crumbs.

Add all but 2 tablespoons crushed cookies to medium bowl. Add cream cheese and salt and stir until evenly combined.

Line baking sheet with parchment paper. Using small cookie scoop, form mixture into small balls and transfer to prepared baking sheet.

Freeze until slightly hardened, about 30 minutes.

Melt chocolate chips, then dip frozen balls in melted chocolate until coated and return to baking sheet. Sprinkle with remaining cookie crumbs. Freeze until chocolate hardens, about 15 minutes.

AUNT TILLY'S GO-TO CREAM CHEESE LOBSTER APPETIZER

1 8-ounce block cream cheese

⅓ cup olive oil mayonnaise

½ teaspoon Grey Poupon mustard

1 teaspoon garlic powder

1 teaspoon onion powder

5 or more ounces fresh lobster meat cut into small chunks

5 slices precooked bacon, cut into tiny pieces

2 tablespoons dry sherry

½ cup shredded sharp cheddar cheese

¼ cup shredded Colby cheese

15 (or so) frozen phyllo cups

Preheat oven to 350 degrees F.

Heat cream cheese and mayonnaise in medium saucepan on low.

Once melted, add mustard, garlic powder, and onion powder. Stir well.

Add lobster meat, bacon, sherry, and shredded cheeses. Stir until well combined.

Remove phyllo cups from freezer and fill with lobster meat.

Bake on baking sheet for about 10 minutes.

Share with guests!

Acknowledgments

Leis, you're incredible. I count myself blessed to be able to work with you. Your enthusiasm for my work reignites my passion and makes me wanna run to the keyboard! No one, I mean NO ONE, has a keener eye than you!

All of those behind the scenes at Berkley, THANK YOU! To the cover designer, Sarah Oberrender, thank you.

Sandy, for sticking with this one and never giving up. I appreciate all your tireless work and dedication, especially on this Maine series, which seemed to take the longest yet is closest to my heart.

To my author friends from "Sandy's Group," you know who you are! Thanks for the tireless support, camaraderie, and sharing in this crazy journey. All I can say is, ride the zone.

Linda, I appreciate you more than you know.

For all of those Facebook friends and cozy groups who have been champions of my work so willingly over the years, including but not limited to Denise Swanson Stybr, Lori Caswell, Dru Ann Love, Meg Gustafson, and Karen Hollins-Stallman. If I missed anyone, it's entirely my fault!

Ryan DeBroux, regarding touch DNA and that a hair follicle is more likely than touch to be found buried under the ground. Appreciate the expertise!

Beth Schumacher, for the care package of special-delivery cookies while I was in the trenches of writing this book. Your kindness will never be forgotten. (See, it's written in print forever now.) And Julie Jo Knief, too. I'll never forget your encouragement via gluten-free Oreos. It's your kindness, though, that sticks with me the most.

Amy and Jean, for your visit and reminding me of home. Amy, especially for the gifts and photos from Maine and the memories shared that quite literally catapulted me back to that special time and place. Amos, those were special days, indeed! Ones that I carry with me deep within my heart and I will never forget.

Heather, for your willingness for first-draft reads and letting me constantly burden you with my cozy mystery, fictional friends, and plucking "the weeds." I love you for that . . . and so much more! Conor, your thoughts and input helped me rethink these characters and sharpen them on the page. Keep reading and editing!

For my pals at Sunset Beach who are a constant inspiration: Brian (Benzo), Andy, Julie, Tall Andy, Kelly, Jill, but most especially Brad. Because without you, Brad, chapters fifteen through eighteen could not possibly have been written, could they? And yes, if you find your name (which means you'd have to have read the book), I'll buy you a drink or a coffee. Yes, definitely a coffee. Or maybe a coconut latte for Jill, from Spork.

Oh, and Lori, Steve, and Miley, for the long weekend of editing/dog-sitting/Airbnb-ing/Brett graduating. Without that weekend . . . this book would probably not be finished.

Jesse, for your constant encouragement of my work and listening to me bemoan it all . . . ☺

Mark, as always. How many ways can I write my gratitude for you? And your undying support? I'm running out of fingers to count the ways . . . except . . . I love you more. Your support means everything to me.

*Keep reading for an excerpt from the
next Mainely Murder mystery,*

MURDER UNDER THE MISTLETOE

The scent of pine boughs permeated the dining room of the Salty Breeze Inn, and the cheery sound of Andy Williams singing "Happy Holiday" filled the air. Meanwhile, a crackling wood fire, built in the original stone-stacked fireplace, kept everyone toasty and warm despite the room's tall timber ceiling.

Kinsley Clark looked away from the festive group of volunteer elves and smiled when she noticed her best friend, Becca, entering the room, plucking snowflakes from her long dark hair. Becca then brushed the hint of snow from her shoulders, causing it to melt off her wool coat.

"You made it!" Kinsley said. Becca's grin grew wide as Kinsley moved to welcome her. "And just in time, too. We could use you at the ribbon station."

"Ribbon station? I hope you have someone to teach me how to tie bows, otherwise you might be in trouble." Becca's golden eyes, which mimicked the center of a sunflower, twinkled. She slipped out of her coat and hung it on the back of a nearby chair before greeting Kinsley with a half hug.

"I'm just glad you're here and safe with us now. It looks like the snow started already, huh?" Kinsley leaned her head on her friend's shoulder for a moment before the two took a step closer to the table.

"Yeah, I'm here, despite the unplowed roads. The snow is starting to really stick out there—and faster than the weather forecaster predicted." Becca's salon-groomed brows furrowed. "Not sure I'm ready for winter to rear its ugly head just yet. We haven't even finished our leftover turkey from Thanksgiving!"

"Hey, now, 'tis the season." Kinsley elbowed her friend playfully. "Life in Harborside, Maine, can't be all warm, sunny beach days," she added. "Besides, I just love the first snow. It puts everyone in the holiday spirit. Which is just what we need right about now to prepare for the upcoming boat parade. Next weekend will be here before you know it. I promised the town council to have Harborside fully decorated by then as it's the town's official holiday-kickoff party and I *will* deliver on that promise!" Kinsley pumped an excited fist into the air.

Becca gestured to the group gathered around the table. "Yeah, looks like you rounded up a good group of volunteers to help this year. I'm sure you'll get it all done."

"Fa-la-la-la-la, 'tis the season for help and cheer! I just love this time of year," Kinsley crooned.

"I wish I could share in your enthusiasm and holiday spirit. I just had my third client cancel for this week; I'm feeling a little bummed," Becca admitted. "Unfortunately, things tend to hit a lull for the real estate biz during the holidays, as snowy winter days don't exactly make clients all that excited to pack up and move." Becca lowered her voice again and leaned into Kinsley. "Which isn't exactly helping my purse strings and my upcoming Christmas shopping list, if you know what I mean. I might just need to get a second job to get me through this winter." She sighed.

"Look no further if it's work you're looking for because I could use some extra hands at SeaScapes. That is, if you're up for it? Besides Harborside needing Christmas decorations, I have several clients lined up who've requested that I prep for their holiday gatherings, too. Seems people are just too busy this year. They're asking for their trees to be put up and their homes to look festive. Honestly, I was wondering how I would get it all done. You might even find a few new real estate clients out of the deal. The job's yours if you want it." Kinsley shrugged.

"Really? You'd hire me? I mean, you're already paying Adam, aren't you?" Becca said, nodding in his direction. "You can't afford to add me to the payroll, too, can you?"

Kinsley lowered her voice to match Becca's. "Well, technically, yeah, Adam's getting paid for today, but that's mainly to help his mom, Alice. I can't bear to think of her as a single mom handling everything on her own this time of year. Harborside's an expensive place to live, and it can't be easy for her. I know Adam gives his mom a portion of his salary, but don't tell him I told you how endearing he is."

"Oh? He does? Aw, what a sweetheart." Becca nodded. "I knew you had a keeper with him."

Kinsley ushered them farther out of earshot. "Anyway, most everyone is a volunteer today. Don't worry, between the profits that the town puts aside to pay SeaScapes and the extra clients . . . there's more than enough work to go around. So not to worry, my friend. I've got ya covered." She nudged her friend playfully again with her elbow.

Becca still didn't look overly convinced, so Kinsley continued, "None of that frowny face. I don't want you to stress—especially over the holidays. It's the best time of the year!"

"Kins, you're sweeter than your aunt's Christmas cookies, there's no doubt about it." Becca threw her arm around Kinsley's shoulder and gave a light squeeze. "I'll gladly take the job at SeaScapes. Decorating sure does put me in the spirit, and it'll be fun. Plus, the best part? I get to hang out with you!"

Kinsley was glad that her good business fortune could help out her friend and put a growing smile on her face. Kinsley's landscape design business—based out of the caretaker's cottage behind her aunt Tilly's Salty Breeze Inn—kicked into high gear during the winter months, even though that was when her gardening work came to a halt. She was solely responsible for all of the town's seasonal decor and used mostly natural elements found locally in Maine, and it was quite a production. Therefore, Kinsley had convinced her aunt Tilly to let her use the inn the weekend after Thanksgiving to coordinate all her decorating efforts. In return, she would transform the Salty Breeze Inn into a magical holiday destination that would make guests want to linger. It was a win-win for both of them and the only weekend of the entire year the inn was closed to the public.

"I'm so glad you're here to help this year," Kinsley said, leading Becca by the arm back to the rest of the group. "We need you here, right, guys?" Kinsley looked around the long dining room table and added, "You all remember my friend Becca?"

A bunch of greetings ensued as folks stopped what they were doing to welcome Becca with a wave, nod, or hello. The volunteers were busy creating the Christmas kissing balls that would be used all over Harborside. The kissing balls, which were made up of round clusters of greenery, were making a comeback. They originated from the Middle Ages and hung from entryways and doorways within a home so that everyone who passed beneath them would be gifted with blessings and good tidings. Over the centuries, though, they eventually transformed into a replacement for mistletoe. They were crafted from rosemary, thyme, and mistletoe, symbolizing love and devotion. Kinsley liked to use more traditional branches from the state of Maine, though, such as cedar, fir, white pine, and boxwood. This made it a more symbolic tradition for the town. These beautiful orbs would soon be hung from the light posts on Main Street and sprinkled around the town of Harborside, including at the wharf and marina.

"Oh, Becca, did I overhear you say Kinsley is sweeter than my holiday cookies? She *is* pretty special." Aunt Tilly beamed as she crossed the room with a plate of freshly baked Christmas cookies. "So I can't say I disagree with you, but you'll have to taste one and see for yourself. These just happen to be topped with a kiss."

"You heard that?" Becca said, astonished, as a French-manicured hand flew to her chest.

"Her ears are like a bat's; don't let her age fool you," Kinsley said with a giggle. "The woman is amazing! Someone's got a birthday coming up real soon, too. Aunt Tilly's turning sixty-three in a few weeks. We'll have to plan a party!"

Tilly clicked her tongue. "We'll have none of that. When you turn my age, you don't need a party to remind you that the clock is tickin'." She set the cookies on the table in front of the group of volunteers. "Here, Becca, have one," she encouraged further, gesturing with her outstretched hand. "Hopefully this should make your effort of driving in the snow worth it," she added, shining as brightly as a Christmas star atop a tree. Kinsley's aunt clearly loved the holiday season, too.

"Ooh, those do look amazing," Becca said, leaning in to examine the plate. "Oh, yes, they're the peanut butter kiss cookies. Just one of the many holiday favorites that you make every year!" Becca exclaimed. "Now it's really starting to feel like Christmas around here." She looked to Kinsley with a grin.

"I know, right? Lucky for us, she'll be baking all season long; this is only the beginning. Right, Aunt Tilly?" Kinsley directed to her aunt.

"You know I can't help myself, darlin'. I've been told holiday treats are my inn's specialty, and I wouldn't want to disappoint any of my guests," she answered with a devilish grin. Kinsley wondered by the look on her aunt's face if she had a new recipe up her sleeve. Either way, mouthwatering desserts wouldn't be lacking at the inn the entire month of December. Which made all the visitors who crossed the threshold *and* Kinsley and her friends quite happy.

"I'll take one of those!" Adam, Kinsley's summer employee, piped up, stealing one from the plate and immediately stuffing the entire cookie into his mouth. He groaned with pleasure as melted chocolate leaked out from the sides of his mouth and he attempted to catch it with his tongue.

"Adam!" his mother scolded. "I raised you with better

manners than that. You're going to choke to death. Take smaller bites! Plus, the way you're huffing it, that cookie is going to get all stuck in your braces," she added with a *tsk*. Alice, too, had been swindled into helping as a volunteer. Adam's mom had been recently hired as a housekeeper at Edna's home next door, which was a full-time job, as Edna Williamsburg owned an oceanside mansion. Alice was also known for making the best bows in town, and she was currently hard at work, twisting and pulling on loops. Meanwhile Adam's young sister, Melody, played with the rolls of wired ribbon at her mother's feet.

Each of the volunteers bustled around the table, managing their specific tasks. Cari Day, who worked at the humane society, was responsible for attaching chicken wire to pieces of floral foam. She then handed those pieces over to Jackie Horn, a busy stay-at-home mom of three, who soaked the foam in a bucket of water to prepare it for branches.

Adam was responsible for cutting all branches to an even six inches long and then stripping the ends off. Kinsley arranged the different evergreens that he'd cut into piles so that each kissing ball would have a well-rounded selection of branches.

Mallory Chesterfield, the owner of the local flower shop Precious Petals, had donated the winterberry, holly, and dogwood, and was cutting them to size to add a pop of festive color.

Pete O'Rourke—the owner of the local tavern the Blue Lobstah, which was located alongside the marina—had stopped by to lend a hand, too. The New England name of the eatery had everyone in town using his Boston slang. Which was why he'd chosen to name his restaurant after his roots. Pete was busy sticking the limbs into the soaked pieces of floral foam and poking his fingers with prickly branches along the way. Occasionally, the group would hear an "Ouch!" uttered from the bar owner's lips and a wounded finger would pop into his mouth.

Tilly provided the group with endless mugs of hot cocoa topped with homemade marshmallows and a dollop of cream. And by the recent look of things, a large supply of cookies. Candy canes were set in mason jars all down the center of the table in case anyone wanted to stir their cocoa or enjoy the peppermint treat as they labored. These numerous delights enticed the volunteers to happily make a reappearance year after year.

"*Peter*, would you mind adding a few logs to the fire while I run back to the kitchen to check my oven? I don't want to take a chance on burning my next batch of cookies," Tilly asked.

Kinsley looked over to Pete and lifted her shoulders in a shrug. Her aunt was the only one in town who called him Peter, and she seemed to refuse to call him Pete, despite multiple corrections on Kinsley's part. He smiled back at her with his winning smile. A smile that lit his face and made you think he'd just won the lottery. He rose from the dining chair and went straight to the task.

"Becca, would you mind joining Alice at the bow-making station? I'll head over to help Pete load the fire," Kinsley said. "I'm pretty up to task at my station."

"Uh-huh," Becca teased with a playful swat to Kinsley's backside. "Like he needs the help. But you go on ahead, my friend." Becca waggled her eyebrows. "It sounds to me like you're just looking for a moment alone with our Boston friend over there."

No doubt, Kinsley and Becca hung out at Pete's establishment quite a bit. And to Becca's credit, Kinsley was the one encouraging it, more and more. Something about that Pete O'Rourke had Kinsley coming back. But it was complicated. They were both remarkably busy with their respective businesses, and time off was hard to come by, so any time spent together meant her hanging on the end of his bar. Something she didn't really want to make a habit of.

"He's my friend. Can't women and men *just* be friends?" Kinsley protested.

Becca batted her eyelashes and made a kissy face.

Kinsley responded with an eye roll before nudging Becca back in the direction of the bows and turning on her heel toward the fireplace. Thankfully, Pete had his back turned, oblivious to the goings-on. He was down on one knee and loading logs into the fire but turned when she laid a soft hand on his shoulder.

"Thanks for keeping this going." Kinsley extended her arms out to feel the heat of the roaring fire.

"Hey, no problem."

"And thanks for helping today; I really appreciate it." She looked at the clock above the mantel and added, "What time do you have to be back at the Blue Lobstah?"

Pete's eye's, the color of blue asters, followed hers, and he, too, snuck a peek at the time. "I hate to leave you hanging, but it's two fifteen so I probably should head out soon. I haven't hired anyone to plow yet this winter, so I guess it'll be me cleaning the parking lot before the night crowd." He grimaced. "I guess I bettah get busy on that!" he added as he turned to load another log into the fire. He stood and jabbed at the new log with the fire poker, setting it aflame.

Kinsley loved when hints of Pete's Boston accent came

out. It usually happened when he was excited or under stress. Right now it sounded like stress, though, so she said, "No worries. I'm finished with separating the branches so I can take over your job and put them in. Again, thanks for sticking with it as long as you have," she teased as she pointed out his wounded fingers. "I do appreciate it."

Pete laughed. "No problem, part of the job." He winked before he set the fire poker back in its holder. "You mind if I take off now then?"

"Not at all! But you're still planning on helping me with the lobster-trap tree tomorrow out by the cliff walk, right? I could really use you for that." She gave his hand a quick squeeze before releasing it and then followed him toward the exit.

"Yeah, I'd be happy to. Just let me know when you need the lift delivered, and I'll make a few calls. I think we'll need a lift to stack 'em, since you were talking about making it thirty-eight feet. I'm tall, but not that tall." He chuckled.

"Will do!" Kinsley said.

The background music suddenly shifted to Mariah Carey singing "All I Want for Christmas Is You," and when Kinsley turned to ask everyone to say good-bye to Pete, she couldn't help but notice the silly grin splashed across Becca's face. Maybe Kinsley's only wish for Christmas *was* for Pete to take special notice of her. But she'd tuck that away for now, like an unwrapped present.

After everyone shared their good-byes with the bar owner and the volunteers got back to business, Kinsley glanced around the table for a moment to watch them work their Christmas magic. The kissing balls were now hanging from wide red bows and filling up drying racks scattered around the room. She couldn't help but wonder if a chance meeting with Pete beneath a kissing ball might happen this season. Little did she know that less than a week later, kissing would be the last thing on her mind, and several of those gathered around the table this very night would be questioned about a murder.

ABOUT THE AUTHOR

Sherry Lynn spent countless summers on the coast of Maine knowing she'd one day return to write about the magical location from her youth. Curious by nature, sleuthing became the perfect fit for her, and she has written multiple cozy mystery series under several pseudonyms. Currently, Sherry lives in the Midwest with her husband, but she dreams about one day retiring oceanside with a good book in her hand.

CONNECT ONLINE

SherryLynnBooks.com
 SherryLynnBooks

Ready to find
your next great read?

Let us help.

Visit prh.com/nextread

Penguin
Random
House